# Dager
# of the
# Tasman Empire

By Teresa Schapansky

# REVIEWERS SAY...

"*Dager* is a hit in our household! Every night we read a chapter and my boys excitedly await the next development in the story. They especially like the old man. We recommend this book to any family looking for mystery and adventure."
*Susan Valeri, President, Powerful Publicity Group*

"After having the fortune to read *Imogene*, I was absolutely thrilled to read *Dager*, and frankly, I'm glad I did. Readers, both young and old, will enjoy these stories of mythical, mystical kingdoms that breathe life back into a popular but dying subject. The author shows apparent growth and expertise in this second in a series. She does such extraordinary things to her characters; she uses her creative imagination to bring their sheer essence and innocence leaping from the pages with a ferocious rush of emotions. The storylines and plots are fresh and exhilarating, with twists and turns that leave the reader breathless, still hungry for more. I'm confident that the author has earned herself a place in the literary world, while her characters find their place into readers' hearts."
*Kimberly Hayes, Freelance Writer/Professional Book Reviewer*

"Dager and his family travel to the new world where they are reunited with their family and friends. Women and men are equal, laws are made and Mod becomes the new leader of the new world. Dager, Lucia, Pagan and the other children will now be raised in a happy environment where mutual respect, understanding and equality for all are key. Children everywhere will love *Dager of the Tasman Empire*."

*Shirley Roe, Allbooks Reviews*

"Once again, the author has searched her incredible imagination and written an adventure story worthy of many readings. *Dager of the Tasman Empire* is an exciting novel that connects a magical world under the sea and an equally fascinating land of heat and dust.

*Dager* is abducted and taken to live in this arid, hostile land with a wicked hag. No child should have to live as he does, but despite the difficulties, he grows and develops wisdom beyond his years. Incredible powers of the undersea folk, their love for all creatures and their sense of justice help them build a new community apart from the injustices of both worlds. *Dager's* undersea family never ceases to search for him and the story of their search brings intrigue and magic into the lives of young readers. Readers are never quite sure what will happen next, while surprises await eager minds, page after page.

This story is written with elementary and middle school children in mind, but will certainly capture

the imagination of all ages."
*Elaine Fuhr, Freelance Reviewer*

"Teresa Schapansky's second book, *Dager of the Tasman Empire* is a book that shows the author is indeed at the height of her powers. The imagery it generates wraps the reader up in the plot. Never once does the action cease to flow, as layer upon layer of excitement builds.

This is a book that fulfils the goals of entertainment for children. Firing up the imagination with a writing style that always keeps the action flowing, Teresa Schapansky has created the foundation for many more solid tales. Children everywhere will be impatiently waiting to read more from this talented writer."
*Warren Thurston, Owner of Boggle Books*

"*Dager* is a hit in our household! Every night we read a chapter and my two boys excitedly await the next development in the story. They especially like the old man. We recommend this book to any family looking for mystery and adventure."
*Susan Valeri, The Powerful Publicity Group*

"Magical! This is the second book I have read by Teresa Schapansky and again, I want more! For me, there is a feeling of love and respect in her writing. Human respect for each other and the environment. There was a passage I read where (not a spoiler) a leaf floated above and whirled around with other leaves. As I read it, it made me think of being in Wonderland. Just a more simple wonderland. I could just see it happening. I could picture the miniseries for kids. The lessons one could learn will help build foundations for so many that now only know what they think is entitled to them. And a bonus is that their imaginations will be put to good use! I will definitely keep these books on my shelf for future use in my business. They can help the young and not so old to do better!"

*Lachelle René ~Reading: It does the body good!*

"I found this enchanting. I read a fair amount of children's books as I am in the process of writing one, moreover, thought I had finished one, so for research really. In this however, although it was written for a different age bracket than mine is/was originally, it has given me pause for thought as to the content of my own. Sure My book has a message, yet a specific one whereas I found this has many. Traditional family values is the one that really stands out though. Something I find is lacking in today's what I shall refer to as, 'nonsensical' world. In my honest opinion I believe there would be a great benefit including this in every young readers' school curriculum...Highly recommended."

*J.P. Willson. Author*

# Dager of the Tasman Empire

ISBN 978-1-988024-37-0

# DEDICATION

This book is dedicated to my children.

This book is also dedicated to every single person that believes in magic, the impossible, the what if's, and in particular, the what for's.

Thanks to Lucas, Adrienne and Gracie, for being my original Dager, Lucia and Pagan.

Thanks to everyone, for understanding my need to leave the surface on occasion.

# TABLE OF CONTENTS

# Dager
## of the
# Tasman Empire

# POND SCUM

The miserable old woman glared at her young charge with those all too familiar steel grey eyes. Instantly he cowered and shrunk back against the wall, causing the hag's mood to soften. But only a little. And even that was short-lived. She straightened and leaned toward him.

"You little pond scum! How many times have I told you? I want this floor spotless!" Her intimidating voice was deep, rough and loud. She threw the pitch fork that only moments before, had been raised high above him like a battle weapon ready to strike, to the ground at his feet. She lifted her heavy skirts, and stormed out of the chicken coop. He heard the lock click shut behind her, and only then did he breathe a sigh of relief. At least she was gone. He knew that no matter how hard he tried, or how clean he got that floor, it would never, ever be good enough to satisfy his master.

The little guy picked up his fork, turned it to its side and began scraping the stubborn chicken droppings from the old, worn out floor. His movements were quick, experienced and rhythmic; and so they should be. He'd been doing this now for more than two years. With calloused hands that had no business belonging to a five-year old boy, he scraped and scratched and pulled the dung to the far corner of the little room, then opened the trap in the floor. In the next moment, the little room was bare, except for him and the fork. Now all that was left for him to do, was wait for her return.

He slumped down onto his bottom, against the wall across from the door and rested. Chances are that he would have nodded off right away, sitting there like that in the dark and quiet, if not for the hunger pains that gnawed ever so constantly at his empty insides.

It so happened though, that he did eventually fall asleep. After all, a child his age could hardly be expected to work from morning until night with no grub nor a break in-between. He dreamt. Did he ever dream, and his dreams rarely changed from one to the next. He dreamt of magical, faraway lands, which during the waking hours, he knew did not truly exist. He dreamt that he was a free boy who had a family that loved him. In his dreams there was no old hag and no stinky, dirty chicken coop. There were only fun and games and most importantly, laughter. Not the wicked laughter that he was sadly used to hearing, either; this was good laughter that came straight from the bellies of kind people. And then as most dreams do, this particular dream came to an end. An abrupt, cruel end. The boy did not wake up of his own accord either, oh no. It was the chickens that roused him. The old hag had left him locked up in the coop, and then proceeded to let the chickens in. He jumped up from the floor and let out a yelp. And then, high above the clucking and pecking noises from the hens, he heard it. Her laugh; her horrible, spine-tingling laugh that surely was not of this earth. She opened the door.

The morning sun was already high in the sky, and was far too brilliant for his little eyes to take in all at once, and he was momentarily blinded by it. She laughed again as she reached in and grabbed him by the shoulder.

"Come now, boy! Did mama go and leave you in the coop all night?" And then she cackled again, as she roughly pulled the boy toward her. He still couldn't see and would have stumbled if not for her holding him up. As it was, she threw him to the ground anyway, the minute he was out of the coop. It would have been a little kinder if he had fallen on his own. The boy's hand landed directly upon a sharp object, which had been hidden underneath the dirt. He looked down at his injured hand surprised, and watched as droplets of his very own blood turned a small piece of the earth an angry shade of red, and then mysteriously disappeared. He glanced back at his hand again, and was even more startled to see that the wound was now gone. As sly as could be, the boy wrapped his small fist around the object and hid it safely within his grasp. And although it was still early morn, and the sky was as blue as blue could be, thunder roared and lightening shot across the sky.

At that same moment, unbeknownst to him or to the hag, in a world that very few knew existed, an old man's hand began to bleed.

And the blind old man, who was an all-important part of a world that very few knew existed, the blind old man who could see far better than anyone with regular vision could, slapped his gnarled and twisted freshly wounded hand to his useless knee, with old, pent up anger. He then rubbed his hands together briefly. And when he pulled them apart, there was not even the slightest sign of blood or injury.

"T'is time! T'is time, I say! I've found the lost 'un. I've found'im, al'ight!" His voice cracked, as it was rarely used these days at all. In fact, he hadn't said a word for two years. Until now. And although he sat alone and spoke to no one, everyone who was supposed to hear him, heard. Most of the men, women and children who were supposed to, dropped whatever they were doing and sped to his cave. All but one family. This one family sat for a moment and reflected. Could it be? Had they heard right? But they knew it must be so, because it was the old man who said it. They cried tears of relief, the three of them stood at once, held hands, then went to join the others. When the rest of them saw this particular trio advancing upon them, they immediately bowed their heads and stood off to the side to let them pass. The three had clear passage all the way through the scores of villagers who had come either because they were supposed to, or because they were curious. The three knelt at the foot of the old man who had spoken, and all became quiet. There was not a single living soul in this Village of Hurtsmire, focal point of the Tasman Empire, who would dare to speak out of turn now.

"Yer here, al'ight. I kin smells ya's." If total silence could ever become quieter, it did so just then. Necks craned inward and breaths were held. For the old man did not speak loud. His voice was old and weak, and came out barely louder than a whisper. But he hadn't ever said anything that did not need to be said. That was just one of the reasons why he was held in such high regard.

It was the head of the family who answered him, as in their empire that was the way it had always been. He held his hat in his hands as he spoke, as if that would make any difference to a blind man. But he knew better; he knew that it did.

"Yes, Da, I mean, sir. We are here. It is I, Mod. I brought with me, my wife, Goy and our daughter, Lucia. You have news for us. We are ready to hear it." The old man let out a wheeze of a breath and slapped his hand against his knee again. He was angry for sure, but not with Mod.

"Dey gots'im, al'ight. Ya needs ta bing'im back now." The old man tried to hide the urgency in his voice.

"Yes, sir. We'll bring him back. Please, tell me what I must do!" Mod was twisting his hat in his hands now, this way and that, as he tried to remain patient with the old timer. The last thing he wanted to do was show disrespect. Suddenly the old man's hands shot forward and stilled Mod's. Goy and Lucia were startled, but remained quiet as female folk should be.

"Now! Nary a mom'nt ta waste! T'is mama got yer lost un!" Mod shook his head, for he couldn't have heard right. The old man still held his hands and hat fast. Mod angrily pulled free of his grasp, respect or not!

"No, sir. Goy hasn't got our son!" The old man hissed at him, for he was growing impatient with the young man who knelt before him.

"NO! Not dat mama! T'is de bad, bad mama got lost 'un!" A great hush fell over the cave. The old man was speaking in riddles, for sure. Tears ran silently down Goy's cheeks as she tried to make sense of what they were being told. The old man continued.

"When de man Croy came and took de boy..." And then he let out another horrible sounding wheeze. The effort to speak was becoming too great for the old man to take. His young handmaiden, Gia, came running toward him with a cup of water. He reached for it just as though he saw it coming. But that was impossible. His eyes were as empty as anything could ever be.

"Yes, sir. We know Croy took Dager. Please tell me, where is he?" The crumpled, ruined hat fell to the floor now, and Mod's hands hung helplessly at his sides. He was almost convinced that the old man had actually lost his mind. And he didn't dare look at his wife to see the tormented expression he knew she'd bear.

"Croy took an' sole' de boy, Mod. De mama buy 'im. De mama not good to yer boy, Mod. Ya git'im now! Ya git'im now!" The old man's voice was gaining in strength, and became louder with each syllable he spoke. The hair on the back of Mod's neck was standing straight up. How he wished he could at this moment, send his wife and daughter away. How he wished they wouldn't hear what he feared the old man was about to say. But it was too late now.

"You go to de point where de rivas meet. You don't folla de riva, no. You go straight nort at de point, Mod! Go straight nort by de first bay of de sea! In de mocket, Mod! Ya find'im in de mocket!" The old man's head fell back against the chair, and he wheezed again. Mod knew he was tiring. He had already surpassed his limit. But Mod wasn't done with him yet!

"When, sir? When do we find him in the market? When?" The old man's head lolled forward again, and if Mod hadn't known better, he would have thought he was staring right at him. Chills ran up and down his spine, for he knew time was of the essence.

"Ya go now. Ya betta go now, Mod. Ya send de gull. De lost'un don't trust ya. Ya gotta send de gull." And that was all that they would get out of the old man on this day. He took a deep breath in, and then wheezed it back out again. His head dropped down upon his chest and he began to snore. Gia came running to his side and motioning with her hands, she silently began to shoo them all away. Even the family, she shooed away. For the old man, the all-important old man who lived in a world that few knew existed, needed his rest.

The old man dreamt as usual. But this dream was not usual, by any means. This dream was special and it was as real as anything could ever be. For in this dream, he spoke directly to the lost 'un.

*"T'is al'ight, boy."*

As the boy lie there on the ground at the old hag's feet, he thought he heard something, but not quite. It was a voice, but to whom it might belong, he did not know. And then the old hag, who preferred to be called 'mama', screeched at him.

"Look at how filthy you've gotten yourself, boy! You'd better hurry now and get cleaned up, for we're going to market today! You'll find some leftover grub in the pigs' trough if you're quick enough." The boy scrambled to his feet and made haste for the pig pen. As he ran, he stuffed the object into his pants pocket, for there was no time for that now. He was too hungry to even care what it was that had pierced his skin and caused him to bleed. And the old hag was right, there was some fresh grub left. The boy yelled as he picked up a stick and smacked the pigs away. They squealed as they ran, but they knew that they must either run or be whipped. And the pigs also knew that it would not take much to satisfy the young boy anyway, and they could return to the trough as soon as he'd had his fill. The boy dug in with both hands, he was so hungry. It was a mixture of grain and corn and sour milk that he ate, and it tasted far better than the dry bread the old hag would feed him later. Her bread was as tough as shoe leather, anyway. As he feasted, under the watchful eyes of the pigs, he heard it again.

*"T'is al'ight, I say, boy."* He stopped chewing for a moment, cocked his head to the side and listened intently now. *"Aye, I'm speakin' to ya. T'is yer very own granda speakin' to ya now."* The boy froze on the spot, but cautiously, with his pale blue eyes that had long ago lost their brilliance, he looked around. There was not another person in sight. Even the old hag had gone into her house, probably to eat salt pork and eggs, and that tough old bread. He swallowed his mouthful and listened again.

*"Al'ight now, boy. Yer not meant for de ol' hag now. She ain't yer mama, no. Yer mama fer real loves ya, boy. She wants ya back. Do ya wanna go back to yer real fam'ly now?"* The child didn't hesitate at all, but nodded

his head up and down. Surely this had to be a dream, but how? He was wide awake. The boy realized that he didn't even care that he was dreaming while he was awake though, for this was the best news that he'd ever had in his life. *"Den ya betta listen up. At de mocket t'day, ya see a gull. Ya neva see dis gull befoe. Ya folla de gull, boy."* The old man thought for a moment, then asked, *"Do ya even know yer name, boy?"* To which the boy shook his head, no. He thought perhaps he didn't have one. Wasn't even worthy of a name, like most boys in his situation. He wasn't free, after all. Again, he shook his head, no. The old man nodded knowingly. It was just as he had expected. *"Yer name is Dager, boy. Ya belong wid us. Not de ol' hag. We loves ya boy and we wants ya back! T'day!"* Dager nodded enthusiastically. He was ready to go. But then he trembled. What if the old hag caught him trying to leave? He'd seen what she'd done to the other boys who had left before. He did not want that to happen to him, no way. The old man heard the boy's fears. *"No, ya can't git caught, Dager. Ya must sneak like ya's neva snuck befoe. In de mocket today, ya's folla de gull to where she go. No matta where she go, ya folla de gull. Den ya be's wit yer fam'ly agin. Don't git caught, boy. I canno speaks wid ya agin t'day. Ya just gotta folla de gull. Ya hears yer Granda, Dager? Ya hears me?"* Dager nodded and then waited for more. But that was all that he would hear from the old man on this day. He shrugged his small shoulders, and then dug into the grub again.

Mod, his wife and child, returned to their little hut and immediately began to pack. They knew where they had to go, but they did not know what they would find when they got there. And Lucia! To send Lucia, their one remaining child. But for the old man to speak it, they knew that there simply would be no other way.

"But, Da! I've never been to the surface before! What if I get caught, and how will I know him?" Lucia began to panic now, and ran from him to her mother. "Ma! Can't you come with me?" Goy sat down on the kitchen stool, and motioned for her daughter to join her. Lucia promptly sat on her mother's lap, and looked deep into her blue, blue eyes.

"You will know him, Lucia, for he is your brother. The old man says he won't trust your father and I. He won't go with us. We need to have Dager back, Lucia. It is an important job that you have." Lucia nodded, but her eyes were still filled with fear. Her mother held her close and rubbed her back. And then she asked her husband.

"Mod, what about the high council? They may not let us go. You know how much they need you here in Hurtsmire." Mod looked to his wife incredulously.

"Need me! Need me? And how do they repay me for the service I do for them? We live in little more than a shack. They provide us with little more than the grub on the table for what I do for them. Surely they can survive without me for a day or two. As far as I am concerned my dear, they have no choice in the matter. It is our son, after all. Our long lost son whose life is at stake." The man paced about the small room as he spoke. And Goy knew that he would not let anything stand between him and Dager now. He threw his hands in the air. "For two years, Goy! For two years father has sat in his cave, searching, and now he's found him. We have to go. The high council can turn us away, for all I care." Goy nodded to her husband, for she felt just as strongly about it as he. There was nothing worse than enduring the loss of a child. And now they were so close to having him back. Lucia sat quietly and listened to her parents speak. She remembered very little of her brother, for it was such a long time ago. Two years to a seven-year old after all, felt like an eternity.

"Will you at least advise them of our departure, Mod?"

"Aye, that much I'll do, Goy. But I will not beg for their permission to go. If it comes to that, we are no longer of this village." And then Mod stomped directly out of their hut. Goy knew he was headed straight to the meeting chambers, and silently she wished him luck. It was up to her now, to finish the packing. She gave her daughter another loving squeeze.

"Lucia, you can do this, you know. You can bring your brother back." Lucia trembled in her mother's arms. She had heard the horror stories about the surface dwellers, and she'd never had even the slightest intentions of going up there, ever. And now on this day, it seemed that she would indeed have to go up, and worse than that, she would in part, be going alone.

"Why wouldn't he trust you and Da? Why does it have to be me?" Her mother thought about that for a moment, and she was a smart woman. Although the very idea made her fret until she felt sick to her stomach, she knew there would only be one reason why her son wouldn't trust anyone other than a child.

"Well, Lucia, it's hard to explain. I think this bad mama that your granda spoke of is a bad, bad person. She must have been very bad to Dager, and Dager being as young as he is, probably thinks that all, or at least most big people are bad! Your father and I will have to earn his trust back, love. And it will be a long journey, I'm afraid, for all of us." Lucia shook her head. It all sounded like way too much work.

"Ma, can't we just leave him there, then?"

"Oh, no, Lucia. The most important reason that he has to come back is because he is our blood. He is your only brother and our only son. He was not meant to go away, oh no. It was that bad Curor named Croy who took him."

"Why, Ma? Why did Croy take him?" Lucia had heard stories about Croy and none of them were good. But, she never understood any of it. Now, at the final hour, she needed to learn.

"Well, love. Croy wanted to be the Empire's Curor. He was always competing against your father. But your father is the one they chose, because it is his blood that has run through Hurtsmire's Curors all along. Croy was cast away from his own land, love. And he figured he'd just move on in here and take over."

"I don't get it, Ma. So why did he take Dager? Dager was just a little boy and not a Curor."

"Ah, that's right. But Dager would be the next Curor. When Dager would become old enough to cure, and your father becomes too old to cure, Dager would step in. By taking Dager from us, the Empire would have no choice but to look elsewhere for a Curor. And where else would they look, but to Croy?"

"But, if Da got too old to cure, wouldn't Croy also be too old?"

"Right again, Lucia. But Croy has a son, too. His son is the same age as Dager is. It would be Croy's son who would take the position, should your father be the last of his kind." Lucia snuggled in closer to her mother's chest. It was all beginning to make sense, sort of. How she wished she'd paid more attention before. Would there be time for her to be taught all that she needed to know?

In the meantime, Mod was cautiously making his way through the dark forest that led to the meeting chambers. The blackish trees were so tall and thick that they created a heavy, foreboding canopy that blocked out most of the light. He hated every step he took in that dreary forest. He hated it because it was in that very forest two years ago, when his son was taken. And he remembered it clearly, as though it had happened only yesterday.

# 2

## THE DISAPPEARANCE

Two Years Before

The highest member of council, the man who sat on the uppermost seat, in the center of the pyramid, stood. And it meant that he and the others had reached their decision. All eyes fell upon him. He reached up with his left hand and twisted one side of his long moustache, as he eyed the two men who knelt before him. With his right hand, he smashed the gavel down so hard upon the podium that it shook.

"I cannot believe that we've had to convene for this trivial purpose." Dramatically, he waved his arms up in the air as he addressed the entire crowd. And then he spoke directly to the man kneeling, who was positioned to his left.

"Croy. You were welcomed our village, within the Tasman Empire, as a man. Not a Curor, just a man. It was on that pretense alone that we allowed you to settle here with your wife and son. Nothing more. Nothing more is possible. You were once a Curor, sure enough. But not anymore, and certainly not in Hurtsmire. You know better than that, man. There is no room for two Curors in the Village of Hurtsmire. My question to you is, can you live out the rest of your days, here in this land, satisfied with that? Can you be just a man?" The councilor reached over to the man called Croy, and tapped him lightly upon the shoulder with his gavel. Croy stood and angrily replied.

"Aye; I can live with that. I can live with the fact that there can only be one Curor in Hurtsmire. But you know as well as I, that I am the better Curor. Does the quality of the cure mean nothing?" Whispers and gasps could be heard throughout the giant cave, as Croy defiantly challenged the councilor. But the councilor was more wise than he, and he laughed openly at the man who stood before him. The crowd immediately became silent again.

"Ha, ha ha. It is a good thing, Croy, that you think so highly of yourself. I do not know that everyone here shares in your opinion, however." He stole a quick glance to the other man, who remained silent and on his knees to his right, and then continued. "We will not waste time worrying about who would make the better Curor, man named Croy. There is no argument there. Mod is the Curor of the Village of Hurtsmire, and that is the way it will always be." The councilor stepped back startled then, as Croy suddenly jerked toward him. His eyes were full of fury, but he knew well enough to keep his oversized, tightly balled fists safely hidden behind his back. His voice had a dangerously threatening tone to it, as he replied.

"No, you are right, sir. No more time will be wasted on this. But let it be known that I am the most powerful Curor. This man who cowers before you and shakes on his knees can never give to Hurtsmire, what I can. It is his family who comes first with him, not the Tasman Empire, nor anything else, for that matter. And when he shows you his true colours, and trust that he will indeed... you will be at my door begging for help. A village such as Hurtsmire, in the Tasman Empire cannot be without a Curor for any length of time, and mark my words. You will be sorry that you chose not to take me up on my overly kind and generous offer." The councilor tried to hide his fear of the man called Croy, as Croy glared at him one more time. Then, as he took to his feet and turned around to leave, he kicked Mod hard in the side. Mod winced, but remained respectfully on his knees before council, as he should. The only sound that could be heard now, were Croy's heavy footsteps as he left. And still, moments after the man was gone, no one dared move. All eyes once again, fell upon the councilor. He regained his composure, wiped the sweat from his brow, then tapped Mod upon the shoulder with his gavel.

Despite the stitch in his now tender ribs, Mod obediently stood.

"Mod! It is a dreadful thing, what you've just been through. You are very important to the Tasman Empire; that should never be in doubt. You will, as your father before you and his father before him did, carry on as the Curor for the Village of Hurtsmire." And then the councilor's voice took on an eerie edge, just as Mod had silently predicted it would. He sighed as he prepared for the ultimatum that he knew was imminent. The councilor laughed mockingly; prompting the other members who sat upon their high and mighty seats to do the same. Mod was careful to ensure that his own face remained true; expressionless.

"But! Mod, if and I do mean if. If we should find out that anything that the man named Croy said were true of your first loyalties to our village..." he paused dramatically, "I don't think I need to tell you what would become of you! You are a powerful Curor, oh yes. That is known throughout the land, indeed. But do not think for a moment that your life is your own. You belong to us, Mod. You live and breathe for the Tasman Empire and don't you ever forget it." Mod stared straight ahead and nodded in agreement. It would be best for him and for his family's sake, that the high council, along with anyone else for that matter, never found out what his true feelings were.

The councilor gave his nod to the drummers who sat across from the pyramid. The instruments sounded and the meeting was adjourned. Mod turned and began to walk out of the cave. How he hated those drums and the so-called order that they represented. Although his head remained bowed, he knew that the rest of the villagers; the ones who had come to the meeting because they were supposed to, and the ones who had come because they were curious, walked completely in tune to the beat of those drums. Mod was very different from these people. Each step he took was his own, and his pace varied greatly from that of his fellow villagers. His steps led him away from the rest, who were most likely going to gossip with their neighbours about the current events. They obviously had nothing better to do with their time.

Mod on the other hand, had important matters to discuss. Matters of the heart, which he had only ever been able to share with two people; one of whom was his wife, and the other was his father. His father, however was the one who deeply understood him, for he had once walked the same, uphill, obstructed path that Mod now found himself on.

Mod shook his head with disgust, as he always did, as he entered his father's dilapidated cave. He despised the hole that the councilors had sent his father to live in after they'd decided that he'd outlived his usefulness. His father of course, knew he'd arrived even before Mod had made the slightest noise.

"Yer here, al'ight! I kin smells ya! Come closer, boy." Mod smiled at the very idea that his father still thought of him as a boy. He'd been married now for six years, and had two children. He'd been Curing since the Year of the Crimson Serpent, and that was well over ten years ago.

"Yes sir. I'm here." Mod agreed patiently, and then went and sat at the foot of his father's mat.

"What of ya den? Yer ready to git now, Mod?" Mod shook his head, no.

"No, sir. I don't think it's time for us to go. I'll wait it out. I'll serve some more time here before I'm done." But the old man knew better. He knew full well, what was keeping his son from leaving the Village of Hurtsmire.

"Ya ain't gonna fool yer own father now, Mod. Ya don't worry 'bout me no more. Ya git wid your wife and fam'ly."

"No, I don't think so. Not without you." The old man sat up and rested upon one elbow as he turned toward his son. His old bones creaked and cracked in protest as he did so.

"Ya kin't take me wid ya's, ya know dat now. How you gonna pack an old fella like me 'round? Don't be a fool, boy. Go whilst ya kin go." Mod helped his father lay back upon his old pillow, and then tenderly packed the blankets back around his feeble form.

As he stood up to leave, he said, "No, da. When we go, it'll be as a family and that includes you. Besides, if you'd just let me cure you a little bit. Just enough so you could see and walk..."

"I fear not, boy. Ya gots ta save dat kinda cure for a guy wid some future left in'im. T'is not for me. Ya don't go and waste de cure on me." It was the same old argument between them, and both knew that neither man would win. Good-naturedly, Mod shook his head at him.

"Alright then, you win. But for now, I must go home and speak with Goy." And then Mod turned to take his leave.

"WAIT, MOD!" Mod stopped dead in his tracks. His father's sudden outburst, so out of character, combined with his panic-stricken tone, caused a tidal wave of fear to ripple through Mod's entire being. He rushed back to his father's side.

"What is it?" He furrowed his brows as he asked, and then searched deep into the old man's empty, white eyes. The old man replied gravely.

"Ya gots ta go and get de boy." Mod was puzzled when he heard this.

"What? What was that you said?" The old man grabbed his wrist and tried to push Mod away and toward the cave's entrance.

"YA GOTS TA GO AND GET DE BOY!" The colour drained from Mod's face as he realized right then that his father was referring to Mod's own son, Dager. His heart literally froze in mid-beat as he pulled free of his father's bony grip. He sped from the cave so fast that the world around him spun and had become nothing more than a blur. And at the same time, he knew full well, in that uncanny way that Curors have of knowing, that it was already too late.

Mod ran directly to his home. Goy was in the kitchen, preparing their evening meal. Lucia sat contentedly on a stool at the table, weaving together her beloved bead mat. Goy saw the horror in her husband's eyes the moment he appeared in the doorway. The fragile bowl she'd been holding fell to the floor, immediately shattering into a million pieces.

"Where's Dager, Goy?" Goy only shook her head, and looked around. She was so startled that for the time being, she wasn't able to think clearly. Mod repeated himself, but louder this time around. "I said, WHERE IS DAGER?" Mod crossed the distance between where he'd been standing in the entrance, to the kitchen in two giant steps. He took his terrified wife by the shoulders and was about to ask her one more time, when very unexpectedly, he felt a series of sharp tugs upon the hemline of his vest. He looked down at the small girl whose eyes were brimming with tears. She pleaded.

"Please, Da! Let go of her!" Until that moment, Mod had not realized that he'd taken hold of Goy as roughly as he had. Quickly, his loosened his grip and transformed it into a loving embrace. He honestly had not meant to hurt nor scare anyone. Goy squeezed him back and then at last, found her voice.

"Mod, I don't understand!" Her chest heaved

and shuddered again. "Dager is playing near the edge of the forest. Did you not see him on your way home, love?" She pulled free of Mod and then scooped their whimpering young daughter up into her arms. She had never seen her husband act so crazed before, and she was a little afraid. Mod fell to his knees and covered his face with his hands.

"Quiet now, I have to think." Goy, with Lucia still held tight to her chest, backed away from the kitchen. She knew full well what it meant, when Mod said he had to think.

All was quiet in their hut now, and stone still. Mod fell back onto his rear and drew his knees up tightly to his chest. He unclasped the ancient chain that hung around his neck, and allowed his serpent medallion to fall onto the palm of his hand. The chain dropped to the floor with a clatter as he clasped the medallion between both hands and squeezed. It warmed up and within a matter of seconds, caused the backs of his hands to glow red, and heat pulsed through his entire body. Mod concentrated harder than he'd ever done before. The vision of his son came quickly to him.

There, sure enough, in the background of his vision he saw his own hut. In the opposite direction, he knew, lay that horrible, horrible forest. Mod's eyes immediately came to rest upon the small, lone form standing in the clearing.

Three year old Dager threw the stone as far as he could. But as usual, he missed his mark. It hadn't even come close to landing within the circle of rocks; his intended target. Dager just knew that if he kept trying, if only he kept aiming at the circle, soon enough he'd get it in. Then he'd be able to play the rock game with his sister, instead of by himself. He ran with his stubby little legs to where the rock had fallen, and he was ready to draw the necessary line in the dirt and start over. As he bent downward, ready to retrieve his weapon of choice, a dark shadow enveloped him, the rock and the ground around him. He looked up and was so startled to see the strange man standing before him, where only a moment ago there had been no one, that he staggered back a step and landed flat upon his bottom.

Mod forced himself to keep his concentration intact. He recognized that shadow. He'd know that dreaded, evil form anywhere. No matter what, he just had to continue watching, to see what would become of his only son. It took all his might, and then some. He fought the urge to jump to his feet, run blindly into the countryside and search; that would take ages. He knew he was too late anyway, and time he could not afford to waste.

The man reached down toward him, and Dager being a trusting sort of boy, naturally assumed that the man's intentions were to help him up. He did not expect it when he was lifted roughly at the waist and thrown upon the man's hip! Dager struggled right away. He even took the rock that was still tight within his fist, and threw it down, onto the man's foot. The man gruffly held the boy out in front of him and stood him up. Dager smiled sweetly. He already felt sorry and hoped he wouldn't get in trouble for having thrown the rock. He was in the middle of thinking just that and smiling, when the man swiftly produced a smelly cloth from within his cape, and forced it over Dager's mouth. The boy's smile disappeared as he was forced to inhale the rotten fumes that covered his face. The man picked him up and put him back upon his hip, and began to walk away.

Dager's head bobbed up and down with each massive step the man took. With heavy, heavy lids he could see that they were heading into the forest; that dark and scary forest that he was not allowed to go into without the company of either of his parents. He turned his head one last time in the direction of his home, and sadly reached his little hand out toward it, before he fell into a deep, drug induced sleep.

The minute Dager lost consciousness, Mod's connection with him was gone. The only lead Mod had was to go into the forest and search. He was lucky to know that much. And if that failed, if he searched that horrible forest from root to treetop with still no sign of his son, he would hunt down Croy. Croy was undoubtedly the man who had taken his son. Although he had no more of the vision, Mod continued to sit there and rock for a while longer. It was all he could do, to not let out a heart wrenching wail, and if it weren't for his wife and daughter being nearby, he would have done just that. How in the world , he wondered, would he break the news to his wife and tell her wife what he'd just witnessed? He tried to remain calm as he wiped the tears from his eyes and straightened out his legs. He finally stood, and on weakened legs, walked out of his home, coming to rest against a tree in his backyard. Finally, when he felt that he'd regained his courage, he made his way back to the hut. Once there, he gathered his wife and daughter into his arms and told them what had become of Dager. Goy wailed as only a mother who'd lost her child could, while Lucia sobbed for the loss of her playmate. Incredibly, over the next two years, while Lucia's memories of her brother had begun to fade, her parents never gave up hope that someday and somehow, Dager would return to them.

Present Day

Mod weaved his way through the last of the trees. He did not keep to the path; he always veered away from it. Not only did he not trust it, but it was the route that everyone was expected to take. He bucked the system every step of the way. Finally, nothing stood before him and the meeting chambers; the dreaded place where in the next short while, his fate would surely be determined. He climbed the high stone steps and pulled on the rope to ring the bell. He rang the bell not once, not twice, but three times; lest there be no mistake that this was indeed, a matter of the highest importance. A sharp, shrill voice bellowed out from the crude lookout window above him.

"I see it's you, Mod. What business have you here? What is so urgent that you feel the need to address the high council today? You don't have an appointment, man." Mod looked up at the mouse of a man with the scrawny voice who'd called down to him. Face to face, he was nothing more than a simpleton. Obviously he felt pretty important, perched up high in the window of the meeting chambers. Without uttering a single word in reply, Mod made eye contact with the foolish man who should have known better, and concentrated. The fool's face immediately softened.

"Right away, Mod! I'm coming, I'm coming! I'll let you in!" Mod smiled. The door in front of him strained against its old and worn out hinges, and was pulled open. Any day now, Mod knew that the door would give up and either remain it its opened state, or stay closed forever. Nothing in this blasted Village of Hurtsmire was ever maintained.

The mouse-like man nodded his head up and down, and motioned for Mod to enter the meeting chambers. He followed along as he scurried through the foyer and Mod smiled again as he realized that his referring to him as 'mouse-man' was more than fitting. All Mod could do now was wait, while the council was summoned. As he stood there, tall and proud like most men do, he knew full well in that uncanny way that Curors have of knowing, that this would be a very long wait. Time was of the essence and so he called out to Goy. He raised his hands to his chest and squeezed his medallion. The image of Goy appeared right away, and he watched as she looked up suddenly. She was so in tune with him, that already she could feel his presence.

*"Mod, what is it? Are you alright?"*

*"Yes, Goy. I am waiting for the high council to arrive. I think it would be best if the two of you go on without me. My father said where to go. You and Lucia will be okay. Just be sure to take enough supplies, love."*

*"But, Mod! Neither Lucia nor I have ever been to the surface. I don't want to go without you, not so far away!"*

*"But go you must, Goy. I promise to follow as soon as I am able. You heard my father. You must hurry."*

*"Alright then, Mod. We'll do as you say. May the Serpent protect us."*

*"No worries about that, Goy. I do believe the Serpent is on our side today."* Unfortunately for Mod, he could not have been more wrong.

# 3

## JOURNEY TO THE SURFACE

Goy clasped her hands together and silently made a wish. And then she finished packing her daughter's small bag.

"What is it, Ma? Were you speaking with my da?" Lucia could easily see it by her mother's telltale, far off expression, but she asked anyway. Goy nodded at her child and replied.

"Aye, love. Your father is going to be a tad late in joining us. We have to go on without him." Goy tightened the drawstring on her shoulder bag and made for the door. Lucia grimaced and still had not budged. "Well then, child! Let's go get your brother!" Obediently, Lucia forced one reluctant foot in front of the other, and followed her mother out of their home and into the light of day. Single file they marched, without exchanging a word for quite some time. Once clear of the village, Goy headed straight for the Clay Peaks that lay just east of the Great Pond. Lucia had the funny feeling that she'd been this far at least once, but she couldn't remember any details.

"Ma, have we been here before?" she asked as they ducked under branches and stepped over fallen logs, leaves and twigs that littered the seldom used path. Her mother smiled.

"Yes, we have, but it was long ago. Often, your father, brother, you and I would sit on the beach of the Great Pond and enjoy picnic lunches. We would spend the entire day skipping rocks on the water and splashing about. Do you remember any of that?" It pained Goy as she dryly recalled that their last visit to the area had been shortly before Dager went missing. And since that day, the family had not been on one single day trip. Rather, they'd waited anxiously near home, hoping for word of his safety or whereabouts. Lucia hustled to keep up.

"No, I only remember this hike, I think."

"Love, perhaps once we reach the beach, you'll remember more." And they trudged on. They had passed not another soul on the journey and Goy shook her head as she thought of the other villagers who were always too preoccupied with themselves to take their children anywhere. Day in and day out, most of them sat in their miserable huts, huddled together over hot tea talking silly nonsense about their neighbours. This one or that one, it never mattered whom; they easily found someone to criticize and pick apart.

Goy and Mod never did fit in with such nonsense, and that had always suited the both of them, just fine. Their decision to not participate in the gossip often made them the hot topic of the day; something they had long ago learned well to ignore.

"Are we there yet, ma? I don't see any beach!" Lucia complained. Her legs were starting to cramp and she certainly felt like she'd just run a marathon. The skeeter and ground bugs were starting to come out too, and had begun to dine on her bare feet, making them itch. She was becoming quite fed up. As she walked, she tried to look and see what, if anything was beyond her mother's form in front of her. But, all she could see was more trail, more logs to step or climb over, and she assumed that most likely there would be more bugs. She shuddered at the very idea of hungry, hungry bugs with sharp teeth, just looking to munch on sweet young flesh such as her own, and wrapped her arms tightly across her chest. Suddenly, just as her mother reached the crest of a hill, she stopped and turned toward her child.

"Come, love. Take a look at this view!" With a sudden burst of energy, Lucia bounded up the hill and stood side by side with her mother, taking hold of her hand in the same motion. Her breath caught in her throat and in that same instant, all of her itches, aches and worries had become a thing of the past. From where they stood, the earth dipped down into an endless green valley. Flowers were in full bloom everywhere Lucia looked, and they were gigantic! The blooms grew upon velvety green stalks; the likes of which she couldn't recall having ever seen before. The colours were not pasty and dull, like the ones in the village that she was used to. This, right in front of her, was nature at its best. Undisturbed, vibrant growth which swayed gracefully to and fro in the slight breeze. The breeze brought with it, a mixture of fragrance, each one unique, but once each scent danced and swirled together, becoming one, it was like breathing in the very essence of a rainbow. Almost in unison, Lucia and her mother inhaled deeply and sighed. The scenery was breathtaking. At the bottom of the valley, almost in the center, standing proud and tall; as though watching over the entire valley like noble caretakers from ancient times, were the Clay Peaks. There were three of them and they were arranged in order of size. Perfectly conical in shape and completely grey in colour. The exact colour of clay. There was no vegetation at all on the Peaks. Just clay, by the looks of it, and more clay. Goy knelt down and wrapped an arm around her daughter's waist. She pointed beyond the Peaks.

"On the far side of the Peaks, lies the Great Pond. That is where we must go, love. What do you think of the valley?" Lucia's eyes were still big and round with wonder.

"Oh, Ma, it's so beautiful! Can you draw it for me someday?" Goy was an amazing artist and drew most things that caught her daughter's eye. Drawing was her passion, second of course, to her family. She'd been drawing landscapes and portraits practically since she'd learned to walk. People were always trying to buy or barter for her artwork, but none of it was ever for sale. Goy drew from her heart, and out of love. Not for fame nor riches.

"Of course I will draw it for you. I don't think though, that even I could ever do beauty such as this, justice. But I will do my best. Anyway, we'd better get going now." She stood and held onto Lucia's hand again, and together they half ran, half walked down the flower lined path that led them to the middle of the valley. The earth was soft and sponge-like beneath their feet. Here, no logs crossed the trail, no branches scratched their legs in protest and there were no ground bugs nor skeeters at all. Lucia was relieved, and she was sure that they had entered into some sort of paradise. Even the sky had magically turned from the softest blue to an unbelievably cool violet. And they continued on.

As they neared the Clay Peaks, the flowers became smaller and less colourful. Pretty, but less. It was the only way Lucia could think to describe them. She was curious and questioned her mother.

"Ma, why have the flowers shrunk and gotten dim?" Goy laughed at her ever inquisitive child.

"The closer we get to pure clay, the less minerals and nutrients there are in the soil.

Nothing can grow on pure clay, and that's why soon there will be just that; nothing but clay. But you'll see, Lucia. Once we pass the Clay Peaks, the flowers and trees and grass will sprout up again. Especially near the Great Pond, because as you know, plants love water. Rather interesting, isn't it?"

"Yes! Ma, you'll have to draw this too, okay?" Goy laughed again.

"Aye, it's a deal. We're almost there, love." Goy knew that soon she'd have to leave her daughter's side, and it was best to prepare her for it ahead of time. The sooner the better, in fact. And as she was thinking just that, she gave Lucia's hand an extra squeeze. Lucia looked up at her mother knowingly.

"It's almost time, isn't it, Ma?"

"Aye, it is. Just remember that we wouldn't ever expect you to do something that you weren't capable of doing." They were making their way between the first and second peak now, and stepped carefully over the mounds of clay that had crumbled over time, all the way from the top to the ground. The ground had become sticky underneath their feet, but it felt soothing and wonderful all at the same time. Lucia squealed with delight. This was even more fun than playing in the mud!

"I know, Ma." Lucia answered half-heartedly, as her main concern at the moment was squishing the wet clay between her toes. Goy tugged gently on her daughter's hand to hurry her along.

"Listen now, love. Once we are on the surface, I will set up camp near our route. I'll point you in the direction of the village, but you must go there on your own. Dager cannot yet see that you are with an adult. You mustn't talk with any surface people. In fact, don't even make eye contact with them. They are not like us, love. The surface people, or at least the ones whom I've heard of, are no good at all." And then, almost as an afterthought, she added, "Perhaps that's why that nasty Croy gets along with them so well."

"Croy! Oh, I'm not going to run into him, am I?" Lucia came down with a sudden case of the shivers as she asked.

"Oh, no. I'm sure Croy will be too busy down in the village to worry about us, love." In fact, with a nauseating feeling in the pit of her stomach, Goy knew it to be true.

Finally, Goy and Lucia were free of the Clay Peaks and the path they were on became surrounded by plant life and beauty once again. The Great Pond lay before them. Lucia was delighted when she spotted three bigger than normal frogs nearest the shore, hopping from lily pad to lily pad. The amphibians either didn't notice or didn't care that their world had been intruded upon by the mother and child, and so they continued their careless frolicking about. Lucia laughed out loud when she saw the bigger frog miss its mark and land with a splash in the crystal-clear water. She watched for it to come back up again, and almost shuddered when it did, for the frog, she was certain, was glaring directly at her. She hurried up to stay closer to her mother and didn't dare look the frog's way again. Surely, she'd been mistaken. But perhaps she shouldn't have laughed when it fell into the water, she surmised. Obviously, she had insulted the frog. She grabbed hold of her mother's ample skirt anyway, just for good measure.

Goy circled the pond and headed straight for a thicket of willows that grew upon the farthest shore. Lucia followed her across the fine sand that circled the water. They were now exactly opposite from where the frogs had been, and Lucia breathed a great sigh of relief. Goy came to a stop in the middle of the willows, and sat right down on the damp ground. She patted the earth beside her, motioning for her daughter to do the same. Instead, Lucia plunked herself down right on her mother's lap.

"Now Lucia, you must listen to me carefully." She hoisted her daughter up and firmly placed her on the ground in front of her. After all, now was not the time for coddling. Lucia looked at her mother intently. "I've already told you to veer away from the surface people. But your brother, I do believe, you'll recognize, right away." Lucia opened her mouth to protest, but Goy would have none of that. She put her fingers to her lips and shushed her before the child had the chance.

"His hair is the colour of pure gold, Lucia. Much the same as yours. His eyes are as blue as the very sea that protects our world. They are the colour of yours, mine, and everyone else we know. When he sees you love, he will follow you back to me." Lucia hopped to her feet and whined.

"How can you be sure? How do you know he'll follow me and how do you know I'll know him?" Goy smiled and reached up for her daughter's hand. Gently she pulled the girl back down to a sitting position.

"There are things we just know, Lucia. Some people call it instinct and some people are fool enough to ignore the things they should know. While you grow, if you learn to trust your deeper feelings and follow your instincts, you will learn that they are, more often than not, correct. For instance, how did your grandfather know where to find Dager? How does he know that Dager would be in the market today?" Lucia scrunched up her nose.

"That's not fair, Ma! We all know that Granda is magical, anyway." Goy nodded in agreement.

"To a certain extent, yes he is magical, for he is a Curor. He has fantastic healing powers, that much is true. But let's just agree that what he knows is half magical and half instinct. For example, I don't think it was magic that told your grandfather that Dager does not trust grownups. I know, it's all incredible, Lucia. But you have to believe. Believe in your grandfather, but most importantly, you must believe in yourself." Lucia's chest puffed out a little and she was overcome with a feeling of pride. She let go of her mother's hand and stood again.

"Alright, Ma. I will believe in myself and all that you've said. I'll bring Dager back to us, and I'll do it today!" Tears mixed with pride and fear sprung from the corners of Goy's eyes as she stood and gave her daughter a hug. Wordlessly then, she led her to the tallest willow that stood in the center of the small clearing they were in. She knelt down and began pulling brush, branches and leaves from the base of the thick trunk. Lucia followed her lead and began to help. In a matter of seconds, they had revealed an opening. A crevice of sorts, that was large enough for little more than a body to squeeze through.

"Ma!" Lucia exclaimed in surprise. She poked her head through the hole and looked down. But all she could see was darkness. Scary, creepy darkness. She got the shivers again and backed away. Goy laughed.

"I'll go first, and it really isn't as bad as it looks! It's just a hollow tree that leads to a tunnel in the bottom of the pond. We'll follow that tunnel, and it will eventually take us to the surface." Goy watched as her daughter trembled again, and she wondered what had happened to the brave child who had stood before her only moments ago. But Goy could spend no more time explaining and convincing Lucia. She tightened the strap of her shoulder bag, and without even a look back, squeezed through and into the trunk, and landed with a soft splash below. Lucia was stunned by her mother's abrupt departure. Suddenly, she heard a branch break behind her. She swung around in the direction of the noise, but saw nothing. She was alone. Wasn't she?

Another sharp crack, followed by the crunching of leaves. Lucia swallowed hard, and then forced her body into the crevice. In the next instant she was gone, and all that was left standing in the clearing of the willows, were the three large ancient frogs. The biggest one winked at the others, they croaked, then in in single file, hopped all the way back to their side of the pond.

Lucia fell with a splatter into the water at the bottom of the old tree. The small crevice grew wider with each paddle and kick that she gave, and soon she was able to turn her body so that she was pointing headfirst. She had not been swimming for some time and was quite enjoying it. She took a deep breath in, allowing quite naturally, the water to fill first her mouth, then her throat and lungs. It tingled at first, but as soon as her breathing became regular again, the water felt no different from breathing in the air. And as she swam on, dutifully following her mother, she wondered about the surface dwellers. It had been said that they were not able to breathe underwater. She could not imagine living a life with those kinds of limitations.

Goy looked back once, and much to her relief,

she saw her daughter paddling along behind. Despite all else, she thought, what an adventure this must be for her. She reached the end of the tunnel, and then waited for Lucia to catch up. As soon as she did, Goy pushed off, skimming the ocean floor with the underside of her body. They had to stay as close to the bottom as possible, for she'd been warned about just how shallow the ocean was at this point. Lucia followed suit, willing herself to concentrate only on following her mother. She didn't dare look at all the wonderful shells and other small treasures that littered the ocean floor, just fractions of an inch beneath her, for then she would become distracted. And Lucia knew better than anyone else, just how easily that could happen to her.

# 4

## BOY MEETS GIRL

After eating the pigs' grub, Dager headed straight for the water trough nearest the barn to clean up. He knew he'd made a horrible mess of himself, and he had to make it right before the hag found out. And while he scrubbed at his clothing with an old corn broom, he wondered about the voice he'd heard. Could it have been a dream? He really didn't think so, for his dreams were a lot different than that had been. And what if at the market, he *did* see a girl he'd never seen before? What then? Should he follow her? Then, as he dried himself off with a burlap sack, he decided that he probably would. As long as he didn't get caught, he had nothing to lose. He then stuffed his hand into the bag of dried corn and filled his pocket with it. He did not know how long he might have to follow the girl and that meant that he also had no idea where his next meal would come from.

"Boy!" The hag screeched for him. Dager dusted himself off with his hands once again just in case, and stepped out from the shadows of the barn. He patted his pocket to make sure there was no evidence of the corn he'd stolen. Lastly, he pulled his tattered shirt farther down over the top of his pants, and headed for the direction of her shack. The hag was sitting in the horse drawn wagon, but when she saw the boy approaching, she quickly jumped to the ground. She went straight for the rear of the vehicle and held up the rope. Obediently, Dager held out his wrists, which she promptly bound together. The rope was not kind to his skin, and began to chafe it immediately. Dager knew better than to complain, and he ignored his discomfort by thinking only about the voice he'd heard earlier, and of course about the mysterious girl.

"What's that yer smirkin' 'bout, boy? Somethin' strike you as bein' funny? Somethin' I should know 'bout?" the hag scowled as she glared at him. She knew something was different about her boy, but she couldn't quite put her finger on it. Quickly, Dager put on the mask she so desired to see. Fear filled his eyes and his mouth drooped into a frown.

"That's more like it, pond scum. You've nothin' to be grinnin' 'bout, do ya?" Dager shook his head, no. Satisfied now that she'd put him back in his rightful place, she cackled and hopped back onto the seat of her wagon. With a slim, leather whip she snapped at the horse's behind, forcing it onward. Even the old gelding knew better than to whinny in protest at her wicked abuse. The hag steered him slowly in the direction of the village. Dager staggered along behind, at the end of the rope he so detested.

Two long miles later, they reached the edge of the village. Market day only came once every two weeks for them, and it was the only chance Dager ever had to go anywhere. Strangely enough, aside from the stinging, raw wrists he was sure to end up with by the day's end, he always looked forward to the outing. It was an opportunity for him to see other people, places and things. A couple of times on previous trips, he'd even made brief eye contact with other boys in the same situation, but to his dismay, he rarely if ever, saw the same boys twice. And girls? To see girls in his situation was almost unheard of. The only girls out and about were of the free variety and were tightly held onto by their parents at all times. The free children of this land were always freshly bathed and dressed in nice, clean clothes, Dager had learned over time. The ones like him, who were bought and sold like ordinary merchandise, were easily recognized by their filthy condition and by the rags they wore.

The hag pulled into her usual parking spot at the end of the dirt street. That of course, was in case she was caught again, stealing and hiding goods in her skirt, and she'd have to make a quick escape. That had happened often enough for most of the merchants to frown uneasily once the hag made her presence known. They would keep a sharp eye on their wares until she moved on.

She hopped down from her seat and tied the horse's rein to the wooden stand, and then made for Dager. He readily held out his hands, and at once, cleverly donned the expression of despair and helplessness. He knew it was most important, especially now that they were in the market, that she suspect nothing out of the ordinary. As she always did, as she untied his rope, she scolded him.

"Ya know well, which shops boys ain't allowed ta enter into. Ya need remindin', boy?" She raised her hand, ready to strike him, but Dager was quick to shake his head, no. Her hand dropped back to her side. "I expect ta see ya when I look for ya, so don't ever be out of my sight. I'll sic the hounds on ya. Ya know the consequences, eh?" Dager nodded, keeping his eyes to the ground. He knew full well how long it would actually take her to round up the hounds, and so he didn't take the threat too seriously. In fact, the lead hound was due to give birth any day now, and wouldn't be any help to her at all. The other two hounds, he'd made good friends of, and he couldn't see that they'd ever do him harm. Foremost on his mind, was that he couldn't wait for the hag to be on her way so he could watch the people milling about. Surely the girl was out there somewhere. And little did he realize it yet, but his heart was set on it.

At the very same time as the hag was untying

the knot in Dager's rope, Lucia and her mother arrived on the surface.

"Oh, Ma! It's so hot up here!" As Lucia complained, she splashed the cool water from the river onto her face and neck. Goy laughed as she used her hands to wring out her daughter's long blonde hair. The water ran down the girl's back, refreshing her at the same time.

"Well, love. I don't think you'll need the dry change of clothes I brought for you, after all. You'll be good and dry under this hot sun, by the time you reach the market." Goy looked around cautiously as she spoke, and breathed a sigh of relief when she saw that there was not another soul in sight, which meant that nobody had seen them emerge from the water. She looked about and saw nothing but the water, sparse grass, and an expanse of hot, cracked earth. She took her child by the hand, swung her bag back over her shoulder, and together they walked in the direction of the pale looking vegetation that grew at the bank of the river.

"This is where I will wait for you and Dager, Lucia. This clump of brush with the tall tree on the end. See it?" She pointed to the lonely, branchless twig of a tree that was gangly and lifeless - more so than the others that stood beside it. Lucia nodded, scrunching up her nose again.

"What if I go the wrong way? I may get mixed up and go the wrong way out of the village, Ma!" They sat down together under what little shade the plants could provide. Lucia quietly watched as her mother pulled the drawstring of her bag loose. The sides fell softly to the ground, instantly revealing its contents. Goy plucked up a small, neatly wrapped package and began opening it, explaining all the while.

"No, you won't go the wrong way, love. I've brought you your very own serpent pointer!" Lucia oohed and aahed. She'd seen them in the possession of the older kids at school, but she never imagined she'd have one of her own. Goy passed it to her child. "Do you understand how it works?" Lucia nodded her head up and down, and then stood up with her precious new tool in her hand.

"Yes, I think so. Don't I spin it on the ground and when it comes to a stop it should be pointing north?" Goy laughed. She hadn't until now, realized just how much Lucia had been learning, simply by watching others.

"Yes, that's exactly right, Lucia!" Goy was still smiling as she watched her child try out the pointer for the first time. Lucia held it up against the light and admired it long and hard. It was hand carved from the finest soapstone ever discovered in the Empire, as all serpent pointers were. It was in the shape of the revered crimson serpent. Sunken deep within the eye sockets were sparkling red rubies. It was the most beautiful pointer that Lucia had ever seen. Lucia gently placed it on the ground in front of her, and gave it a quick and even spin. The pointer spun wildly, its eyes flickering bright in the sunshine; and finally came to rest, pointing beyond the brush they were nestled in. Goy clapped her hands.

"Yes! By my calculations, that's the exact direction the pointer should be indicating, Lucia. I think you have the hang of it well enough."

She passed the wrapping to Lucia so she could safely bundle it up and stow it in the little apron of her dress. Once Lucia had it tucked away, her mother passed her two more bundles and explained.

"These packages contain dried fruit and some nuts, Lucia." Lucia stepped backward, as though accepting them might bring her bad luck. "No, love. You must take them and keep them with you. What if for some reason you are delayed in coming back to me? What if you're not delayed, but Dager needs grub? It is simply a precautionary measure, my child," and for extra conviction, Goy added, "your father would expect you to have them with you." That in particular, happened to be the nudge Lucia needed. She stepped forth again and took the grub from her mother's hands. She tucked the bundles into the apron alongside her pointer.

"Is there anything else, Ma, that I may need?" Her little voice rang with an edge of sarcasm and she just about rolled her eyes into the back of her head. She stopped short of it as she remembered that doing so would provoke a good scolding. But this was all becoming way too complicated, way too fast for the little girl. She had been under the impression that this was to be an in and out kind of mission and having to bring grub along no longer made it seem that way. Goy reached out and took her child by both hands, looking her straight in the eye.

"No, only this." She then handed her daughter a small canteen of water. Lucia slung its strap over her head and left shoulder, so that it hung comfortably under her right arm. "Just remember to stay as clear of surface dwellers as you can. Once you've caught Dager's eye, lead him out of the market and down the road back here to me. And don't forget, Lucia. We love you with all our hearts." Goy pulled Lucia tight to her chest and gave her a giant hug. Lucia squeezed back almost as hard. They pulled away at the same time, and Lucia turned and skipped away in a northbound direction. She turned and gave her mother one final wave, right before following the bend over the hill, on the old dirt road. As soon as Lucia was out of sight, Goy unfolded her easel that she'd collapsed and stowed away in her bag. She set it up and began to sketch. If anyone should come around and ask what she was doing, sitting on the bank of the river, she would be able to answer quite honestly, "Why drawing, of course!"

It seemed to take forever before Lucia reached the village that the dirt road led to. Her legs were aching now and her body was pouring icky, unfamiliar sweat. The ground beneath her feet was so hot that she didn't dare let them touch down upon it for long. In an attempt to keep her tender soles from burning, she skipped along as much as she could. There had been just one intersection in the road, but she barely hesitated at it, as she knew that she was supposed to keep going straight ahead. Finally, once she reached the village, she was surprised to see how big it was! Villages in her empire consisted only of a few pull-along carts upon which people sold or bartered their homegrown grub or crafts. These in front of her were large, permanent structures made of wood, with see through windows and doors! The really good thing about them, was that they provided the ground with ample shade, and her poor feet immediately felt relief from the heat. There were no goods in the street that she could see; all that cluttered the street were lots and lots of surface dwellers.

The first thing she came upon was a large, ugly, brown four legged beast with a big nose, a long tail, and long dark hair which grew all the way from the top of its head to the base of its neck. Lucia veered far away from the creature, but kept her eyes on it, in case it made any sudden moves toward her. She was relieved to see that it was stuck to the spot by a rope. Not only that, but surely the big cart that it was attached to from behind would slow it down, should it ever decide to give chase. More curious yet, was the rope that hung from the back of the cart, which was not attached to anything at all. Lucia decided that surface dwellers were strange indeed.

Speaking of the surface dwellers, Lucia was being ever so careful to not look any of them straight in the eye. Aside from the odd way of dress and the clumsy looking things which they wore upon their feet, they looked harmless enough. Unknowingly, she might have assumed that they were not a lot different in form than the people of the Empire. However, she knew better than that. She knew from all the learning she'd done, that their appearance was a disguise. Deep down, they were hideous beasts not to be trusted for a second.

She passed all sorts of them as well as a few more of the beastie carts, as she made her way through the crowded market place. Mostly the surface dwellers consisted of adults, although there were a few boys straggling about. They were dressed far worse than even the poorest people who lived where Lucia had come from. She shuddered at the idea of ever having to wear such rags.

By the time Lucia made it to the middle of the village, she felt very strange when she became aware that there weren't any little girls around at all. Not even one, and she was near panic when she realized how obvious her presence must be. Nonetheless, she kept walking forth.

There were, altogether little more than half a dozen boys she'd walked by, but with their mournful, downcast gazes it was impossible for her to find a boy with blonde hair and brilliantly blue eyes. But, she was determined to keep her end of the bargain and do all that she possibly could do to find Dager. She walked all the way to the very last building, looking for him this way and that, and then turned around to go back from where she'd come. She stopped for a moment, and took a small sip of water from her canteen. And as she did so, she worried about her predicament. Granda said Dager would be at the market on this day, so where was he, then?

Dager shuffled his feet in frustration. He'd been looking everywhere for the mysterious girl, all the while keeping in full view of the old hag. And that hadn't been easy! He climbed up onto the back of his master's cart to sit a while, when something very bright and out of place caught the corner of his eye. He lifted his arm, shielding his eyes from the hot, midday sun, blinked hard and looked again. Sure enough, he saw a strange, brightly dressed girl, and she was walking in his direction! She just *had* to be the one the voice told him about. He hopped down onto the ground and began to move her way.

Lucia saw the boy right away, the one who seemed to be heading right in her path. But sadly, his eyes were not like hers at all, and his hair was certainly not the colour of gold. It was more like the colour of dirt. Dirty dirt. She was a mere six feet away from him when very unexpectedly, someone grabbed her from behind!

"What's this we have here, mate?" The man who'd grabbed Lucia growled to his grubby friend. Her captor spun her around so the both of them could take a better look. Lucia's heart caught in her throat. She was so terrified that she wouldn't have been able to speak or yell out no matter how hard she tried. The grubby friend ran his fingers through her clean, blonde hair, and then replied gruffly.

"Me thinks this lass forgot her mammy somewheres! Where's your mammy, lassie?" And then he moved his face to within inches of hers; so close that she could smell his rank breath. The skin on his face was rough, dry and cracked; reminding her of the dirt beneath her feet. Lucia gagged when he breathed heavily into her face and she was instantly convinced that something must have died inside him, to cause him to smell so incredibly bad. And by now, her all-important mission in finding her long, lost brother was as far from her mind as anything could ever be.

"HEY!" The men were just as startled as Lucia was, by the little boy with the big voice who'd pushed himself in between the girl and the grubby friend. The captor tightened his grip on Lucia's shoulders, as though this were no more than a game of finders keepers, and she was the prize. Lucia's eyes widened when she saw that this was none other than the boy with the pale eyes and dirty hair who'd been walking toward her. Why, he couldn't be any older than six, but he was acting so courageous. The grubby friend leered at him.

"What'cha want, scum? This here's none of yer business." The boy stuck out his chin at the man and placed his hands firmly upon his hips. It was obvious that he was not going to back down. Then he scowled and bravely spat on the ground between them, as though drawing a line in the sand.

"Yeah," he replied, "It is my business. This lass belongs with the hag. I'm sure you know the hag?" And he directed his eyes toward the hag's horse drawn wagon. Upon seeing the wagon and realizing to whom the boy was referring, the captor released Lucia. The boy continued, "And it's my job to look after this lass while the hag shops." Then he turned to the frightened, wide-eyed girl and asked, "Want me to get her for you now?" The men shook in their boots, backed away and then suddenly disappeared into the crowd of people. Lucia and Dager were left facing one another. Lucia remembered well how she had been instructed not to talk with any surface dwellers, but she quickly decided that talking to just this one boy would be okay. After all, he'd probably just saved her life.

"Thank you for saving me," she stammered quietly, as she was still quite shaken up. The boy eyed her up and down, but said nothing. He was still trying to decide if this was the girl he was supposed to follow. She eyed him back, smiled weakly, and then asked.

"What would those men have done with me if you hadn't come along?" The boy shifted his eyes to her strange, bare feet, before replying.

"They'd have taken you home probably to be a kitchen lass for their wives. Why aren't you with your owners?"

"Owners? I don't have owners!" Lucia answered indignantly; though that wasn't the only thing she was upset about. Firstly, it seemed that they boy she was seeking was not in the market after all. Granda surely had been mistaken. Secondly, she had almost got herself snatched up! She'd already experienced enough of the surface to last her a lifetime, and her grandfather would just have to find another way to bring Dager home. Now it was time for her to say goodbye to the grubby little boy with the pale blue eyes.

"I have to go now. My ma is waiting for me." She told him as she looked at him long and hard one last time. She tried to smile, for she was extremely grateful for what he'd done. "Thank you for freeing me from those awful men." Dager nodded and backed away; he could tell that she was seconds away from taking her leave. If she really and truly was the one, was it possible that she didn't know that he was supposed to follow her? And her mother was waiting for her? Did that mean that she was also waiting for him? *His* ma? His real mother that the voice told him about?

"That's okay," he replied slowly, for he was thinking about too many things at once. "Just be careful and hurry on to your ma before anything else happens." He turned and headed back for the hag's wagon, climbed onto the back of it, and watched her go. He had a decision to make, and fast. He looked in the direction of the shop he'd last seen the hag enter, and there was no sign of her coming out yet. Dager knew, in a brand new way of knowing, that it was now or never. The girl was still in sight, but barely, and he figured that if he really hurried, he could catch up. Dager jumped down from the wagon one last time. As he made for the hag's gelding that was tied forlornly to the wooden stand, he dug into his pocket and pulled out the handful of dried corn. The horse almost let out a laugh when he saw him approach, for he was glad to see the kind boy who always took the time to brush and speak to him. He whinnied some more and then nibbled at the corn that lay on the boy's flat, outstretched hand. As he chewed, he looked up and into the boy's eyes. And when he did so, his mouth froze in mid-chew. The boy's eyes had changed. They sparkled anew, and the pale, lifeless colour that they had always been had suddenly changed to a bright blue. The horse stomped his foot, jumped, whinnied, and nodded his head, and then continued chewing.

Dager jumped back when the horse let out his little jump and nod. Did the horse know that he was leaving? And when he nodded at him, did that mean that he approved? Dager shook his head, for he knew that his imagination was only getting the best of him. His hand was empty of corn now, and he lovingly ran it down the length of the horse's long and horribly neglected mane. He leaned in close, so much so that his face was resting upon its nose, and then he whispered, "I am sorry. I'm going now, and I don't think I'll be back. But if I do? If I can come back? I'll free you for sure. You can run the wild outback with the rest of your brothers and sisters. After all, families are meant to be together, right?" As Dager spoke, hope flashed across his face and his eyes sparkled an even brighter blue. The horse nuzzled up against the boy, and then returned to his chewing. Dager stole another quick look to the shop, and then he took off running. He followed the pretty, but strangely dressed girl out of the market place. He knew that later, if he got caught, there would be consequences. After all, weren't there always consequences? But on this particular day, Dager did not plan on getting caught.

5

# THE ESCAPE

Dager stalked the girl, as an animal in the wild might stalk its prey. The major difference of course being, that he would not harm or eat her. He was so enchanted by her; she had the brightest blue eyes in the world and he had to see where she was going and perhaps to whom she belonged. To his family? To his real family? Would that mean that this girl was his sister? Needless to say, it appeared that she didn't belong to anyone at all. The voice could have been wrong.

No adult held her hand, and as plain as day he could see her bare back due to the open-back dress she wore, and it bore not even one faded nor new whip mark. And although he had never seen clothes like hers before, it was her scar free back that encouraged him the most. It was very much unlike his own. He wondered what it might be like to have never been on the receiving end of the sharp side of a whip.

As he followed her, slipping into alleys, ducking behind wagons, squeezing in and out of people who hadn't any cares, he noted that this girl was not worry-free. She didn't appear as joyous as he would have expected a free child to be. She was almost as skittish as he, so much so that he wondered if she were trying earnestly *not* to be followed. This adventure so intrigued him that soon his dreaded consequences were as far away from his mind as anything could ever be.

"Hey!" Dager yelled, for the second time that day. The girl whirled around. She was completely surprised to see that the grubby little boy who had saved her, was following her out of the village. Politely, she stopped and waited for him to catch up. As he did, his eyes were downward, focused completely on her bare feet again, which were beginning to burn up again since she'd stopped moving them. Lucia shifted uneasily from one foot to the other. Annoyed now, she rolled her eyes into the back of her head.

"What do you need? Why are you following me?" She just knew that she could not lead this surface dweller back to the river. How could she convince him to turn around and go back to where he'd come from? And then she watched as he removed the tattered shirt from his back and placed it on the ground between them. Dager knew how sore her feet must be from the hot earth, and he wondered where her shoes were;

after all, as poor as he was, he at least had shoes. Grateful to the boy for the second time that day, Lucia immediately stepped onto it. She felt instant relief from the heat, and then as she looked absently over her shoulder, in the direction she should be going, she repeated.

"I said, what do you need?" Dager smiled sheepishly at the girl who still hadn't bothered to give him a sideways glance, and then he replied.

"Well, I haven't much time to explain," and as he spoke, visions of the hag rounding up the hounds flashed through his head. What if she used someone else's hounds? Hounds that Dager had not made friends with? He knew it was possible, and by now he was thinking the worst. "And I know it's odd, but I think I'm supposed to follow you today." Lucia sucked in a deep breath. This grubby boy just couldn't be her brother! She turned her head and peered into his eyes, and as she did so, she gasped and her hand flew straight to her mouth. His eyes were no longer the mournful, lifeless eyes that they had been only moments before. Could this be Dager? No, she decided. It must have been the shade of the buildings that had disguised his eyes earlier. She still did not think that this was the right boy. Having made up her mind about that, she regained her composure, and then as a matter-of-factly, told him.

"I don't think so. The boy who is supposed to follow me has golden hair like mine! Your hair is not blonde!" She looked sadly at him, for he looked desperate. She wished there was something she could do to help, but at this point she knew she'd be lucky enough to get herself back to the water, let alone bring a stray boy along. Lucia stepped off of his shirt, picked it up and handed it back to him. "Thanks again, but I must hurry off." And then she turned and began skipping away. Dager balled up the shirt in his hands and hurried after her.

"Now I *know* I have to follow you! What is your name?" He caught up and walked by her side. Lucia laughed impatiently. She really didn't have time for this, and she turned to the boy, eyeing him crossly.

"I think the question is, what is *your* name? Tell me yours and then I just may tell you mine!" Dager had not expected her snappy reaction, and he hesitated, but only for a moment. He'd never before had the opportunity to speak his name out loud, and after all, he'd only learned that he had one, that morning.

"My name is Dager." Time stood still and Lucia stopped dead in her tracks. Automatically, Dager threw his shirt back onto the ground for her to stand on.

"What was that you said?" she asked seriously, sounding very much like her father would, in a state of affairs such as this. The boy looked nervously over his shoulder. After all, the hag would be returning home this way any minute now; turning east at the intersection he and the girl had just crossed.

"I said, I am Dager!" The two children stood facing each other again, much the same as they had in the market place when they were nothing more than strangers. Lucia's hand flew to her mouth again. She *had* heard right! Blonde hair or not, it had to be Dager, for how else could he know that name?

"Oh!" Lucia managed to sputter. She watched him look nervously over his shoulder again. "Is someone going to look for you?" And now she shivered as she remembered the two awful men. Dager bobbed his head up and down.

"Uh-huh! Can we go to where we're going and soon?" She nodded and grabbed him by the arm to hurry him along. As she did, he winced and pulled it back. Lucia furrowed her brows together and took hold of his arm again, but this time by the elbow. And it was then that she saw why he'd drawn it back as sharply as he had. His wrists, on both arms in fact, had been rubbed raw. She cringed as she realized how painful his wounds must be. She knew that she had to get him away from there, and fast.

"Hurry!" she ordered, and both children broke into a run. They ran farther from the village and closer to the point where the two rivers met. Once Dager felt they were far enough from the intersection to be seen, he slowed down to a walk. He watched as Lucia took a long, badly needed drink from her canteen, and he wished that he could do the same. But he did not have a canteen, and the idea that she might share with him had not even once crossed his mind. He was to say the least, surprised, when she stuffed the stopper back in and threw it to him. He caught it with both hands, raising his eyebrows at the same time.

"There's enough in there for you, go ahead and finish it!" Lucia commanded, as if sharing were a perfectly normal thing to do. Then she reached into her apron and pulled out the bundles of grub. Dager drank eagerly and then politely handed the canteen back to her. At the same time, she thrust one of the bundles into his hand. He brought it up to his nose and sniffed. It smelled very good, but he was not about to open his until she opened hers. Unfortunately for him, she didn't seem to be in a big hurry to do that.

"Why did you look so surprised, Dager? Weren't you thirsty, too?" Lucia couldn't begin to understand the kind of treatment that her brother was accustomed to. Dager didn't know how to explain his reaction, but he did the best he could.

"On hot days, mostly the hag would drink a lot of water from her jug," he began, and as he relived it, his mouth became dry and his tongue stuck to the roof of his mouth. He swallowed hard, and then continued, "but I wasn't allowed to have any. She doesn't share anything, unless it is something that has gone bad and she doesn't want it anymore. And she *always* wants her water." Lucia gasped and thought long and hard for a moment, remembering her Granda's words about *'de bad mama'*.

"How can you not have water? Everyone needs water!" Lucia looked at him from the corner of her eye, unsure as to whether she believed him or not.

"Oh, I had water, alright, just not from her jug. I drank from the troughs. The pigs, hounds and horses always have lots of water!" he smiled as he spoke, for he was thinking about the animals who'd kept him company for as long as he could remember. Suddenly he realized that he didn't even know what to call her, and he asked again, "Hey, what is your name?" Lucia laughed out loud and began untying her bundle. Dager did the same and was very pleased to see the dried fruit and nuts. He hadn't often seen the likes of this kind of grub, and he dug in greedily.

"My name is Lucia, silly!" She reached over with her free hand and tickled Dager in the ribs. Now it was Dager's turn to laugh out loud. Although she could remember little about him, how her memories were beginning to tingle and spark, and she thought that quite possibly, she did remember his laugh. "Do you know who I am to you?" she asked him sincerely, when she stopped laughing and chewing. "And how did you know that you were supposed to follow me?" They walked a few more paces before Dager answered. Lucia could see the gangly tree off in the distance now, and she knew that soon she'd better prepare him to meet their mother.

"Lucia? I think you are my sister." he looked at her hopefully, and much to his relief, she smiled and nodded at him. "A voice told me this morning, that while I was in the market today, I would see a strange girl. The voice told me to follow her." Dager's legs were aching now, and his feet were sweating, although not burning nearly as much as Lucia's. He looked absently at his surroundings. He'd never, ever been this far away from the hag's property before, and he couldn't help but listen for the barking of the hounds. "If we are going to see your ma, then she's my ma too, right?" And then, in a smaller, almost frightened voice, he half whispered, "*My* mama?" Lucia reached over and intertwined her fingers through his. They walked just that way; hand in hand for a short distance before Lucia replied.

"Yes, my ma is yours, too. And yes, you are my brother!" She looked over at him and saw that tears had welled up in his eyes. A great big lump suddenly formed in her throat at the very sight. Rather abruptly, he let go of her hand and they both stopped walking. Lucia yanked his shirt from the crook of his arm and stood on it, and with newfound patience that siblings ordinarily possess, she waited for his response. She could see that he was struggling to find the right words.

"Lucia, why did she sell *me* to the hag, then?" His voice became louder and shrill with each painful word. "Why did she keep you and sell *me*? Is it because I'm just a boy? And now she wants me back?" As he asked, he pondered the idea that he may not want to go back to a family that would so easily give him up. Lucia was completely stunned at his questions. Why did he think such nasty things? Is that what he'd been told? She began to cry. She sobbed for him and for the two years he must have spent believing those horrible things.

"No!" she wailed, and rubbed her eyes clear with the backs of her hands. Dager eyed her suspiciously.

"What then? Tell me!" he defiantly stuck out his chin again, the way she'd seen him do earlier, when he'd faced off the two awful men on her behalf. For a brief moment she thought he might even spit on the ground. She moved her feet back a few steps, just to be safe.

"Oh, Dager." She was so upset that she still sobbed and her chest heaved, but she forced herself to settle down long enough to tell him the truth. "Ma and Da did not sell you! An awful man named Croy, who lives in our land stole you! Our grandfather, whose voice I think you heard this morning, has been looking for you the entire time!" Dager's eyes couldn't have opened wider for anything. Could it be true? Had the old hag lied to him? And then sadly, he realized that she had. Every horrible thing she'd ever told him had been a lie and despondently, he knew that all Lucia was telling him was true. He reached his arms up around her shoulders and hugged her. He was used to hugging his animals; this was very different. Lucia hugged him back, and then in the next moment, pulled free of her brother, and stepped off of his shirt. She handed it back to him, and as she looked him straight in the eyes, she could easily see the brilliant blue that had at first, been missing. It seemed that the more truths her brother learned, the more his eyes were returning to their natural state.

"We can talk as we go, okay? But for now, our ma is waiting for us so we have to hurry on!" She sniffled back the last of her tears and they continued on their journey. The distance between the children and the gangly tree was becoming less with every step they took. Lucia knew that she'd never in her life, be happier to see her mother. But in the meantime, she still had some explaining to do with her brother. Dager silently walked by her side.

"We're not of the surface, Dager. We come from a land far greater than this. And way less hot!" Dager looked up at his sister quizzically. Not of this land? There was a different land than this one? He had always assumed that this, right in front of him, was all that there ever was and all that there ever would be. And then, as quick as a flash, he recalled his dreams. Did he dare ask? He threw caution to the wind and suddenly blurted out.

"Lucia, is our land not too hot and not too

cold?"

"Yes."

"Our family, is it a happy one?"

"Well, kind of. Our parents are very kind and very good, but they've been awfully sad ever since you were stolen. I know we'll be a happy family again, now!" Dager's heart caught in his throat. Is that what his dreams had been about all along? A world he had convinced himself never truly existed. Were those dreams his actual memories?

"Do they laugh, Lucia? Really laugh like they mean it?" Lucia scrunched up her nose at that very strange question, for she'd never considered there would be another kind of laugh. She answered him honestly.

"Yes, they do!"

"Is there *magic* in our land, Lucia?" he held his breath while he waited for her reply.

"Well yes, of course there is!" Dager's mind raced. He'd held onto his foolish dreams of nonexistent lands for as long as he could remember. Was that what they really were? Memories?

Now they only had the last hill to climb before they would be in full view of the river, and of course, in full sight of their mother. Lucia stopped, and Dager looked at her questioningly.

"Dager, our granda is worried that you won't trust our parents. You have to know that they are not like whomever it is that you've been with. Granda calls her the bad mama." Dager shook his head.

"I can't believe it. How does he know so much? The hag made me call her *'mama'*. I thought, until this morning, that just maybe she was my real mama. But Lucia, if our parents are anything like you, I don't think Granda has to worry!" And Dager had never been more sincere. This last hour, which he'd spent walking and talking with Lucia, was already like a dream come true. And he really felt, straight from the bottom of his heart, that things could only get better from now on.

"See that tree?" Lucia pointed to the gangly tree ahead, beyond the hill in the road that lay before them, much the same way their mother had pointed it out to her, but from the opposite direction. Dager nodded and she continued. "That tree is on the edge of the river bank. Our ma is waiting for us there. Are you ready to meet her?" Dager nodded eagerly again. He'd never, ever been more ready for anything in his whole life.

6

## THE CURE

By the time the regular council members had taken their seats, Mod had been standing there waiting for so long that he was very nearly at his wits' end. The highest member would naturally be the last to arrive. How could he make such a grand entrance, otherwise?

As soon as the highest member took his place, Mod respectfully moved from a standing to a kneeling position, lowered his head in the customary manner and waited. He heard the gavel land with an angry smack upon the podium. He gritted his teeth and braced himself against the high member's imminent wrath.

"Mod! Back so soon!" he snorted a wicked, mocking chortle at the Curor, whom he felt was, and forever would be, completely under his control. Mod, the ideal puppet whose strings he had command of; or so he thought. Mod ignored the slow-witted comments and listened to the patter of feet entering the cave. He knew they belonged to none other than the meddlesome villagers who were arriving now and making themselves comfortable. They had come only because they were curious. They had come to listen in on a meeting which, in the first place, was none of their business whatsoever. This large audience, Mod knew, would please the council members greatly, as they sat proudly on display, high above everyone else, on their beloved pyramid. A midday show. Something exciting to break the monotony of their humdrum, every day existences. The drums sounded, and then there was nothing left but uncomfortable silence. The gavel struck again.

"I see you've come on your own, Mod. Are you not playing with Croy, today? After all, wasn't he your partner the last time you saw fit to disturb me?" The councilor guffawed again and bowed to the applause that his spectators had awarded him with. They were indeed, enjoying the show. The councilor tapped Mod upon the shoulder, allowing him to stand. Mod wasted no time in doing so. He stood and deliberately looked at each council member in turn.

"Nay. Croy is no friend of mine. I've come to you to ask permission to leave our empire for only half a day's time." Mod ignored the sounds of mockery and laughter which had suddenly filled the cave. He raised his voice a notch, so he could be heard above it, as he continued. "My father has found my son. I wish to bring him home to us." The high member smacked his gavel down hard, and Mod returned to his knees and bowed his head.

"Mod! Are you such a fool? Are you to stand before me, fully aware of the rules which govern this village, and boldly ask for permission to break them? You? Our powerful and mighty Curor wishes to break the rules?" The cave was silent once more, and the member tapped Mod on the shoulder again. Mod stood and replied.

"I am no fool. You all know that my son, the next Curor in line, was stolen from Hurtsmire two years ago! What is best for the Village of Hurtsmire is all that I have in mind, Councilor. If Dager does not return, the lineage will be broken. My wife cannot bear another child. Dager is the only hope for the future of this great village." Mod ground his teeth together as he told his boldfaced lie. His only wish was to have his family together again. To speak untruths went completely against his grain, but he knew that in this instance, there would be no other way. The councilor gave him such an accusatory glare, that Mod had to wonder if he could see right through him. The gavel landed hard upon the podium again, and Mod fell to his knees.

Unexpectedly, from somewhere amidst the scores of people behind him, came a sudden ruckus. And then footsteps. Heavy footsteps. Mod recognized them right away. Croy soon knelt beside him and bowed his head.

"Croy! How dare you interrupt our meeting! Although I am not surprised that you could not keep away from an exciting event such as this one!" The high member could barely contain his glee. A round of applause rippled through the villagers again. As far as they were concerned, the show was getting better by the minute. The drums sounded, signaling silence again. The high member, eyeing the spectators, chose to entertain them some more. "Aye, man called Croy. I will allow you to share with us, what is so important that it could not wait!" he tapped him on the shoulder with his gavel. Croy, eager to oblige, stood.

"I've only come to you Councilor, because I believe that the future of Hurtsmire is at stake. You cannot honestly believe for a minute, that Mod wishes to return his son for *you*? His best interests do not even include this village. What he proposes to do, is to leave the village in an unprotected and vulnerable state while he holidays on the surface. For all we know, he could be away indefinitely. What guarantee could he possibly offer of his immediate return?" Croy looked intently at the high member, who had begun to twist each end of his moustache, this way and that. And that, Croy knew, was always a good sign.

Mod hung his head in resignation. By the end of this meeting, he knew that he would either be cast aside as his father had been, or he would have no choice but to quit his position as the Curor for the village. The high member nervously paced back and forth in front of the two men, before replying.

"You do have a point, Croy," he nodded enthusiastically then, as a brand new possibility occurred to him. A dramatic scenario that would surely go down in history. He tapped Mod on the shoulder with his gavel. Mod stood and grimly stared straight ahead. He could not, at this moment, bring himself to acknowledge the presence of the man called Croy. The high member smiled gleefully.

"Let us allow Mod to decide for himself, Croy. Mod! What is it going to be? You know that no reason is good enough for this village to be without a Curor for any length of time. If the return of your son depends on your departure, then I have to say that it is impossible. And would that not mean that once you were done curing for us, the Village of Hurtsmire would have to look elsewhere, anyway? What say you? Should Croy step in now, at this moment, as Curor for the Village of Hurtsmire, or would you rather stay until the end of your term?" Gales of laughter could be heard throughout the cave once more. In fact, the giggles, chuckles, and guffaws were so fierce that Mod was sure the floor was vibrating. His answer to the high member's question was simple, for he'd already made his choice the moment his father had found his son. Now it was his turn to smile. He turned to the high member.

"From this day forth, Councilor, I cease and desist all curing for the Village of Hurtsmire, in the Tasman Empire. The best of luck to you with your new Curor named Croy. I am sure you'll all be very happy together." And then he looked at the new Curor, who obviously had no real idea of what he was in for. Croy could not have been more surprised. He had not expected Mod to give up his title so easily, and without so much as a fight. "Now, if you will excuse me, I must go and bring my son home." Mod turned to leave, but stopped short when he felt the gavel rest upon his shoulder. He whirled about and once again faced the high member who had instantly turned an angry shade of red. He was enraged, because he had not received the reaction nor the results he had expected. Mod appeared not the least bit upset and it looked as though he had gotten exactly what he wanted all along. At that moment, no one dared blink for fear of missing a single thing.

"Mod! You think you can just come and go as you please? Is that what you think, man called Mod?" Mod stepped closer to him and replied vehemently.

"In fact, I do. I'm just a regular villager now, am I not? Everyone else in the village does as they please, do they not? What would make me any different, now?" The high member retorted with a satisfied gleam in his eye.

"The difference between you and them Mod, is that they all have a home. You do not. Not anymore. Go and live with your beloved blind, crippled father in his pathetic little cave. Your home, as of this day, belongs to Croy and his family. Now get out of here."

And now it was Mod who laughed. He laughed at the fools sitting high upon the pyramid and he laughed at the spectators who'd come for the sport of sitting in. He'd never in his life, felt more liberated than he did now, as he put one foot in front of the other and began walking away. He held his head up high and proud as he stepped foot outside the cave for the first time ever, a free man. And as soon as he was far enough away to not be seen, he ran like the wind to his father's cave.

Mod was out of breath when at last he turned into the opening of the cave his father called home. Even before he reached his side, he could tell that the old man was fast asleep. Mod smiled, because he knew that his timing was perfect. Even the handmaiden was not yet around to tend to the old man's needs, and Mod smiled again, because he knew that once he was through with him, the old man would not be in need of her services anymore.

Quietly, he knelt at his father's side, removed his medallion from his neck, and squeezed it tightly within the palms of his hands. As soon as he felt the heat radiating through his body, he let the medallion fall softly upon the old man's chest, then placed his palms over the old man's closed eyelids. His father didn't even stir as the heat, along with the cure, passed from his son's body to his own ailing one. Mod concentrated with everything he had, and when he was done, he felt confident that he had succeeded. Gently then and still not disturbing the sleeping old man, he lifted his hands away from his father's eyes. And although it looked as though nothing had changed, Mod knew better. He knew that from this moment on, everything would be different. He smiled again as he retrieved his medallion and returned it to its proper place against his own chest, and then crept out of the cave. His father would need his rest now, more than ever before.

Mod made for his own hut and earnestly tried to keep from worrying about Goy and the children. If anything at this point, had gone wrong, he'd surely have felt it by now. For the time being, Mod had enough to do. The first order of business, now that his father was cured, was to pack up a few things while he still could. He didn't imagine that Croy would waste any time before claiming Mod's hut for his own. Mod pulled his cart from its spot in the backyard to the front door and began to load it. At first he piled only the necessary things that he and his family would need for survival. Their belongings were meager anyway, and it did not take him long to gather them. Lastly, he packed up whatever was personal in nature, and before he knew it, he was done. Very little littered the floor of the hut that he and Goy, Lucia and Dager had once called home.

Mod struggled with the cart, and lugged it up

the path that led to the Clay Peaks that lay just east of the Great Pond. He may have to return for the old man later, but for now there was no more time to be spent with him.

"Lucia?" Dager's heart was in his throat, as he spoke his sister's name, and his voice had become so quiet that it was barely audible. Lucia turned, stopped in her tracks and looked to her brother, who was now standing very still.

"Whatever it is, Dager, can't it wait? Ma is just over that hill!" she peered deeper into his eyes, and it was then that she heard them. Unfamiliar, scary noises that made her skin crawl, and goose bumps formed full force on her arms. It was the wild, vicious sounding barking of the hounds. "Dager! What is that? What do we do?" she looked back in the direction from where they'd come and she could see growing clouds of red dust billowing furiously up into the sky. Dager's mind raced. He too, was terrified.

"Is our ma alone?" he stammered, and his lips quivered with each word.

"Yes, why?" Lucia's eyes were big with fear. Could this be the hag; the bad mama coming after them? Could she possibly be worse than those two awful men were?

"Then we have to lead them away from her. I don't know what our ma is like, Lucia, but I don't think she'd be any match for the hag and the hounds." He grabbed her by the arm and pulled her backwards, in the direction of the noises! She yanked herself free; she was so frightened. Why was Dager pulling her back there?

"Dager, what are you doing? The hounds are that way!" Poor Lucia still had no idea what hounds even were, but she so hoped that they weren't anything like those hideous, hungry looking beasts attached to carts that she'd seen in the village. Dager roughly took hold of her arm again.

"Lucia! Do you want the hag to get Ma, too?" Finally, Lucia understood and offered no more resistance. They forced their scared stiff legs to break into a slow-motion run, back toward what could only be their impending doom. Lucia hoped they'd turned back in time, before their mother spotted them. It would break her heart, she knew, to see her own two children getting all snatched up. In her haste, Lucia lost her footing and stumbled. She fell face first onto the hot ground. Her once bright sundress and apron were now a dirty, reddish brown. Dager helped her back to her feet.

"Lucia, you have to trust me." She only had time to nod, before the hounds appeared like monsters through the dust; flying toward them angrily. They snarled and growled, and stopped in their tracks within mere inches of the children. Further off, Lucia saw a beastie cart coming their way. Strangely, the beastie cart was not at this moment, her greatest worry. For the time being, it was the hound who held within its powerful jaws, a mouthful of the hem of her dress, that was causing her the most distress. She was even too scared to breathe. She watched wide-eyed as Dager reached his hand toward the four legged creature and ruffled the hair on the top of its head! The hound immediately let go of Lucia's clothing.

"It's okay," he explained. "This one is Millie. She won't hurt you; she only wants you to be still until the hag gets here." Silently, Dager reprimanded himself for having wasted so much time. They should have run like anything, far away from the village, the entire distance. But no, they talked. And sometimes they even stopped walking and argued. Who knew how far they might have gotten if only they'd hurried.

Mod parked the wagon amongst the willows, near the Great Pond. He backtracked and stood at the water's edge, then pulled from his shirt pocket, an old, worn snakeskin pouch, and then shook it. With his free hand, he held onto his medallion and waited. In a matter of seconds, he saw them. The three ancient frogs were making their way, hopping from lily pad to lily pad toward him. The biggest one, the leader, came to a stop at Mod's feet. Mod slowly lowered himself to a kneeling position so he could look it in the eye. The frog croaked back at him impatiently. Mod loosened the drawstring at the top of the pouch, opened it wide, and then emptied its contents onto the ground for the scaly beasts to feast upon. The frogs immediately started to lick up the crippled flies.

"My wife and child have traveled through here, aye?" To which the biggest frog nodded in agreement. The two others paid Mod no mind at all, concerning themselves only with the treat that lay before them.

"And I trust you will let me know if anyone other than a member of my family comes through this way?" The frog again nodded at Mod, and then took another fly and stored it away in his cheek.

"Everything is as it shall be, then. You will be watching my wagon as agreed?" When the three frogs all croaked together in response, Mod knew it would be so. But the flies were gone now, meaning that he'd just run out of bargaining power. He would get no more out of them until he returned with a fresh supply. He didn't blame the frogs for it, for this was the way it had always been. Nothing was ever free in the wretched Empire. Mod returned his now empty pouch to his pocket. He watched them hop back to their side of the pond, and as he did so, he took stock in how lucky he'd always been to have them on his side. He turned to make his way back to the willows, when he felt it. Blood curdling fear. Mod fell suddenly to his knees, closed his eyes and held onto his medallion with both hands. His vision came quickly to him. The vision of this daughter, his long lost son, and the ragged woman who had to be none other, than the bad mama. In the next instant, his wife appeared front and center. Mod knew that he had to stop her.

Goy was becoming agitated. Her easel stood before her, but the artwork that sat upon it had no dimension; it was completely uncharacteristic of anything she'd ever drawn before. She replaced her quill into the inkwell, and then set her supplies down on the ground next to her feet, and drew in a deep breath. And it was then that she heard the animals. At that same instant, she also knew that something had gone horribly wrong. She bolted up from her makeshift stool, tipped the easel in the process and sent her sketch flying through the air. She was about to run like the wind toward the village, when she heard him. Goy stopped dead in her tracks.

*"No, Goy. You mustn't go, yet."*

*"But, Mod,"* and she answered in such a way that only her husband could hear. He did not wait for her to finish. He had to stop her before it was too late.

*"No! I fully understand that the children are in trouble. You won't be of any help on your own. Just wait for me by the river, I'm coming!"*

Poor Goy had no choice but to obey her husband, because a woman of the Tasman Empire would never consider going against her husband's word. She dropped noiselessly to the ground at first on all fours, and then inched along on her belly until she could peek through the trees, to where the animal noises had come from. In order to prevent herself from crying out, she bit her bottom lip so hard, that she drew blood. Off in the distance, she spotted her children right away. How Dager had grown! He certainly was no longer the toddler as she'd last seen him. She wished she could just scoop up both children into her loving arms and make all the bad go away. But for now, sadly, that was not to be. Chills ran up and down her spine as she watched the hag grab onto Dager by the collar and lift him up, high into the air. Goy's nails dug helplessly into the earth beneath her, and a drop of blood from her lip spilled onto the ground, and then mysteriously disappeared. And although the sky was blue and as clear as clear could be, thunder roared and lightning shot across it.

At that same moment, unbeknownst to Goy, or to the hag, or to the children, in a world that very few knew existed, an old man's lip began to bleed.

And the blind old man who was an all-important part of a world that very few knew existed, the blind old man who could see far better than anyone with regular vision could, awoke. He licked his lips together, surprised at the moisture he found there. He recognized the taste immediately. Blood. And then he sat up with a start. Something was different; something was wrong. Definitely wrong. It wasn't just the blood, or the visions he'd just had about Mod's wife and his grandchildren. There was more. He propped himself up onto his elbow and with the other hand, smacked himself in the leg. Ouch! It hurt! The old man shook his head and hit himself again, and again, it hurt. How could that be? He hadn't had any feeling in his legs for years. And then he knew. He knew it had to have been none other than Mod, who'd gone and spent an entire cure on his own old, worn out body. The old man sat bolt upright in bed now, and then with surprising ease, swung his legs over the edge of his mat. And then very slowly, he opened his eyes.

# 7

# GIA AND PAGAN

Lucia still didn't dare move, even though Millie had let go of her dress. She folded her arms across her chest and tucked her hands deep into each armpits in order to protect them from the hounds' sharp teeth. That was, until the hag picked up her brother by the back of the collar. Lucia jumped and took a step back, scared out of her wits.

"Pond scum. Ya musta taken a likin' to sleepin' in the chicken coop, hey?" She shook him roughly before letting him fall to the ground in a heap. Millie, the hound, raced to his side and began licking his face. The hag paid no attention to that. She had averted her eyes to Lucia, and was staring at her with an evil gleam. And then she nodded, as if she'd finally realized what was actually going on. She cackled, high and shrill.

"Well, scum. Maybe ya gone and done a good thing for once in your rotten life. Where did ya find her and did her owners see ya go?" Lucia fervently shook her head to protest, but one look from Dager stopped her from crying out. She watched Dager's expression turn pitiful.

"She was lost is all, mama. I couldn't see any owners, but see? She don't talk none." Lucia shook with fright now and glared at him. What if she forgot and started talking? Her tears spilled over, down the length of her dirty face. Right about then, she didn't look a whole lot different from any other surface dweller in that particular situation. The hag moved closer to her. Lucia visibly trembled and then took another small step backwards, further away from both the hag and Dager.

"Alright then, boy. She'll take a while to warm up to the mama. I can see that 'cause I weren't borned yesterday." She pointed a big, fat finger at him as she threatened. "She's your job. She goes to rot, it's on you, boy. She does good, ya both'll live to see another day." With that, the hag stomped over to the back of the beastie cart and pulled a loose rope from the back of it. She proceeded to tie it up alongside the other rope; the one that hung from the back, that wasn't at that moment, attached to anything at all. She then picked up the original rope and held it out in front of her.

Without an ounce of hesitation, Dager was on his feet and hurried toward his sister. He took her by the arm and pulled her with him, to the hag. As soon as they were close enough, he let go and held both of his wrists up in front of him, side by side. Within seconds, the hag had him bound. Lucia watched him wince as the rope settled back into the well-worn grooves in his wrists. And then, because she was a smart girl, she did the same as she'd seen Dager do. She held up her wrists for the hag to bind. The hag took a close look at Lucia's bare, scar-free arms now, and she cackled with delight.

"We got us a fresh one, pond scum!" She smiled a toothless smile at the young girl, before tying her up. "That's a good'un, alright. No retraining to do. Start'em from scratch, like I did you boy, and turn'em into a keeper." The hag rambled on and on about the good'un Dager had found for her, as she made her way to the front of the cart and took her seat behind the horse. With one sharp crack of the whip, she turned the cart around to make its long journey homeward.

Now that they were behind the hag and out of her sight, Dager dared to look at his utterly distraught sister. He truly felt bad for her, being a new recruit in his situation, but he also knew that she wouldn't ever have it as bad off as he. She was a girl, after all, and would be treated with slightly more care than he had ever been.

"It'll be okay," he whispered carefully, and although he knew there was no chance that the hag could hear them speak, he kept an eye on her anyway; only sporadically glancing at Lucia. She whispered back hoarsely.

"Okay? Okay? What about this, is okay, Dager? Now we'll never get home and our parents will have no children left at all!" she sobbed and cried a whole new set of tears. It was all her fault, too. She just knew it. In the meantime, Dager's heart was breaking for her. And what could he possibly say to make her feel better? Not a thing.

The children spent the rest of their journey in silence. The only sounds that could be heard were those of the horse plodding along, the wagon banging, the wheels squeaking, and their own feet as they kicked up more dust. Lucia's feet were in absolute agony as she had been on them for hours, with little rest. Dager's feet chafed against his ill-fitting shoes, but he was more experienced at tolerating pain than his sister was. And besides that, his mind was busy; racing with thoughts and schemes. The main thing on his mind, was not his sore feet or his rope-burned wrists, but planning their escape.

Dager fought back the urge to smile. He felt rich with the knowledge that once he was truly free of the hag, and he was sure that time would come; he had a place of his own to go. A home! A real home! And even though, according to his sister, it was down south and in a foreign land, he was very determined to go there. Nothing and nobody would stand in his way.

Gia, the young handmaiden, entered the cave at the same time she always did, with the old man's early lunch. Every morning she would wake up, and wonder if the present day might be his last. His breathing had worsened, especially over the last fortnight, and his appetite had dwindled down to one half cup of broth per meal. Only the day before, he'd spat out yet another tooth, onto the spoon she used to feed him with. She knew with sickening dread, that his death would come soon. But on this particular day, he did not greet her with his usual, "Yer here, I kin smells ya!" and that was when she knew for certain that he was gone. It would be a pity in more ways than one. Not only had she grown fond of him, and she'd miss caring for him terribly, but it meant that she must seek employment elsewhere, and as soon as possible, too. After all, her small wage was all she had to rely on in order to support herself and her young child. Tears filled her eyes immediately, and so she wiped them clear and forced them to adjust to the dim room.

What Gia did not expect to see was his empty mat. What had he done, somehow hobbled off somewhere to die alone? She shook her head, no. That was impossible. His arms couldn't possibly be strong enough to drag his worn out body anywhere. She set the cup of broth aside, knelt down on the cold, hard ground by his mat, and began to weep.

The next thing that Gia certainly did not expect, was the sudden hand which had come up from behind and rested itself gently upon her shoulder. Her mind raced. Who stood there? Friend or foe? She had heard no one enter the cave after her, which meant that he or she had deliberately snuck in. The tiny hairs on the back of her neck stood straight up as she reached behind and flung the strange hand away. In the same instant, she was back on her feet and had spun around to face whoever it was. Her mouth opened wide when she saw the man who stood before her. She was shocked.

The old man smiled at his young handmaiden and gave her a small, friendly wave. Gia somewhat regained her composure and stepped closer to look him up and down. Surely it could be none other than the old man she'd spent the last three years tending to. But how in the name of the serpent could this be happening? She stammered.

"But sir, the serpent..." He shook his head at her, and pointed toward the mat.

"Sit down, child," the old man ordered. Gia sat down with a thump directly upon his mat. He walked over and sat right by her side. She was still wide-eyed and stared at him with amazement. He rubbed his legs, and then as he began to explain, she realized that along with everything else, his speech had improved as well.

"Firstly of all, Gia, the serpent has nothing to do with anything. The council has always maintained that the whole Tasman Empire, and everyone in it, owes everything it is today, to a silly reptile that does not even exist. It is wrong."

He narrowed his eyes at her, and he knew that he held her attention fast, like never before. She was an incredibly loyal and good person, and it was his wish to keep her as near to him as he possibly could. Maybe it was to be his turn, after all this time, to care for her. Gia nodded, silently urging him on.

"My son has cured me." Gia's hand flew to her mouth in surprise.

"But sir, it is forbidden!" And she began to think that she was sitting beside a true abomination. He laughed softly before replying.

"According to whom? The only people who have said such a thing are the members of the high council! And who put them in charge, anyway? Why, they did. And all they've ever really done, is instill fear into the hearts of every single villager." He waited a moment before adding, "Look at me and listen to me, Gia, and then tell me if you see that a great wrong has been committed!" He was still smiling, genuinely. And now it was she, who chuckled at the absurdity of it all. In the last two minutes, he had already convinced her that everything she'd ever been taught, was in every way, shape and form, wrong.

"You're right, sir. But now what? What is the next step? I know there is one. You and Mod must have a plan?" she begged him with her eyes. She now had a strange feeling, that a large part of her destiny... or rather, her and her daughter's destiny was sitting next to her, in that dark, decrepit little cave.

"Secondly, my friend, you can stop calling me 'sir'. I think you have more than earned the right to call me by my first name, Brand. And thirdly, yes, there is definitely a plan." Although the old man had little doubt, he added, "If you wish to be a part of it, that is."

"Do you have to ask, sir... I mean, Brand? Somehow, I think you already know the answer to that." And she stared intently now into his eyes as she spoke. The dead, white look in his eyes had been replaced with a blue brilliance which matched her own. Brand stood, and offered her his hand to help her up. She accepted, and was quite taken back at the brute strength he now possessed. Her eyes were still filled with wonder and awe. Her heart, which had lost hope of a decent future long ago, was now overflowing with excitement and threatened to burst right out of her chest.

"It is as I expected it would be. You will have a new life with us, if that is your desire. Speak not a word of this to anyone. We certainly cannot afford for the word to get out just yet. Gather up only your most important belongings and your child, and meet us at the Great Pond. Do you know the way?"

"Aye, I do."

"And so it shall be done."

Gia's heart raced with anticipation as she took leave of Brand and his cave. She headed straight for her hut that lay at the end of the main path, and began to pack. Sadly, Gia had little that she wished to bring. Mostly, she packed for her daughter; five-year old Pagan's dresses and her favourite doll, landed first into the shoulder bag. For herself, she brought her sewing kit and beadwork. Gia took one last look around the bare walls that she hadn't ever been able to afford to decorate, the window openings, which she could never cover up, and the lumpy dirt floor that had never provided her with warmth or comfort. She was not aware that the doll had slipped out of the bottom seam of the bag, and so she smiled as she walked out the door. She knew that there would be no regrets.

"Ma!" Pagan squealed with delight as she peeked over the fence and saw her mother hurrying down the path toward her. The child pushed through the other children, straight to her caregiver and pulled her along to the gate.

"Ma's here! I can go home now, Nanny!" The nanny humoured the little girl and followed along. She could hardly believe her eyes when she spotted Gia nearing the yard. It wasn't nearly time for her to fetch her child, yet. She grimaced, as she realized it meant that Gia would owe her fewer chores at the end of the week. And what was that, a skip in her step? The nanny's curiosity was most definitely aroused. In the meantime, Pagan threw open the gate and ran to her mother. The nanny harrumphed, defiantly placed her hands upon her hips, and confronted the young woman.

"This does not mean that you get out of the

week's cleaning, you know." Gia laughed openly, which along with the skip in her step, was completely out of character. She saw the look on the nanny's face and quickly recovered. Her expression sobered immediately.

"Oh, no. Don't worry, I'll be here at the usual time. It's just that the old man fell asleep right away, and I've already finished the cleaning for him." Gia spoke through gritted teeth, and hoped the nanny could not see through her boldfaced lies. She continued, "I'll put in the same amount of time for you, as I always do. It's just that I thought I might as well spend this extra time today, with Pagan." Gia took her daughter by the hand as she smiled sincerely at the nanny. Pagan could tell that something was up with her mother, and although she didn't know what exactly, she decided that she liked it anyway. She hadn't seen her mother smile so big for a long time!

"As long as you know the score. Most women with extra time on their hands would spend it having tea with other women, not wasting it on their children. But, it's none of my business, now is it? You are a peculiar one, however." At that moment, one of the nanny's charges approached her and asked for a snack. She swatted the tot away as one might do to an annoying fly. The child whimpered and ran off, but the nanny acted as though nothing had happened at all. Gia cringed at the very idea that this woman was in charge of so many children. She smiled, as she answered.

"Yes, I've been told that I am different. I am well aware. I'll see you later, then." And Gia, still holding her daughter by the hand, turned on her heel and left the nanny standing there, speechless. That however, would not last. Gia knew that the nanny was already itching to gossip about this latest conversation to anyone who came along.

"What is it? What's the big old hurry?" Pagan asked as she and her mother rushed away. Gia stopped right in the middle of the hut lined path, and knelt down, facing her daughter. She ran her hand through Pagan's beautiful light brown curls, as she replied in hushed tones.

"How about an adventure? Why don't we go for a walk, Pagan?" Pagan grinned from ear to ear. This would indeed be an adventure! Her mother worked so much for the old man and the nanny that they rarely had time to take walks together.

"Aye, Ma! A long one though. It's got to be a long walk, or I won't go," the little girl insisted. She'd already decided that in order to get the most out of this special occasion, the walk had better be on her own terms. She folded her arms across her chest, stomped her foot onto the ground and raised her eyebrows at her mother. To her complete surprise, Gia nodded in agreement.

"If that's how you want it Pagan, that's the way it will be. Now let's get on with it, then!" And away they went. Straight beyond the rest of the huts, the villagers who took absolutely no notice anyway, and that much closer to the new life that awaited them on the other side of the Great Pond.

By that time, Brand had packed his few belongings as well. There wasn't much from the cave that he desired to take, and so his load was also light. The main thing for him to make sure of, was that he left the village, undetected. And of that, he was hardly worried. It would so happen that whoever's path he crossed on his journey out, would forget they'd ever laid eyes upon him. That was just one of the advantages of being a Curor.

He pulled his outer hood low over the top of his head, so that it just about covered his brow. Around his waist, he wrapped his tool belt tight, inside out so its contents lay snug and noiseless against his skin. His blanket, he folded many times, into a narrow rectangle, and saddled it over his shoulder. And, much the same as Mod had done earlier, and then much the same as Gia had recently done, he took one last look around his home. He knew that he would be a very happy man, if he never laid eyes upon it again. He stepped out into daylight for the first time in years. In the first minute, his sensitive eyes squinted against the soft sun, and in the next, they had adjusted. He smiled as he stepped forth from the cave, and toward his new life.

The time that Goy spent waiting for Mod's arrival went by slower than she ever before, would have thought possible. The last she saw of her children, was when they'd been tied up to that awful contraption and led away to who knew where. Anything could have become of them by the time Mod arrived. It was all she could do, to obey him. Then, just when she had almost decided to go against his wishes, she heard him splashing about in the river. She ran to the river bank just as he stepped foot on solid ground.

"Oh, Mod," she embraced her husband, and she felt glad that she had waited for him, after all. Mod hugged his wife back and together they walked to the clump of brush.

"Which way, Goy?" She pointed in the direction she'd seen her children go, and then asked.

"What will we do, Mod? The bad mama is a horrible woman. Poor Lucia! What will *she* do?" Goy had promised her daughter that nothing would go wrong. She was wrought with guilt and frustration. Fresh tears ran down her face. Mod reached over and with the palms of his hands, tenderly wiped them away.

"This is nothing, Goy. A little obstacle. The worst is over; the worst is over by far. Don't worry about Lucia, my love. I have the feeling that Dager will take good care of her. He won't let harm come her way, I'm sure of that." He looked closely at his wife, and saw the dried blood crusted upon her bottom lip. He placed his hand upon his medallion, and the vision appeared; the whole sordid account came to him as clear as day. The agony she'd been through, the helplessness she felt when she was unable to protect their children. He frowned.

"What do you mean, the worst is over? What happened with the high council?" And then, just as she asked, she realized that she had an extremely good idea, just what had gone on. She nodded in understanding.

"That's not important right now, Goy. Right now, we must go and get our children, and bring them home. For far too long I've gone with the flow, and I've done exactly what's been expected of me, or what I've been told to do. Not anymore." He stood up and reached his hand toward her. As Goy took it and stood at her husband's side, she knew that something had changed inside of him. She knew all that he had just said, was true. This *would* be a new life. A different life. A better life. And then together, Mod and Goy took their first determined steps toward rescuing both of their children from the horrible hag.

# 8

# LUCIA AND THE DARK

The hag steered the beastie cart off the road, down her driveway and into her yard. Lucia saw all sorts of animals that she'd never before known existed. The pink, noisy animals scared her the most, even more than the hounds or the beast that pulled the cart. She shuddered with fright. Dager saw Lucia's pale face turn a shade whiter and he could tell how afraid she was. There was at this moment though, nothing that he could do for her. The hag pulled the beastie cart to a dead stop right in front of her shack, hopped down from her seat and made her way to the children.

"Does she understand talk, pond scum?" The hag asked him as she untied his rope. She hadn't heard the girl utter a single sound and had begun to worry that she might be simple. But Dager caught on to her concerns right away, and decided that would be the best direction to go. He knew that she preferred the children to be dumb, but not too dumb.

"Maybe," he answered thoughtfully, "she don't talk, but she might know it. She don't nod or even shake her head, Mama." Dismally, he kicked the ground at his feet and hoped she believed him. The hag untied Lucia's rope, and then took her by the shoulders and stared closely at her face. Lucia kept her eyes cast as low to the ground as she could.

"Well, let's give it till tomorrah. Let the girl get used to the place and then tomorrah I'll put her through the paces. You tend to her till then. I ain't got time right now. I gots ta sort through today's finds from the market." Dager nodded at the hag, backed away, and then ran toward the barn. He so hoped Lucia would do the same, and when he turned to look, he was glad to see that she was not far behind. She was running like anything after him, but stopped short when she saw her brother hop the fence into the pen that held the pink, noisy animals. Dager motioned to her with his hand to follow, but she just couldn't. Her feet were glued to the spot. Finally, he gave up and climbed the fence back out of the pigpen. Because she was new at this, he would let her get away with it, just this once. She could have it her way. He shrugged his shoulders for her benefit, and then led her into the barn, where there were no animals other than the occasional hound.

"Don't you like pigs?" he smirked at her, once they were safe inside. He was joking good-heartedly, but she didn't know that. Her face was full of rage as she faced him.

"How dare you! How dare you make it sound like I'm simple!" she mimicked him then, and did a good job of it too, straight from his weak little voice, to his expression of doom. She acted as if she actually was Dager, speaking to the hag. *"Maybe,"* she began, and then paused dramatically. *"She don't talk, but she might know it. She don't nod or even shake her head, Mama."*

Finished with her little performance, she kicked the ground at his feet so hard that dirt flew into the air. Dager couldn't help it; he laughed out loud at her antics. Lucia suddenly realized how funny she must have sounded and looked, then laughed too. After all, it would do her no good to stay angry with Dager, her brother and her only ally. Together, they laid back on a bale of hay, side by side. One was just about as exhausted as the other, from the day's events.

"Okay, really. I'm not mad anymore, but why did you want her to think that I'm not very smart?" she asked as she began to tug at the twine that held the bale in place. Dager rolled onto his belly and leaned on his elbows, facing her. He explained as best he could.

"Well, you're not the first child I've had to get for her. And there were more before me. If she thought you were smart, she'd be harder on you, to make you want to stay. Also, if she thought you were smart, she'd want more from you." Lucia nodded at his thoughtfulness. She was impressed.

"Okay, that makes sense. But why did you tell her that I *didn't talk none*?" she mimicked again as she asked.

"Because I didn't want you to say something you shouldn't, by mistake. What if she asked where you came from and you had to describe it to her? What would you say?"

"You're right, Dager. I never thought of that at all. But now that we're talking about it, would you like me to describe where we come from, to you?" Dager nodded eagerly. He couldn't wait to see it for himself, but for now hearing about it would have to do.

"It's not as hot at home as it is here. But it isn't cold, either. At least not until nighttime, when the wind blows. It rains sometimes, but not often." She paused and looked at him. He only nodded back eagerly again, and she continued. "And the trees are big and thick with lots and lots of leaves. So many leaves, that you can't really see through the trees. The green is greener than any green that I've seen up here."

"What do you mean, up here?" Dager looked at Lucia quizzically. Did she really come from the south? A green land in the south? Lucia looked serious. She had the feeling that he wouldn't believe what she would tell him next.

"Somehow, and I can't explain how, but our land seems under this one. Under and over." her brows furrowed together as she tried to figure out the best way to describe it to him. She groaned in dismay. "Okay, I'll start from the beginning. When Ma and I were on our way to get you, we had to go on a long walk, farther than the Clay Peaks and the three big scary frogs, and the Great Pond!" Dager had never heard of such places, although frogs were certainly common. He waited patiently for her to finish. "Then we cleared some brush away from the base of the trunk of a big tree, jumped down into it and swam here!" Dager laughed out loud. What was she talking about? Lucia became even more determined now, to describe it, than ever before. There was nothing worse, as far as she was concerned, than to have someone doubt her word. "Dang it all, Dager! You don't believe me!"

Just then, the lead hound waddled into the barn. She was whimpering in agony as she made her way to the darkest, farthest corner. Dager smiled happily.

"What is it, Dager? What's wrong with that hound?" Dager took Lucia by the arm and pulled her with him slowly, to the hound's side. The hound moaned when she saw her friend approach, but growled at the strange and unfamiliar girl who was by his side.

"It's okay, Mindy." And then Dager pulled Lucia's hand slowly toward the hound's muzzle. Lucia squeezed her eyes tight and braced herself for the worst, all the while wondering why her brother was about to sacrifice her hand. To her alarm, the hound sniffed and then licked her. It tickled and Lucia let out a sigh of relief. Dager explained.

"She needs to smell you to know you." he said, as he proceeded to rub the animal behind the ears. The hound snuggled in closer to his touch, and then winced in pain.

"What's wrong with her?" Lucia still had no idea what the hound's troubles were. But Dager knew. He'd seen it time and again, first with the pigs, and then with the cow. Now it seemed, it would be Mindy's turn.

"She's going to have babies, Lucia!" he couldn't hide his excitement. And for that moment, all of the troubles that plagued him and his sister, were furthest from his mind.

"Babies! How do you know?" she looked at the hound from top to bottom, but she still couldn't tell. Dager gently lifted one of her hind legs and revealed the hound's hairy, bulging belly to his sister.

"You see here?" he asked as he pointed to each teat. Lucia smiled, a little embarrassed that her brother was pointing to the animal's boobs. "No, it's not a funny thing, Lucia. It's a great thing! Under each bump, is a puppy, a baby hound! A real puppy just waiting to be born!" Lucia was amazed that Dager knew so much.

"But, when? When will they be born?"

"Soon, Lucia. Tonight for sure. Maybe Mindy will let us watch, but for now we should leave her alone. I've seen that the other animals like to be alone when they're ready to do this stuff." Lucia nodded, although she was disappointed to have to leave Mindy's side. She and Dager walked quietly back to the bale of hay and laid back down upon it. Lucia was glad to be off her feet again for any length of time. Speaking of feet, she looked curiously at Dager's.

"I've been dying to know. What are those big, clumsy things on your feet? Don't they get in your way?" she giggled as she imagined herself wearing such things. Dager smiled at her.

"These are called shoes, and I see that you don't wear any. Don't you wear shoes in the south?" Lucia felt herself becoming upset again, because he still did not understand where their home was. She decided to leave that alone for the moment; at this rate she'd never be able to explain it properly.

"No, we don't wear shoes at home. The ground is mostly soft and it sure isn't hot." And then Lucia began to worry about the next day. The day that the hag said, she'd put her through her paces. She rolled over onto her belly, much the same as Dager was. By now, both of them were covered with bits of hay.

"What is the bad mama going to make me do, Dager?" Lucia couldn't even begin to imagine what was in store for her. She'd never before seen the likes of the hag, even in her worst nightmares.

"Oh, don't worry much about it, Lucia. Girls have it pretty good, compared to boys. Boys are no better than the dirt beneath your feet. Especially boys like me. Girls like you don't come around often. I'm sure she'll just have you cook and mend and tidy up after her, is all." he envied her almost, but only a little. He really liked being a boy, but he wished he wasn't a boy in his particular situation. And that situation, he knew, would be changing sometime soon, anyway. That bit Dager had said about boys though, didn't sit right with Lucia.

"What do you mean, boys are like dirt? Is that why you thought Ma sold you? Because up here, boys mean nothing and you thought that's why she sold you and not me?" It was then that Lucia realized that they had not finished this conversation earlier, when Dager had started to cry. Dager said nothing, for he was still embarrassed over his unusual shedding of tears. It wasn't like him to cry, and especially in front of anyone else. He silently promised himself that it would never happen again.

"Dager, where we live, it is the boys and the men who come first." Dager's mouth gaped open as though that was the most astonishing thing he had ever heard.

"What?"

"Aye, you heard me. For example, Ma needs Da's permission to do anything out of the ordinary. Da doesn't ask Ma if he can do things, but Ma has to ask Da. Girls aren't treated bad or anything like that, but it just seems that we are not as important."

"Really?"

"Really. Even my... I mean *our* grandfather. I can only speak to him if he speaks to me first. And Ma hardly says anything to him. It's just the way it has always been." Dager thought about that long and hard. It sounded like the roles were reversed, down south. Almost reversed, as it didn't sound like there were any nasty old hags down there.

"What about the man who took me? Who is he?" Lucia rolled her eyes into the back of her head as she replied.

"Oh, him. He's the bad Curor who took you away from us. He wanted to be the Curor, but Da was already the Curor." Lucia tried to look matter-of-factly about it, but she realized that it would be just as futile as trying to describe the way home.

"What is a Curor?" Now that question, Lucia could answer, at least a little bit better than she could his previous questions.

"A Curor is a healer. A Curor is the most important man in our village. Our da is the Curor." And then she beamed at her brother proudly. "You will also be a Curor." Dager sat up suddenly and made a strange face.

"And what if I don't want to be a Curor? They can't make me be a Curor if I don't want to be one." Then he thought for a moment, before asking in a smaller voice, "Can they?" Just then, Mindy moaned. The children looked briefly over at her, but it didn't seem that anything was happening yet.

"I think they can. I think you have to be a

Curor because Da is and Granda was. But you'll have to ask him."

"Do you think our father will come and look for us now, Lucia? Da and Ma?" Lucia shivered as she thought about that.

"I don't know. I don't think Ma could find us alone, and Da is not allowed to leave the Empire." Dager made another strange face.

"You mean the most important man in the village isn't allowed to go where he wants?" Lucia nodded.

"Aye, that's what I mean. Our empire cannot be without a Curor. Da won't leave because if he did, Croy would try to take his place as Curor." And although Lucia wished that their father would come after them, she knew that it was highly unlikely. Any chance of escape would probably be up to her and Dager.

Mindy cried out again, but this time it sounded different. This was a long, drawn out cry, followed by panting. Lucia and Dager made eye contact. He nodded.

"It's time, I think. We can go over, but we have to move slowly, and then be very quiet and very still." They climbed down from the bale of hay, and made their way toward Mindy. As they went, Lucia happened to notice that it was becoming dark in the barn. It was beginning to remind her of Granda's cave. She looked outside the barn door and was startled to see the sky turning black. She grabbed her brother by the arm and pointed to it. Dager was startled now, too! What did she see that he didn't? He stared and stared into the ever darkening night, but he saw nothing but a few bright stars shining against the midnight blue.

"What is it, Lucia? What do you see?"

"Well, that's just it, Dager. I see nothing. The sky is getting as dark as Granda's cave!" she moved closer to him and snuggled in under his arm, which was not an easy thing to do, given that he was a good four inches shorter than she. Now Dager was really perplexed. Did she say cave?

"Of course it's getting dark. It's getting on nighttime now, and soon, we won't see a thing out there."

"What? How can the sky go out? And when will it be back again?"

"Lucia, it gets dark every night and it gets light again every morning!" he looked at her for a moment, as though she really were simple.

"Oh." Lucia didn't seem convinced and appeared quite content under the protection of her brother's arm. As Dager pulled her along to the hound, he wondered even more about the green land down south that never got dark. He was beginning to wonder how much of what she said, could possibly be true.

The children approached the hound, and squatted carefully beside her. She gave another long, painful cry and then there was another sound. A slurpy squishy sound that was over just as quickly as it had begun. Dager and Lucia looked on, as Mindy reached toward her back end and under her tail, and then with her teeth, carried out what looked like a small, wet rat. Rats, Lucia knew all about. They ran rampant in their Empire. They snuck around at all hours doing what she was convinced, had to be the serpent's work. She was sure they were evil. She wrinkled her nose up at the small creature, while Mindy licked its face clean.

"Has Mindy had babies before, Dager?" she whispered as softly as she could.

"No. She's only one and a half years old. This is her first litter," he whispered back. And not once did either child move their eyes from the incredible sight that was unfolding before them.

"Then how does she know what to do and how to do it?"

"I don't know. They just all know what to do. Even the pigs and the cow knew what to do when their babies came." Mindy's panting began again, and the children stopped talking. Their breaths were held as they watched her push another one out. This one was not as black as the first. It looked as though its feet were white. Mindy proceeded to lift this one close, as she had done with the first, and licked it clean.

"What are baby hounds called, Dager?"

"Puppies. They are called puppies. Don't you have hounds in the south?" Lucia clicked her tongue impatiently, when he again called home, the south.

"No, we don't have hounds. We have rats and frogs and roos. Also there are a lot of bugs and bush goats and other things too, that I can't think of right this minute. And I've never seen any babies get born. But baby rats are called baby rats, and baby frogs are called tadpoles and baby roos are called baby roos. A baby bush goat is called a kid." She hoped that at least some of what she said impressed him. But he was too busy, again watching Mindy push out another puppy.

By the end of the birthing, Mindy had given birth to six puppies. Three of them were straight black, one had socks and two were a black and white mix. Their little eyes were squeezed tight, but they didn't seem to have any trouble finding their mother's milk, despite that. Mindy was exhausted, but she kept right on licking and cleaning her babies, one by one. And once she reached the last one, she'd start at the beginning again.

It was late now, and Lucia and Dager had pretty much talked and watched Mindy, from afternoon until bedtime. Lucia fell fast asleep on the bale of hay, and she dreamt of home. Dager fetched the horse blanket for both of them, and laid down beside her. When he dreamt, it was of the magical, faraway lands, which just a short while ago, he believed did not truly exist.

9

## A FAMILY REUNITED

Pagan's mother came to a sudden, dead stop once she reached the crest of the hill. She saw a whole new incredible world stretched out as far as the eye could see. Never before had she seen such beauty; in fact never before had she even suspected that such beauty was possible. She'd heard about the valley and knew how to get to it, but she'd never once had time to explore it for herself, for she'd always been too busy with work to worry about such things. She hoisted her equally wide-eyed girl up and settled her down comfortably upon her hip. The girl wrapped an arm around her mother's neck as she sucked in a deep, wondrous breath.

"Ma! Real flowers? Are those big flowers really real?" Gia laughed at Pagan, before she replied.

"Aye, they are. Aren't they something? And the grass, do you see how green the grass is?" Pagan nodded her little head up and down in answer. They stood there for a moment, much the same way that Goy and Lucia had recently done before them, and stared. The landscape appeared as though it carried on forever. The soft, floral scented breeze whipped around and around Gia and Pagan, inviting them onward. Gia set the girl back down upon her own feet, and knelt down beside her. Pagan frowned at something on the ground that had caught the corner of her eye. She reached down and picked up a crumpled brown leaf. Gia watched as the girl held it up against the contrasting backdrop of the luscious green valley below, and she smiled as soon as she realized that Pagan was comparing the two. Pagan threw the leaf back down to the ground and took hold of her mother's hand again.

"Well, Ma," she cried, as though she had just reached some sort of important, life-altering decision, before she repeated what her mother had said to her, earlier, "let's get on with it, then!" Gia squeezed Pagan's hand and giggled with delight. She was more eager than Pagan knew, to begin this new life, and so hand in hand, they made their way down into the valley. And not once, did either of them look back.

It all happened exactly as Brand had expected it would. He marched up the path and away from the village, and in the eyes of the villagers, nothing was out of the ordinary. Not a single, miserable soul recognized the hooded figure. No one could have guessed that he was the same all-seeing, blind old cripple from the cave, whom they'd long before held in such high regard.

His steps were light, yet quick. He had somewhere to be and there wasn't a moment to waste. In no time at all, he was hiking along the same trail that Goy and Lucia had traveled upon, followed by Mod, and then Gia and Pagan. The earth beneath the old man's feet was beginning to show long overdue signs of recent use, and it seemed to smile up at him. He took this as a sign of welcome, and he smiled back.

Once Brand reached the crest of the hill, he stopped to rest. He felt an odd, warm sensation near his foot, and so he knelt down to examine its source. It was none other than the crumpled, brown leaf that Pagan had recently discarded. Immediately, the vision of Gia and her small daughter appeared to him, and he knew that they would make it safely to their mutual destination. The newly enchanted leaf floated up from the ground, and spun three times right in front of his eyes. His gaze followed it, as the breeze pulled it up, high into the air. It joined other leaves; some brown and crumpled, some colourful and new. They danced together briefly before floating downward to the valley below. Brand laughed out loud at what he'd just witnessed, and he knew it was just the first of many such displays to come. He stood and stretched for a moment, and he felt so alive that he half-ran, half-skipped down the trail. And as he did, he silently thanked his son for the cure. He did not do it in such a way so that Mod could hear him; he knew better than to disturb the man who was in the midst of desperately trying to reunite his own little family.

From a horizontal position, Mod reached skyward and pushed away the sticks and dead branches he had used the night before, to provide him and his wife with shelter while they slept. Theirs had indeed been a restless sleep, but why shouldn't it have been, with the two of them wandering around in a strange, hot land in search now, not only of their long lost son, but their daughter as well. Of course they slept fitfully. He hoisted himself up on one elbow, leaned over and planted an affectionate kiss on Goy's forehead. She opened her weary eyes and squinted toward him.

"Aye, thank you, Mod. I needed that." She brought her arm up across her eyes to shield them from the already scorching morning sun. "How can the surface dwellers stand this heat?" Mod laughed, before he answered.

"They are used to it, love. Perhaps they'd find our land too cold? Not that I care how they'd find it anyway, after all." He pulled himself up and sat, straddled on the fallen tree that had acted like a barrier against the elements all night long. He looked around, but for as far as he could see, all that lay before him was more angry looking, hot cracked earth. He thought about it for a moment, and then told his wife, "It's no wonder we hear that they are an angry lot. The ground they walk on is not a happy one. The sun is hot and unbearable, the earth is ailing, and there is little to no plant life. What other kind of people could live here, I wonder!" Goy nodded in agreement as she hoisted herself up and sat alongside her husband. She took her canteen from her shoulder bag, and shared its contents with Mod.

"We're almost out, I see," Mod stated with a worried look, "we'll have to find a place to refill it before the day is done." He handed the near empty canteen back to Goy, who then tucked it away. She threw her bag over her shoulder, stood, and stretched.

"Shall we, Mod? Shall we go and get our children, now?" she looked strangely at her husband then, for he hadn't budged an inch, but instead patted the log beside him, urging her to join him there. He wanted her to sit back down. Sit? How could she sit when her children were out there somewhere? But, sit she did, for that was what her husband expected her to do.

"Now do you see, Goy? Do you see how we've been conditioned?" he looked her straight in the eye as he asked, and he could see the confusion brimming there.

"Mod, I don't understand. What does being conditioned have to do with retrieving the young ones?" she was fidgeting and trying very hard to control her impatience.

"Despite the fact that you want more than anything, to start walking down that road," and he pointed to it for emphasis, "you sat down because I asked it of you. Who is it that decreed that no matter what, a wife must obey her husband? And why has it never been the other way around?" Suddenly, Mod had perked Goy's interest enough that she now wished to sit, but only for a moment, to find out what her husband was really trying to get at. She took a deep breath, and then replied warmly.

"If you must know, I was brought up to believe that men are much more important than women are, Mod."

She felt slightly embarrassed about admitting such a thing to her husband, for they had never discussed such matters before. "And that's the way high council expects it to be. Do you remember the time that woman..." and she paused for a moment, remembering. It was something that had occurred long before her time, but the story had been passed along from woman to woman throughout the generations, as an example of sorts. Goy hadn't yet told Lucia though, and she didn't know if Mod knew about it. She looked at him, and judging by the blank expression upon his face, she guessed not. He shook his head no, and then she continued. "The woman was fed up with her husband's orders, and so one day while walking home from the market, she spoke to him without first being spoken to, and then had the nerve to walk ahead of him, all the way down the path! In front of the rest of the villagers, too!" Mod still looked incredulous. "Mod, I can't believe you've never heard about this! High council ordered her stoned to death by her own husband for her actions!"

Mod began to laugh, but not at his wife. He laughed at the desperate lengths the high council had gone to, in order to preserve what they viewed as a harmonious and idealistic village within their empire. Goy furrowed her brows together, for she did not understand Mod's reaction. He was quick to recover.

"Oh, Goy. We couldn't afford to talk about this before, but from now on everything will be so much different; you'll see. Do you really want to raise Lucia to be so pathetically submissive to her husband, or to any other boy or man for that matter? And can you see us bringing up Dager in such a way that he'll feel superior to his wife or to any other girl or woman?"

"Of course not, Mod! But do tell me, what choice do we have? It so happens that we live where we live and things are the way they are. We can't expect that it's possible to change the minds of an entire village worth of people!"

"No, that's not at all what I'm saying. First of all, my love. Let me right a grievous wrong. There was no such woman ordered stoned by the high council. That was a story made up by council to scare the daylights out of any woman who ever thought she had the right to speak before, or walk in front of a man. My father told me about it ages ago, and I guess I simply did not realize that the story was still alive and well and flourishing in the village. Secondly, I don't expect that we can change that village. And if we could, would we want to? Is there more than a handful of people who live in Hurtsmire, whom you would consider worth saving?" Goy thought for a moment, and then shook her head, no. Mod continued. "I expect to begin a new village. A village led in the beginning by one man, born from honesty and righteousness!" Goy's hand flew up and covered her mouth. Never before in her life, had she heard such foolishness.

"A new village! Mod! And who will run such a place? And where do you expect to put it?" Just before Mod was about to reply, he heard the frogs. *Croak, croak, croak.* He brought his hand up and laid it upon his chest, closed his eyes and held the medallion tight. And then he saw them. The fleeting vision of two people; his father's handmaiden and her daughter were playing in the water, near the shore of the Great Pond! The frog had done right by him, and alerted him as agreed, of the strangers' presence. All would be well, Mod knew. He smiled, opened his eyes, and turned to his wife.

"The new village has already begun, my love. My father will lead!" Goy sucked a deep breath inwards. How could that be... and then she knew exactly how it would be possible. She realized that if Mod hadn't already done so, he intended to cure the old man.

"But, Mod. It is forbidden to do such a thing. To commit such a crime would bring the serpent down upon you." her teeth were clenched tight as she whispered those words, almost as though she feared the serpent itself might hear her.

"No!" Mod stood now, and threw his hands upon his hips. He had a lot of re-teaching to do, apparently, and it would begin with his very own wife. "Goy, there is no serpent. And the only reason the high council has never allowed a Curor to cure without orders or permission from them, is so they could forever be in control. Do you really think that providing a spent old man with a new lease on life is criminal? And what if you fell over this log and broke your neck? Would it be so wrong if I cured you, or would it be better that I hung my head and accept fate as it is? I think not." He paced for a moment, and then spat. "Serpent, my foot. Imagine a serpent as large as day, slithering into our village and gobbling up those who have committed even the slightest infraction? No, Goy. They have had us praying to a nonexistent creature that we've been taught to fear. That's all. The high council leads through fear and fear alone. It's no way to live, now is it?"

And now it was Goy's turn to stand. As ridiculous as praying to a serpent sounded, she saw this moment as an opportunity to move toward rescuing their children. After all, they could talk as they walked. Besides, she didn't have to wait for Mod's permission anymore; he'd said so, himself. She smiled a little, stuck her chin out defiantly, and then began to walk in the direction of the road. She had no doubt that she would enjoy getting used to this new way of life. Mod laughed out loud, and then hurried to catch up with her.

"Mod, I think that what you and your father are doing is a fine and noble thing. I can imagine it all, in my mind's eye. Bringing up the children equally, to respect one another whether they are boy or girl. But, you didn't answer my other question, love. Where would you put such a place?" As they walked, Mod reached over and took his wife's hand into his own. It was something that he hadn't done for quite some time, and he smiled as he saw her cheeks redden.

"I think the new village should begin in a sort of paradise, don't you? An eden, if you will."

"Eden? What is an eden, Mod?" The truth was that Mod didn't know exactly what it was, but he had heard that such a place was as close to perfect as perfect could ever get.

"That, I can explain to you at a later date, love. The village will be placed between the Clay Peaks and the Great Pond." Goy squeezed her husband's hand. She hoped that very soon, the children would be safe and sound in their possession, and she looked forward to their new future together, with a wide smile and a full heart.

"It all sounds too good to be true, Mod. But, what about school? Do you intend on there being a school in our new village, and if there will be a school, will you allow girls to attend?" she held her breath then, hoping beyond hope that his answer would be yes. She'd always thought that girls were just as capable of learning as boys were; but they'd never been allowed such an opportunity. As she waited for him to reply, she spotted what appeared to be, a farmyard in the distance. She judged it to be not more than another ten-minute's walk away. She pointed to it and asked, "Mod, is that it? Is that where the hag lives?" He'd seen it too, far before Goy had pointed it out.

"Aye, love. That's where we shall find Lucia and Dager. When we get there, you just follow my lead," and then, so it did not sound like an order from a man to his wife, he asked, "is that alright?" He saw her nod in agreement, before he continued. "About the school, absolutely girls will be attending. From age five onward, the same as the boys. The first job the teacher will have, will be to catch the girls up to where the boys are. And it may be that we'll need separate classes for that, or we'll need more than one teacher." Goy was so relieved to hear this that she was near tears. How happy she felt for Lucia and all the other girls who would come to live in their village! It would be a new beginning for a new generation. And she silently hoped that she might also pick up on some learning at the same time. As if Mod had read her mind, he continued. "There will be classes for the adults too, Goy. For men and women, both!"

They walked the rest of the distance to the hag's driveway in silence. Mod was planning his strategy and Goy had a lot on her mind. A new home, and most importantly, she was about to have her boy back again! How hard might it be, she wondered, to introduce him back into the family. Would he struggle? Would he fit in? What if he blamed her and Mod for having been stolen? A million and one scenarios were playing out in her mind and she was feeling quite stressed.

They stood there for a moment at the end of the driveway, looking at the run-down, litter cluttered yard, and both Mod and Goy shuddered to think that this is where Dager had been living. The home, or at least what they assumed to be the home, was only half roofed. The shingles had either been blown away or torn from the structure. Burlap sacks partially covered the windows, and the front door was falling off its hinges. The haphazard stairs leading to the front landing were either missing altogether, or were broken and strewn about.

Near the big barn, was a fenced off pen which contained little pink animals, and they could see larger animals in the distance. Mod stared angrily for a moment at the chicken coop, but of course he did not know what the building contained. What he did know, what he felt more than anything, was that his son had spent a great deal of time in that little house. And most of it was not good. Then a smile flickered across his face, for in his heart, and heavily outweighing the bad, he felt his son's dreams; in particular his most recent one, which had taken place in the chicken coop. Mod knew that Dager had good dreams. Dreams of home possibly, and perhaps that was what helped to keep him sane over the course of the last two years.

"There." Mod said sternly, as he pointed to the barn.

"What? There?" Goy realized what Mod was really telling her. "Are you saying that the children are in there?"

"Yes, they are. I think we'll go there first to see them. The hag, we can deal with later." And then with quiet, light steps, Mod and Goy walked to the barn. Luckily for them, the hounds were not around and so the hag would not yet be alerted that she had company. The barn door was ajar, and they stepped noiselessly into the building. It took a moment for both pairs of eyes to adjust to the dim, but adjust they did. The first thing they saw was a small animal in the corner, lying down and apparently asleep. Goy realized immediately that the poor thing had recently given birth, and she smiled at the rat looking things that were contentedly nursing upon it. All of a sudden, Mod sucked in a deep breath and pointed to a hay bale. Goy nearly cried out with joy when she saw two little heads poking out from under a blanket. She and Mod stood quietly for a moment, and watched their children sleep. But only for a moment, for Goy could not bear to be still any longer. She rushed to the hay bale and knelt down beside them.

Mod joined her there, as Goy whispered hoarsely, "Lucia, Dager! Wake up! It's time to wake up!" she wanted so much just to grab Dager and hug him until they both tired of it, but she knew better than to force herself upon him. Instead, she turned to her daughter, reached over and with gentle fingers, moved the stray strands of hair from her face. Both of the children blinked hard and opened their eyes at almost the same time, but it was Lucia who first greeted their parents.

"Ma!" And then she was even more surprised when she saw her father. "Da!" He was the last person Lucia expected to see. She reached up and rubbed the sand and sleep from her eyes with her fists. "How... what... how did you find us?" she looked at him worriedly, for she knew that no matter what the reason; he should not have left their empire. That aside, she was very happy to see them both. Dager sat straight up and remained quiet as he stared at the two adults. Goy gently shushed Lucia.

"Keep quiet, love. We don't want the hag here, at least not yet." And then she directed her attention to her little boy. "Hello, Dager," she said, as she cautiously extended her hand toward him. Goy held her breath and she wondered if it were or if it were not the right thing to do. Dager looked at his mother's hand for a moment, and then turned to Lucia. Lucia smiled happily and nodded to him. He stared at both parents then, and he could easily see the similarities between them and his sister. He could tell they were family. He wondered if he also resembled them, and then he looked at their feet. Just like Lucia, they wore no shoes! But most importantly, they really did look kind. Oh, so kind. Just like in his dreams. In fact, he was sure these *were* the people from his dreams. Dager let out a smile, and then reached his hand toward Goy's.

"Hi... Ma," he hesitated for a second, and then looked at Mod and greeted him the same way. "Hi, Da." His voice was small and quiet. In part, because he worried that the hag might barge in at any moment. His eyes narrowed slightly and he wondered how effective the four of them might be against the hag.

Mod and Goy were pleased by Dager's positive reaction to them. Goy wished she could erase the last two bad years and replace them with good ones. There was so much she needed to know about him, the little boy who sat before her, virtually a stranger.

"Dager, love. We've missed you a great deal, and we're very glad to see you again." Goy's hands were back on her own lap now, and she rubbed them nervously against one another. She was surprised at her own self-control. Much to her relief, the boy didn't seem to be the least bit resentful toward her or Mod, or even Lucia. This was a good sign, and exceeded her expectations by a long shot. The child remained quiet, and so she continued. "We'd very much like to take you home with us, Dager. Would you like that?" Dager was enjoying hearing the sound of his mother's kind voice and as such, didn't utter a word. He nodded and smiled. Lucia on the other hand, was becoming impatient and couldn't stand the idea of spending another minute on the dreaded surface.

"Ma, let's go!" she hopped up from the hay bale and grabbing Dager by the hand, pulled him along with her. In no time, they were by the door, ready to take their leave. For the first time since their arrival, Mod spoke to the children, but in an extremely soft tone, so as not to frighten his son.

"No, not yet. Come sit a minute, children." Lucia knew full well to obey her father's word and so rather reluctantly, she pulled her brother back to the hay bale. The two of them sat down, side by side.

"Lucia, I can tell that you and Dager have spent the last day getting to know each other a great deal." Both children nodded eagerly at him. "That is good. Dager, I feel that you are comfortable with us. Am I right?" Dager nodded again, and smiled shyly. Mod then pointed to Dager's pocket. "May I see it?" Dager looked at his father blankly, but only for a moment. He had completely forgotten about the sharp object that he'd cut his hand on. After the events of the last few days, it felt as though that had happened a lifetime ago. Goy and Lucia knew nothing about it, but they remained quiet as they watched and waited. Dager thrust his hand deep into his pocket and brought out the tarnished metal piece. Mod gently took it from him, then turned it over and over in his own hand, before giving it back.

"I know you probably don't remember this, Dager, but when you were a wee boy, your grandfather lost this piece of his medallion," and then Mod pointed to his own medallion, to show Dager what a medallion was. Dager didn't remember, and looked from his father, to the metal piece in his hand, and then back to his father again. "The day Croy took you from us, you found this and put it safely away in your pocket." In actuality, Mod had watched it happen in his vision, but how could he explain that to the boy? There was no way he could understand that yet, and it was in his best interest that Mod kept things as simple as possible. "Yesterday morning, when you cut your hand on it, you bled onto the ground. That was the first time since your arrival on the surface that your blood spilled onto the ground." Dager nodded, but he didn't understand what that had to do with anything. "The moment your blood touched the earth, your grandfather knew where to find you." Dager nodded, remembering now that it was only moments after he'd cut his hand, when he'd heard the strange voice that seemed to have echoed throughout the sky. His grandfather's voice.

"Yes, that was him who talked to me, wasn't it?" Mod slapped his hand to his knee excitedly. He was thrilled to be speaking with his son at long last, and happy that his son understood.

"Aye, he spoke to you. He told you about the girl, didn't he? Your grandfather searched for you the entire time you were gone, son. The fact that you bled from his medallion is more than a coincidence. It was meant to be. Do you understand?"

"A little. Lucia said there is magic where we come from. Is it magic? Did magic make me bleed?"

"Maybe it was magic that made you bleed, and it was certainly magic that connected you to your grandfather. Can I see your hand, now?" Dager stretched out his arm and displayed the palm of his hand for all to see. There was no sign of blood or injury, and it was just as Mod expected. He smiled. "Just as I thought, Dager. You are a Curor, just as I am and just as my father before me. You are destined for many great things, of that we can be sure." Dager beamed proudly. He really didn't understand half of what Mod was telling him, and he wouldn't for a long while to come. But for now, all he needed to know was that he was truly part of a family. A genuine, happy family with parents and even a sister; just like in his dreams! "Come here, boy!" Mod opened his arms wide and without hesitation, Dager scampered into them. As they embraced, the boy pinched himself. He couldn't help it. And when it hurt, he knew that his dreams really had come true. From this day on, he would be a free boy who had an entire family that loved him. And then he heard them laugh. His parents and Lucia laughed easily and happily. It was not the wicked laughter that he was sadly used to hearing, either. This was the good variety of laughter that came straight from the bellies of kind people.

And then, right in the middle of their long overdue and joyous reunion, they heard it. Chills ran up and down Dager's spine as he heard the hag screech his name. Could it be, that this dream was meant to come to an abrupt, cruel end, just like all the other dreams had? He blinked hard as he looked in turn at each person in the barn. There was a hush of silence, and Dager could feel each and every beat of his own heart. He thought for sure, that it might burst right out of his chest. And then they heard it again, angrier and louder than the first time around. So loud that it reverberated off the walls. The sound was so unnatural and wicked that even Goy shook with trepidation.

"POND SCUM!"

# 10

# MAYBELLE P. BONNADOOLIO

Gia pointed to the lone figure in the distance, which was steadily making its way toward them. "Look, Pagan! See who is coming to join us!"

Pagan looked up the hill at the tall approaching form, from the little mound of sand she'd been playing in, and asked, "Who, Ma? Who is that man?" Gia giggled; for she knew that there was no way in the world, her daughter could recognize Brand in his new and improved condition.

"Why, that's the old man I've been tending to, love. He's all better now, see?" Pagan nodded, but absently turned her attention back to the sand. She'd never had a whole lot to do with the old man, for whenever her mother had tended to him, she would be at the nanny's. She'd only actually seen him three times, and each time he'd been lying flat out, covered with a blanket and motionless. Gia hopped to her feet to greet him.

"I see you've made it, Gia!" Brand made small talk and smiled at the young woman.

"Are you kidding? I would let nothing stand in my way. What can I do to help?" she asked, as she knew there was much to be done, but she had no idea where to begin. Brand waved at Pagan as they passed her in the sand, and he and Gia sat down together on the higher, dry ground, not very far from where the child played contentedly.

"At this point, nothing. I am going to summon some people. People whom I think will be interested in joining us here. Before long, we'll have scores of workers. There will be builders and teachers and weavers and the like, to help us build our new village," he replied, as he turned and smiled at her, and as he did, her eyes opened wide in astonishment. His teeth had grown back in! She could easily see that most of the wrinkles and lines in his aged face had also disappeared. This man who sat beside her suddenly appeared twenty years younger.

"But sir... I mean, Brand. There must be something I can do. I may be just a woman, but I can manage." she looked at him hopefully as she asked. She wanted so much to contribute. He smiled back as he replied.

"Oh, yes. You are definitely a woman, Gia. But you are not just a woman; you are every bit as important as any man, and don't you forget it. Not just any woman would care for an old man the way you have done, Gia. I will never forget the patience and kindness you continuously demonstrated to the old cripple that I once was. It will not now, nor will it ever be, overlooked." Gia blushed and looked humbly down at her feet. Never had she been paid such compliments. At least not since the high council had sent her beloved husband away, more than four years before.

"Thank you, Brand. And thank you for inviting us to be part of such a wonderful new world." Pagan looked up then, curiously.

"What new world? What do you mean?" she clapped the wet sand from her hands and plunked herself down upon her mother's comfortable lap. With a twinkle in her eye, Gia answered her inquisitive child.

"Well, Pagan. How would you like it if we lived here? How about if you never had to go back to the nanny's again?" Pagan squealed with delight, and looked from her mother to the old man who suddenly didn't seem so old after all.

"Really, Ma? We can live right here in the green grass and the big flowers?"

"Yes, we can. Pagan, we're never going back to the village to live. This will be our new home!" Pagan bounced up from her mother's lap and danced this way and that, for joy. With tears of happiness welling up in her eyes, Gia watched her child as she returned to the mound of sand that was beginning to look more and more, like a hut.

Brand stood then, and stated, "I need to be alone for a while, Gia. I'll be in the thicket of willows should you need me, but for now I have to summon the others. While I'm at it, is there anyone in particular that you would like to be included?" Gia shook her head, no. Other than the old man and her daughter, as far as she was concerned, she was completely alone in the world. Brand understood, nodded, and left for the willows. And Gia? She sat right down in the wet sand beside her daughter and played.

Brand sat near the tallest willow, the one with the hollow trunk, which was in fact the entrance to the dreaded surface world. He saw his son's overloaded wagon half hidden in the bush a little farther off. He knew that all was well on the surface and that was good, for he needed to concentrate now on providing for his village. And what would the village be called? He'd already decided that in all fairness, the name of it would eventually be brought to a vote. A vote which would include all new villagers; every single man, woman, and child. The old man brought his knees up to his chest and squeezed his medallion between the palms of his hands. In no time at all, he had made contact with some very important people. Not only some of the villagers from Hurtsmire, but with some of those from the surrounding communities as well. There were four entire families from Hurtsmire who replied that they would be more than eager to pack up and move. And then he added two cousins from a nearby community, and a niece and her family from another. Brand was happy with that. Small numbers to begin with, but as things naturally tend to do, the new village would eventually blossom and grow. Soon, and very soon, there would be enough good, contributing people upon which they could build.

He wasn't done summoning yet; for there was one more man that he intended to include. And because Brand had never met him, connecting with him would take a great deal of time and energy. Brand concentrated with all his might on the vision of Gia and her daughter. It was not long before his vision took him far away. As far away as the village called Chadwhip, which sat on the farthermost border of the Tasman Empire. A remote community, so disconnected that it would take any regular person weeks to reach it on foot.

The young, thickly-bearded man appeared before him as clear as day. He was a servant in the office of yet another corrupt government. The old man spoke to him softly, so as not to scare him off. Finally the young man's eyes flickered brightly, and then he nodded in response. He would leave for the new village as soon as possible.

Brand was exhausted now. Even though he was in excellent physical condition, his skills were rusty and he'd had to exert twice the usual effort to employ them. His current task done, all that was left for him to do, was sit and wait. He clambered to his feet, steadied himself and then returned to the shore. He sat on the dry ground and as he waited, he watched the mother and daughter pair build their miniature village, and then he basked in the glory of life and all that was new.

Mod was the first to jump to his feet. His blood boiled at the very sound of the hag yelling for his son in such a humiliating manner. Wouldn't the hag be surprised at the sight of him and his wife! He couldn't wait to confront her. He reached down for his wife's hand, and then helped her to her feet. He glanced over at his son, who was quite noticeably afraid. Mod patted the boy reassuringly on his arm.

"Son, there is no reason for you to dread her anymore. Let's go and see this almighty hag. Let's go and see what this bad mama is made of, shall we?" Dager looked up and saw the passion radiating from his father's eyes, and it was at that very moment, that he knew he had nothing to fear. How could that old woman do anything to him, now? He had a gleam in his eye as he replied.

"Okay, but I will go first." A brilliant scheme had begun to form in his mind. He hurried away from Mod and stood in full view of the hag, in the doorway of the barn. The hag squinted against the wickedly hot sun, and saw him standing there. She screeched.

"Don't just stand there, pond scum. Bring the lass out, she's mine now!" she ordered as she cackled with glee, for she'd already dreamt up an entire day's worth of chores for the girl to work off. After all, the lass could hardly expect to be fed and sheltered for free, could she? But, Dager continued to just stand there. Arrogantly, he then took two steps forward, put his hands upon his hips and spat on the ground toward her. He answered in the toughest, gruffest voice he'd ever used.

"NO!" The hag could hardly believe her ears. What did the scum want, a good beating or perhaps another day or two locked up in the chicken coop? She'd show him. She hopped down from the landing, careful to step over the broken and strewn about steps, then rushed menacingly toward him.

"What's that you said, pond scum? Mama is sure she ain't heard ya say no." she had decided to give the boy one more chance to reply properly, but just the same, the consequences of his first refusal would be severe. Very unexpectedly then, she saw movement behind the boy, and she looked over his shoulder just as the lass stepped out of the barn and into the hot sun.

"He said, no!" Lucia screamed at the hag, and then reached over and took a firm hold of her brother's hand. The hag's shrill cackle rang out again. Oh, what a fine day this was turning out to be. It would take more than a dozen children teamed up together, she knew, to hold a candle against her wrath. So what chance did these two think they stood? None. Oh, the fun she would have.

"Lassie, you can talk! I ain't got no clue as to what malarkey my boy's bin fillin' yer head with, but ya ain't nowhere nears makin' a wise choice here. Now ya step aside so I kin give the boy what's comin' to 'im.'"

With that, the hag covered the distance between her and the children, in no time. She moved so quickly that the children stepped back suddenly and lost their footing. It was a good thing too; because the hag's hand was high in the air, ready to strike Dager across his head. As it was, Mod shot out of the barn and with lightning speed, grabbed the hag by her upraised arm. The hag shrank back and tried to get away from this strange man, but he held her fast. Her chin quivered at first, but she soon recovered and her expression turned as mean as ever.

"I think your days of hitting this boy are over, hag." Mod glared at her, and stood right in between her and his children. She clucked her tongue through her missing teeth as she watched a plain looking woman emerge from the shadows and gather the children up and into her protective arms. The nerve.

"Nay! Nay, I say. Them's my kids and ya ain't got no business here, stranger. Y'all take yer woman and git!" The hag tried vainly to show courage, but it was becoming obvious even to her, that she could not break free of the amazingly strong man. Worse, he showed no sign at all, that he would let go of her arm any time soon. The hag commanded, in a voice that sounded weaker than she liked, "And whilst yer at it, unhand my arm!"

"I'll let go, when I'm good and ready, hag. By the way, did Dager ever ask you to let go of his arm?" The woman rolled her eyes into the back of her head. Surely he had confused her with someone else. She looked him straight in the eye, cocked her head, and informed him.

"I ain't known no Dager. What'ya talkin' 'bout? Thar's never been no Dager in these parts. Ya best git 'fore I call my husband now. I'm tryin' to save yer skin here, man!" her voice had become louder and more shrill. This time, it was Goy who stepped forward. And in a voice calmer than even Goy herself imagined possible, she addressed the hag.

"I'd like to introduce you to *my* children. Did you hear that? *My* children. This boy's name is Dager, not pond scum. And this here, is Lucia. They have names. They are people and they deserve to be treated with respect." The hag flinched as though she'd been struck and tried again to step away, but Mod's grip on her arm would not allow her to move even so much as an inch. Goy was not finished with her.

"And husband? You have no husband. You're a liar. You are a liar and a coward who abuses children." The hag glared hard at the woman who had confronted her. She would never admit to any of that. After all, she'd only ever done what needed to be done. And she treated children no differently from how she herself had been raised, which was in fact, right in this very yard. Dager and Lucia stood off to the side, watching quietly. Lucia had never heard her mother use such a tone of voice before, with anybody. She was impressed. Mod turned on the hag again.

"I know where you will go, hag. My family and I have some preparations to make before we go home. And until then, I know exactly what to do with you." Mod winked at Goy and the children, and then half-pulled, half-dragged the woman to the chicken coop. As soon as she realized where he was taking her, she tried in vain to dig her heels into the unforgiving, hard earth. It was a futile attempt, at best.

"NAY! Not in there! I can't go into the chicken coop! I'll die, for sure! You can't kill a poor old woman like me!" But it was too late; her begging would do her no good on this day. Mod swung the door open, threw her in and locked it tight. He heard her sob for a moment, and then any sounds she tried to make were quickly drowned out by the clucking of the excited, overcrowded birds. Mod returned and faced his family, who were standing stone still, and staring at him with their mouths agape. Dager was worried.

"She won't really die in there, will she, Da?"

"Oh, no. But perhaps she'll think twice before locking another helpless child in there, son. Don't worry; I will not cause her harm, although I admit that I think I really could. After all she's done to you..." his voice trailed off, as he reached behind Dager, and lifted up his tattered shirt. Although Dager did not understand what his father was doing, he stood still while his father examined his old wounds. Curious, Goy raised her eyebrows and started for the direction of Dager's backside, but Mod raised his hand to stop her.

"No, Goy. You don't need to see this, my love." Goy stopped in midstride and began to fidget with her hands again. Lucia knew that this was the perfect opportunity for a well-timed distraction.

"Ma, come with me and see the baby... ra... I mean, what are they called, Dager?"

"Puppies," he answered quietly, and watched his sister pull their mother back into the dim of the barn. Mod ran his hand up and down Dager's scarred back.

"Son, I am deeply sorry that this happened to you." Tears welled up in his eyes as he examined the damage done to the boy, by the hag. Dager replied honestly.

"It's alright, Da. She hasn't done it for a long time, not since I learned about the consequences." Mod nodded at his hardened little boy, but he was still sad. No child after all, should ever have to be on the sharp side of a whip.

"I'm going to make it right for you, boy. Just stand still." Dager did as he was told and his father kept one hand on his back, while placing the other on his medallion. Magically and within minutes, the beatings were little more than dull, painless memories, and all physical signs of them had completely disappeared. Mod pulled the shirt back down to cover Dager's back, reassuring him as he did so. "This doesn't go on at home, you know."

"I know! Or at least I think I do. I've dreamt about it. Laughter and games and magic, right?" Mod laughed and hugged his son.

"Aye, that's pretty much it. Although there is more to it. Nice places to live, good grub, fresh water and the company of loved ones. And school! How does that sound to you?" Dager smiled up at his father, who tousled his hair, lovingly.

"Just like a dream, Da. It sounds like a dream!" Dager was eager to join his mother and sister, and so he asked, "Want to see the puppies, the baby hounds?" Mod nodded and the two of them disappeared into the barn. After all, there would be plenty of time to make the long journey home, now that the hag had been taken care of, and now that they were all together again. Besides, Mod surmised. He was not really ready to leave, for the hag hadn't been locked in the chicken coop, long enough yet.

As they approached the hound and her babies, Mod and Dager could hear Lucia explaining to Goy.

"Dager knows all about this kind of thing, Ma! He's seen other kinds of babies get born the same way!" Dager's cheeks reddened a little, and he wondered what the big deal about it was. He knelt and sat down near Mindy's head, and then cradled it tenderly in his lap. The hound rubbed her nose up against his hand. Mod wrapped an arm around his wife, and they all sat together quietly watching. Mod could tell that it would not be so easy, for his son to leave the animals.

"Dager, you really like these animals, don't you?"

"Well, yes! Mindy is my friend. And the horse too, and the pigs... we all live together. Or we used to," he corrected himself, once he realized that he wouldn't really be living there, anymore. He wondered out loud. "What will happen to them once I go? Who will brush them and talk to them and be their friend?" he worried then, and admonished himself for not having thought about the well-being of the animals sooner.

"Actually, I've been thinking about that." Dager raised his eyebrows and looked at Mod, who was smiling at him, wholeheartedly.

"You have?" Dager stammered, quite surprised.

"Aye. The hag will never raise a whip or a boot to, or backhand another living being for as long as she lives, I'll see to that. And she'll spend the rest of her miserable life, making up for all the harm she's caused." Dager couldn't believe it. How would that ever be possible? The hag surely didn't have a kind bone in her whole entire body!

"She will?" His father nodded, and Goy beamed at them both. Lucia knew exactly what their father was capable of, and none of what he was saying surprised her. She was busy anyway, and her complete attention was focused on the baby hound with the white feet.

"Aye, she will. And do you know what, Dager? In time, she'll come to like it. She'll be a better person for it, in the end." Dager was in disbelief, and despondently, he replied.

"Yes, maybe. Or until she gets another boy to do it for her." Dager felt pity for the next boy; for he knew there would be another, and then another and probably another after that, who would have to endure all that he himself, had gone through.

"Oh, no. There will be no more children here. I'll convince her of that, as well. You don't need to worry about the animals or any more children, Dager. It's as good as done." Dager was confused as he looked from one parent to the other. Goy knelt in close toward him.

"It's true, Dager. Your father is a powerful Curor. All will be right, before we take our leave on this day." she reached over and held him by the hand. And then for a little while longer, they all sat and watched Mindy take care of her babies some more.

A good while later, Mod knew it would be best if they soon made way for home. He didn't wish to spend another night on the horrid surface, and he was pretty confident that his family felt the same way.

"Goy and Lucia, may I have your canteens?" Goy untied her shoulder bag, and handed him hers. Lucia took hers from her apron and passed it to him as well. "Dager, would you care to come with me? You will need to show me where the hag keeps her fresh water!" Dager gently moved out from under Mindy's head and joined his father. They walked out of the barn and both strained to see under the glare of the hot sun.

"It's in her house, Da. And there's bread, too. It isn't good bread, though." Dager smiled apologetically at his father, at the same time wishing he had something better to offer; like the grub his sister had shared with him. Now that tasted good!

"That's alright, son. All we'll need is water, for we're heading straight home. We can eat once we arrive there, and I'm pretty sure there will be more than enough for all. Besides, we wouldn't want to spoil our appetites!" he followed his son into the rundown shack. It looked as though it may have been a nice home at one time, but at present it was a disgusting, disorganized mess. Mod wondered how the hag herself didn't get lost in it. They made their way through to what probably at one time, had functioned as a kitchen, and he filled the canteens from a jug. The water looked clear, Mod thought, and coincidentally, Dager explained.

"I fetch fresh water for her every day, from the well, Da. So I know it's good. But, this must be yesterday's water." Mod nodded.

"Aye, it's good." He said, as he recapped the canteens, then together they hurried from the house. "Now we have one piece of unfinished business left, Dager," he smiled as he looked over to the chicken coop. Dager smiled back.

"The hag?"

"Aye, the hag." Mod handed the canteens to his son to carry, and together they crossed the yard to the chicken coop. The chickens had settled down now, and all was quiet from inside.

"Hag!" Mod called out, and the old woman was not happy as she replied angrily.

"What?" Mod winked at Dager, who was still not sure how this would play out. He tried to smile again, but as he did, he took a few steps backward.

"I'm going to open the door and the two of us are going to have a talk, okay?"

"I ain't talkin' to no stranger," she replied haughtily, as though she were in control of the situation.

"Aye, as you wish it. Then we'll go, and well, good luck to you, I guess." It was as though the world had suddenly stopped spinning for the hag, and all was still. She remained silent for a brief moment, but she soon realized that she really was stuck between a rock and a hard place.

"Alright, alright. Have it yer way. I'll talk with ya a bit." Mod and Dager heard her shuffle through the hens as she made her way to the door. Mod reached up and undid the latch, and in the next instant, she'd thrown the door open and jumped out. She lost her footing and landed flat on her back on the hard, hot ground with a thud. She was covered in filth. Quickly, Dager locked the coop back up, before any of the chickens were able to escape. Roughly, Mod grabbed the hag by her sleeves and pulled her to her feet. He moved his face to within inches of her own, and spoke to her in a soft and controlled tone of voice.

"There are some conditions here that your freedom depends on, hag," he spat, as he pulled her over to the water trough, then forced her to sit on the edge of it. She was too scared to complain and she looked back at him with big, round, hopeful eyes. Mod knelt down in front of her so they were at eye level, and Dager only looked on from a safe distance, a few feet away. "First, you will apologize to my son for all that you've done to him. And it had better be sincere." Tears welled up in her eyes. She had never, ever been made to do such a degrading thing. And to a child! Why, it had never been heard of. Nonetheless, she could see that she had no choice in the matter.

"I'm sorry, boy." she looked at him directly and for a moment, Dager almost thought she meant what she'd said. But, then he saw that old familiar cruelty flicker in her eyes, and he scowled. Mod turned to him.

"Was that good? Are you happy with that, Dager?" to which Dager nodded. After all, why prolong this? He knew that she'd never mean it anyway, even if they spent the next hundred years asking her.

"Good then. Now look at this," he ordered the hag to look at his medallion; which she did, for not knowing any better, she didn't see the harm in it. That just so happened to be her first and last mistake. The moment she laid eyes upon the medallion, she was completely spellbound. Her will to fight disappeared in an instant, as had most everything else she'd ever known or been. The medallion sucked every ounce of strength from her body and when it was done, all that was left was an empty, poor old pitiful looking woman. Dager was sure she'd shrunk in size, right before his very eyes. Mod had only just begun.

"Woman!"

"Yes?" she looked at Mod with a new, bright glint in her eyes as she asked him; she was curious to know how this strange man and boy had suddenly happened to be standing right in front of her. Mod waited patiently for her to find her bearings.

"What is your name?" and then, in a voice so musical and syrupy sweet and high-pitched, which Dager never imagined could ever come from her, she sang out happily.

"Why, I am Maybelle P. Bonnadoolio! Do I know you, son?"

Quietly to himself, Dager tried to pronounce her last name; he couldn't do it, and tried to stop his sudden case of the giggles with the back of his hand.

"Of course you do, Maybelle! My name is Mod, and this is my son, Dager. We are your old friends. Do you remember, now?"

She looked at him and smiled warmly. "Yes! How could I forget sweet boys such as yourselves? Would you care for some tea?"

"No, you already gave us tea, and it was lovely."

"Oh! Good, then," she looked genuinely pleased that the man and his son had enjoyed her tea. Dager stepped in closer to take a better look. He couldn't believe his eyes, or his ears. He pinched himself again, and it hurt like it had before. This just had to be real.

"What can I do for you then, Mod and Dager?" she reached over and squeezed Dager affectionately on his cheek. "My, my, you are a sweet young thing. But I do declare that you are in desperate need of soap and a warm bath!" Dager frowned at the woman who had rarely, if ever, allowed him something as luxurious as a bath.

"Maybelle, we need to go soon, but there are a few things we need to discuss, first."

"Oh, Mod? Going? I really wish you wouldn't go. We've been having such a wonderful time, haven't we?" distraught as she was, she busied her hands and began to fold flat, the pleats of her overly voluminous skirt.

"Aye, we have," Mod began. "We'll be back someday, I promise."

"Well, as long as you promise and let me know so I can prepare some more tea, and perhaps a decent meal?" she asked coyly, as she fluttered her eyelashes.

"Aye, I'll do that. Now as for the important matters..."

"Yes, Mod! What is it that we need to talk about?"

"The animals. They must have fresh grub and water every single day."

"Of course they do, silly man."

"And they need attention. They need your company. The horse needs brushing every morning and every night. The cow needs to be milked by you, every morning and every night. The pigs love it when you sing to them in their pen. They need you to sing to them so they can follow the sound of your beautiful voice!"

"Yes, Mod, I know all that! Every single day. I love my animals. They are my friends. And who else would do all those things, but me?"

"That's right, just you. And Mindy has had her babies, you know!" The hag clapped her hands with joy.

"Oh, how lovely. I think I'll sleep in the barn with her for a few nights, to keep watch. We wouldn't want anything to happen to her or those precious puppies, now would we?"

"No, they are very special to you. You are so good and kind to all those around you, Maybelle. People and animals are lucky to know you."

"Yes, I know. I love all kinds of things."

"And children."

"Well, of course I love children!" she winked at Dager. "I was a child once myself, and it was just wonderful."

"Yes it was, but children don't live here."

"Oh, no. I'm not that fortunate to have children live here. It's just me and my lovely animals and of course you and Dager, when you come to visit."

"That's right, but we have to go now. I think you were on your way to collect the eggs."

"Of course I was, you silly man. Now how's about giving a sweet old woman a hug, before you go?" she asked, as she'd given up on trying to convince them to stay, and resigned herself to the fact that soon she would be left alone. She sighed. "I suppose it's just as well anyway, because I have a lot of chores to do." Mod hugged the woman, and he and his son watched her fetch the egg pail from its hook on the side of the chicken coop. As far as Maybelle was concerned, they were as good as gone; she skipped along without a care in the world, lost in a new and mysterious blissful trance. Dager was amazed. He and Mod turned and headed back for the barn, where Goy and Lucia waited. Before they reached the door, the old gelding ran up to the fence alongside the father-son pair. Dager smiled and dashed to the bag of dried corn that sat waiting in the shadow of the barn's wall. It saddened him to know that setting the horse free, as he had promised it earlier, would not be a wise thing to do, but at least he was now assured that the horse would be cared for properly. Mod watched his son hold his hand out flat to the horse and feed it. He remained quiet as he watched the exchange.

Once in the barn, Dager rather hesitantly said his goodbyes to Mindy and her puppies, and then at last the family of four was off. They headed down the road, toward the river, and in doing so, shortened the distance between Dager's old sad life with the hag, and his optimistic new beginning with his real family that loved him.

# 11

# INTO THE FOREST

Most of the new arrivals came with little more than the clothing on their backs. They knelt at the feet of the old man. He urged them to rise and get to work, for there was little time for formalities and still much to be done. His new, strong and youthful presence awarded him even more respect than ever before.

The few children that accompanied their parents, joined Pagan and they played together at the shallow edge of the pond, while young mothers joined Gia at the shore. The men had begun to gather fallen logs from the forest to help build temporary shelters, until more permanent structures could be erected. Those who were highly skilled, went deeper into the forest to fall the older, larger trees that could be used in later construction.

Once the women saw that the children would be satisfied playing in the water, they delegated a pair of teenage girls to watch over them while they went off to gather grub. They carried nuts and berries in the aprons of their dresses, and began to prepare the evening's humble feast. Word had already spread through the small crowd, of the upcoming arrival of Mod and his family.

Brand was pleased by the goings on around him. The dining area was laid out, with the exception of the food, which would of course be served at the last minute. He could see, in the outlying area around the Great Pond, makeshift shelters made ready in preparation for the evening's end. He was looking around at the eager new villagers with intense pride, when unexpectedly, he felt a sharp tugging upon his vest. He looked down at the source; it was none other than Gia's child, Pagan.

"Well now, what can I do for you?" he asked, as he picked her up and placed her on his knee. She did not answer. She reached up with both hands, and rather boldly ran them from his cheekbones, all the way down to his stubbly chin. She examined the creases in his face, shivered a little, and then folded her hands and smacked them down sharply on her own lap. Her big blue eyes searched his face for a moment longer, before she demanded to know.

"Are we going to have a party, old Granda?" she then smiled at him, hoping his answer would be yes. But she didn't allow him enough time to reply. "Is it a birthday and will there be gifts?" Brand laughed at the inquisitive child.

"Aye, we're going to have a party. But no, there will be no gifts," he thought for a moment, and then, "how old are you, Pagan?" She held up all five fingers on her left hand, and with the other, she rubbed her sleepy eyes, made a sour face, then yawned. "Well, what do you know? We're having a party for Dager, and he's five, too!" She wiggled excitedly on his knee.

"Five like me?" and she held up her fingers again, just to make sure. Brand nodded. "Where is Dager, old Granda?" And she began to search the faces of the other children, who looked like they might be five. Brand shook his head.

"Oh, no, Pagan. Dager is not here yet. His family will be bringing him here soon. You don't know this little boy, for he has been living in a place that is far, far away." The little girl nodded her head, and settled down again. She lifted her legs, and curled up into a ball. Brand cradled her within his arms and in no time at all, and very obviously without a care in the world, Pagan fell fast asleep.

The highest member of council, the man who sat on the uppermost seat in the center of the pyramid, stood. His hands were balled into tight fists at his sides and his teeth were clenched with rage. All eyes fell upon him. He thought for a moment, and then reached up with his left hand and twisted one side of his long moustache. Initially, he hadn't believed Mod's threat to abandon his village; but for hours now, there had been absolutely no sign of him, his wife or daughter. The highest member of council was outraged, to say the least. Suddenly then, with his right hand, he picked up the dreaded gavel and smashed it down so hard upon the podium that the gavel broke in two. The pieces flew high into the air before landing on the audience. No one dared move an inch. This infuriated him even more and he began to shake. The villagers, who had come because they were curious, were now regretting their decision to attend.

The highest member of council raised his arms high above his head, and it looked as though he was about to take flight. He yelled out, in his thundering boom of a voice.

"GUARDS!"

Ten heavily armed men suddenly appeared from out of nowhere and proceeded to kneel before him. He took a sip of water from his earthenware cup, and stepped down from his position. In a move never seen before, he paced. Back and forth, back and forth. It was quite unnerving for the guards, who had volunteered their services, and they began to sweat bullets. Their heads remained bowed, low to the ground; not one of them dared look up, for fear of making eye contact with the highest council member. The raging man's head snapped upwards, and for some reason only known to him, he regained his composure and returned to sit atop the pyramid in his uppermost seat. The silence was nearly unbearable. Anticipation hung so thick in the air that it was almost visible. He twisted his moustache again, and then yelled so all could hear.

"Mod has gone ahead with his stupid, stupid decision and in doing so, he has betrayed the Village of Hurtsmire! He is nowhere to be found. Therefore, the only conclusion to be made here is that he has gone against my wishes. No! Correction! Our wishes! The wishes of each and every one of you!" he pointed his finger toward his audience, lest there be no mistake to whom he was referring. "He has betrayed us. Left us vulnerable to attack. No man who is loyal to his service would do such a thing. He will be punished, and mark my words. He will pay dearly for his wrongdoing. Did he really think that we would just let him walk away?" he paused then, and rather disturbingly, with both hands, played with his moustache again. To anyone wise enough to know better, it would seem that this man had lost his grip on reality. But on this day unfortunately, it would not appear that anyone wise enough to know better, was present. Missing his gavel, he slapped his hand down hard on the podium. Too hard, for he flinched and pulled it back, and then rubbed the palms of his hands together.

"CROY! If Croy is present, he would do well to step forth." Rather dramatically, and as though rehearsed, Croy's form appeared in the doorway. His heavy steps carried him all the way down the aisle, and he stopped just behind the row of kneeling guards, whom it seemed for the time being, had been forgotten. Respectfully, Croy knelt and hung his head. No one could see the evil smile that formed on his lips, for he, as did everyone else in the room, knew what was coming. The drums sounded, and then each of the council members stood. Croy was waiting to be touched upon the shoulder, his signal to stand. Finally the high member ordered.

"Stand, man! Can you not see I haven't got a gavel?" Croy stood obediently. He bowed to each member of council in turn, and then waited again, to be addressed. He did not have to wait long, for the Village of Hurtsmire was in dire need of a Curor.

"Croy of the Tasman Empire!"

"T'is I." Croy replied.

"You know why you've been summoned on this day, do you not?"

"Aye, I do."

"And will you accept the position of Curor for the Village of Hurtsmire? Are you aware of all that acceptance of such an esteemed position entails?"

"Aye, I accept, and I am aware."

"Your life will no longer be your own. You live for the high council of the Village of Hurtsmire. Anything and everything else that you once held dear, will now be of secondary importance."

"Aye."

"From now on, you live and breathe for the

good of the village and you will do our bidding. Do you submit to us?"

"Entirely. I live and breathe for Hurtsmire. It is and always has been, my destiny." The council members took their seats again; all but the high member, who was not yet done.

"All of you..." he waved his arms toward the audience, who was at this moment, filled with dread. None of them had wished for Mod to step down as Curor, and many of them thought it would never come to pass. They had always enjoyed the banter and the disputes between Mod and Croy. Now, having Croy actually appointed to such a position did not exactly fill them with hope for the future. "... bear witness on this day to the appointment of our new line of Curors. Let us rejoice in this new beginning and welcome Croy as the new Curor for the Village of Hurtsmire, of the Tasman Empire!" Because it was expected of them, the villagers all stomped their feet in response. The drums sounded, and the high member sat down. It was done. Croy turned and retraced his steps down the aisle, and took his leave of the cave. He had much to do, after all - the first of which being, to move his family into the Curor's home.

In the meantime, back in the Meeting chambers, the high member had the drums play again, and all of the villagers were swiftly dismissed. The drums beat faster than usual, urging the people to leave quickly. Soon, the only people who remained were the council members, the drummers, and the guards.

"Guards." The guards stood, relieved at last to receive their orders. "You must journey to the surface and find Mod. Bring him back to me, alive." The lead guard, the one with the most seniority was the only man allowed to question council, and so he asked.

"And what of his family, sir? We can only guess that they are together. Do you wish us to capture them, as well?" The high member fiddled with his moustache before replying.

"His family is no threat to us. His father is on his deathbed. In fact, how they moved him out of the village without notice is beyond me. Regardless. The women, well they can scorch on the surface for all I care. They're no good to us here, anyway. We have enough women to worry about." He twisted his moustache rather wickedly now, as he considered further. "But, if you can fetch a good coin for the pair of them, I suppose any money collected could prove useful," he rubbed his chin for a moment, obviously delighted with his most recent decision. "Aye, that's what you shall do! Leave the old man wherever you happen to find him, and sell the woman and child. The money will come in handy on your return back, anyway. Any leftovers, you will bring back here for the village purse."

"And the boy, sir? What of the boy?" The high member laughed.

"If, and I do mean if they retrieved the boy at all, he is of no worry either. He is too young to cure, and so it's not likely that he will ever have the chance to follow in Mod's footsteps. If they've fetched him at all, you may sell him along with his mother and sister."

"Aye, it will be done," the lead guard replied faithfully. "And the route we would take, sir? Which route would you have us use?"

"Well now, it's occurred to me that Mod most likely took the route the old man told him to take. Naturally then, we would have to assume they would come back the same way. Not if we cut them off, however. Supposing you guards get to the point where the rivers meet before they make it back. You could stop their return to the village. Find a place to camp out, while some of you look after Mod, and the rest of you will sell his family..." the high member's expression was wicked, as he shook his head, correcting himself. "Nay! Nay, I say." The guards leaned in closer. "Take Mod with you so he can watch his wife, daughter and son, being sold off, one by one. It's only fitting, isn't it? The betrayer, betrayed? Aye, I like it. Make it so." With a slight wave of his hand, the guards were dispatched. The drums began, but their sound was quickly muffled by the intensity of twenty heavy marching feet that headed out of the dim cave and into the light of day.

Brand jumped. Just a little, but enough to

disturb the slumber of the little girl who'd been resting upon his lap. Pagan was not pleased and she was not afraid to let him know it.

"Old Granda! I was having a nap!" she declared haughtily as she folded her arms across her chest. He smiled at the cranky young thing, and then stood her up on her feet.

"Aye, Pagan. So you were. It's time for you to go and play with the others now," and then he gave her a look. The look was hardly unkind, but it was stern enough that she quickly decided it would be best to obey him. She ran back to the shallow edge of the pond and rejoined the handful of children that still played there. Brand closed his eyes and held his medallion tightly against his chest. Something was wrong; very wrong, indeed. In that uncanny way of knowing, he knew that time would not be on his side, on this particular day. He looked quickly over at the women that were rinsing grub off, in the water. He spotted Gia right away, and called out to her.

"Aye, Brand?" she dropped what she was doing and ran to his side. The look on his face was almost panic stricken, and it worried her.

"Gia, you and the women must take all of the children into the forest and hide. The guards are on their way. Go deep into the forest, and don't come out until I tell you it is safe." All colour drained from Gia's face, but she nodded and ran to alert the others. The berries and fruit were thrown into the middle of the pond, where each piece either sank, or was quickly gobbled up by eager birds. The women and children fled into the forest, almost in single file fashion. Gia ran back to take up the rear, and with twigs and sticks, she wisely swept away most of the telltale footprints left behind. Within minutes, very little evidence remained that women and children had ever been there.

Brand breathed easier knowing they would all be out of harm's way. And then he called to the men who were setting up the shelters for the night, and gave them their instructions. The other skilled men who were deep in the forest falling trees and gathering deadfall, he didn't even worry about; they were not expected back for hours. All that was left now for Brand to do, was sit and wait patiently. Fortunately for him, that was a skill he had mastered very well.

In the meantime, Gia, the other women and the children had run through the trees, crossed small valleys, climbed a cliff, and made their way over two large hills before finally coming to a stop at quite a large flow of water. Gia so hoped that they were far enough away so they couldn't be heard or seen, and the noise from the babbling brook would surely drown out any sounds the children might make. They were being shushed at every turn, but just the same, it would be difficult for them all to remain perfectly still. The women allowed the children to play quietly. They had no trouble keeping busy; throwing leaves and twigs into the water, racing them, and following them downstream until they floated out of view. Some of the women wrung their hands, some paced, some giggled nervously, and the others simply watched the children play. Unfortunately for them, waiting patiently was not a skill they had mastered very well.

# 12

## BACK TO THE BARN

*Croak, croak, croak.* For Mod, there was no mistaking that alert. He stopped for a moment, then listened again.

"Wait, Goy." Goy and the children stopped in their tracks. They had almost reached the point where the two rivers met. She didn't want to stop; they were so close now, to returning to their own land. Goy recognized Mod's tone of voice, and gathered her children protectively into her arms.

"Dager, your father has to think for a moment," she whispered. Dager didn't understand why everyone had suddenly become so quiet and serious. They all watched Mod as he sat right down on the dirt road, and brought his knees up tightly to his chest. He held onto his medallion and closed his eyes.

*"Mod! Turn around."* It was none other than his father, that spoke to him.

*"Da, what is it? I heard the frogs. Who is trespassing into our new village?"*

*"The guards, Mod. It seems that high council has no intention of letting you off easily. I fear they are coming for you. It is not safe for you to return to the Tasman Empire. You must take your family and hide."* Although Mod was not entirely surprised, his mind raced.

*"I will not hide from them, Da. They will not ever give up searching, if this is what they've set their minds to do. If I start hiding now, I'll spend the rest of my life running. That's no way to live."*

*"True son, but for now, you must. You must take your family to a safe place. Once they're tucked away, then you and you alone may return to face your enemies."* Resolutely, Mod knew that all his father said, was right. He would not risk his family's safety over his own foolish pride.

*"Aye, Da. So it shall be done. And you? Are you well?"*

*"Aye, I am well. Even though you shouldn't have cured me, I'm glad you did."*

*"It was meant to be. Your last days were not meant to be spent rotting away in a cave."*

*"What about Dager? I know he's with you. How is he?"*

*"Dager is very well, Da. I am proud to have him as my son."*

*"All is well and good then, Mod."* Mod heard Brand suck in a deep breath. He waited. *"They're here now, Mod. Make haste. Hide your loved ones, son."*

Mod opened his eyes and looked over to his

family, who were still quiet and waiting for his word. How lucky he was to have them. He would go to the ends of the earth to keep them from harm. And his father? He worried more for the guards he was up against, than he did for Brand. There was no need for concern there.

Brand just sat on his stump and watched the ancient frogs as they hopped from lily pad to lily pad, finally coming to rest in the middle of the pond. They sat so still, that they almost couldn't be seen at all. A hush fell over the valley, followed by intense silence; a feeling of dread and doom. The breeze had stopped blowing, the branches of every tree and beautiful bush, motionless. Leaves which had been floating joyously through the air, dropped noiselessly to the ground.

The sensitive soles of Brand's feet felt the first vibrations of the approaching guards. He looked down and saw the ground actually move with each heavy footfall. Small pebbles, twigs and broken leaves bounced at three-second intervals. He glanced over at the workers, who, as instructed by him earlier, began to whistle as though they hadn't a care in the world.

The lead guard frowned at the scene displayed before him. Workers? By the Great Pond, building huts? He shook his head, for surely he was seeing things. The workers seemed to take no notice at all of the approaching sentries. It unnerved the man slightly, but he continued leading his guardsmen forward.

More disturbing, was the man who sat upon the stump, near the shore of the Great Pond. He appeared to be resting, and he did not so much as flinch, when he looked up and saw the guards approaching. The lead guard knew that something was not right with this particular situation, but he couldn't quite put his finger on it. Not yet. Was it an ambush, that they were walking into? He nervously looked this way and that. He saw no evidence of an ambush.

The lead guard stopped his men about ten feet from where Brand sat. The workers whistled in the background and continued with their work.

"I say, sir! What business have you here at the Great Pond?" the lead guard demanded.

"I am resting. And what business have you here?" Brand looked the lead guard straight in the eye as he calmly replied, without the slightest hint of fear.

"We are looking for the man named Mod. He has betrayed the Tasman Empire. Do you aid and abet traitors here?"

"Oh, no. We would never do such a thing. We are in fact, building a new village. A village for respectable, hardworking people. Not for traitors, oh, no." The lead guard laughed out loud at that.

"Have you a permit from high council to build such a village?" He was sure that the man did not.

"Oh, no. We don't have a permit. This village will not be governed by high council or by any other foreign authority."

"Surely you jest, sir. Such an act alone is cause to charge you with treason. I should bring you in, this instant!"

"But you cannot. You are seeking Mod. You don't have time to waste by dragging an old man such as myself back to the meeting chambers."

"You're not so old. And what do you know of the meeting chambers? I've never before laid eyes on the likes of you. You've come from another community. I'll bet you were cast out." Brand stood up, and he was a good four inches at least, taller than the lead guard. He moved closer to the guard, who took a step back.

"You don't recognize me? Surely you remember the old man who was stripped of his status the moment he lost his sight? You were there when I was cast aside to die in a rotten cave. I certainly remember you." The lead guard's mouth opened and then shut, opened, then shut again. He could not make a sound. Brand continued. "It is my son whom you seek, and he is no more a traitor than I am. Surely you can think that out, for yourself." Brand reached up and placed his hand upon his medallion. Six pairs of eyes unwittingly followed the movement and were from that moment on, captivated. Brand smiled at the lead guard and the remaining three, who were not so easily fooled. But the lead guard was still speechless.

"It seems to me, that you will be making the

rest of your journey with fewer men than you started out with. If you insist on allowing the high council to continue pulling your strings, and if you truly believe that you must track down Mod, I will not stop you. That is something you should decide. But as for these men..." The lead guard looked behind him at the six men who now had no intention of going anywhere, and he sighed deeply. He was aware that the man who stood before him held great powers, but he still had trouble believing that this was in fact, the old Curor. Determined to complete his mission, he stepped to the side and ordered his men to follow. The four guards marched directly passed Brand and the workers, and then disappeared into the trees. In doing so, they became a little bit closer to the willow, which would eventually take them to the surface.

"We have to go back." Mod told his family, as he stood up and dusted himself off.

"Go back! Go back? Mod, you can't be serious." Goy blurted. Dager and Lucia didn't make a sound as they watched and listened to their parents.

"Council has sent the guards after me, Goy. And that means, that they are after us, in fact. I have to bring you and the children to a safe place."

"Safe place! Safe place? Mod, there is no such thing as a safe place on the surface. You know that as much as I do. And besides, we must return the children now, to their own climate. See how they sweat!" Goy was grasping at straws now; willing to say or do anything to convince her husband otherwise. "We can hide in the forest near the Great Pond, Mod! They'll never find us there!" Mod shook his head at her. There would be no returning to the Tasman Empire on this day.

"Believe me, Goy. If there was a way for us to return home and hide out until this situation is resolved, we would most certainly do it. The guards have already reached the willow by now. We can't go back. And just so you know, the children will not perish from sweating." Goy wanted to scream out of sheer frustration, but she controlled herself for the sake of the children. And if what Mod said were true, she knew they had no time to spare.

"Well, that's it, then. Come children, and hurry." The family turned around and headed back on the road they all detested so much. Lucia had open sores on the bottom of her feet and she winced with each step she took. Mod took notice of this and allowed his daughter to ride upon his back. It was rough up there, but at least her feet were no longer stinging in pain. Dager hurried alongside his parents. Goy had no idea where they would end up.

"Mod! Where are we going? There is nowhere to hide!" she looked forlornly at the bald landscape which couldn't possibly provide them with cover, and the thought of taking shelter with any of the surface dwellers did not appeal to her in the least.

"There is only one place we can go, Goy." And having said that, he led them back toward the hag's driveway.

"No!" Goy stopped dead in her tracks. "You can hardly expect to bring Dager back to *her*!" Dager didn't want to interrupt, but he knew he had to.

"Ma." Goy looked down at her son, who was pleading with his eyes. "Please, Ma. We have to go back to the hag. There are a lot of places to hide on her land," he tried to smile, to let them all know it would be fine. Lucia burst into tears. He continued, "the hag is different, now."

"Different?" Goy had no idea what her son meant, and she hadn't any time to find out. Mod was already running fast toward the barn with Lucia still safe upon his back. Goy and Dager followed.

"Up into the hayloft!" Dager directed, as soon as the four of them were safely inside. Sleepily, Mindy watched them creep quietly by her and the nursing puppies. She was not worried, for she knew that these people were her friends. The cool shade of the building was a relief for Dager and his family, and the straw floor was much kinder to the bottoms of their feet, than the road had been. They climbed the rickety ladder, one by one, and hid amongst the bales of hay. Just as they settled in, the guards had arrived in the yard.

"Whatever can I do for you, you handsome young men?"

For Dager and Mod, there was no mistaking the sing-song hum of the new and improved Maybelle P. Bonnadoolio's voice. Goy and Lucia were completely perplexed. Dager pulled on his sister's apron, urging her to follow him. They slid along the floor until they could peek out from the cracks of the old, shrunken wallboards. Lucia's breath caught in her throat when she saw the guards, to whom the hag was speaking. The hag! That sounded nothing like the hag she knew! She and her brother watched as the hag lifted her skirts midcalf so that she could meet the guards halfway down the driveway. She straightened out her hair, and pulled her shoulders back. Dager could even see her eyelashes, now fluttering wildly out of control.

"I said, what can I do for you? You are such a sweet young thing," she forced her arm through that of the lead guard, and leaned against him lovingly. He pulled away suddenly, and let her arm fall back to her side.

"Unhand me, woman! I am the lead guard of the Tasman Empire and I demand that you treat me with due respect." The hag smiled sweetly, and cocked her head to the side.

"Oh, you are such a silly young man. And look at the rest of you. You all must be parched. I insist that you stay for tea," she said, as she seemed to take no notice of their weaponry, or their odd way of dress; but she did see their hot, sore looking bare feet.

Teresa Schapansky

"And my goodness. You've all lost your shoes! Come now inside, with me. Maybelle will make you all better." Despite their important mission, the lead guard knew that his men could use some thirst quenching, and the hot cracked earth had certainly not been kind to their feet. He signaled his men, and they all followed the hag into her house. It was a wretched looking building from the outside, but at the very least, it would provide them with shelter from the angry sun. The delicious aroma of freshly baked biscuits wafted out from the windows and made the guards hungry.

The lead guard was surprised to see that the ruined, broken condition of the outside was in no way an indication of how the inside was kept. The foyer was neat and tidy and smelled of a recent scrub. Her coats were hung in order of size near the door, and strange looking footwear was lined up perfectly in a row on the floor. The living room, which bordered the front entrance, consisted of comfortable looking furniture; each piece adorned with hand stitched doilies and cushions. This house was obviously kept with an incredibly loving hand. The lead guard felt sudden and unfamiliar feelings of affection for the hag. He watched her disappear into the kitchen, and then immediately turned to barked orders to his three remaining guards.

"You men wait here. Sit and make yourselves comfortable." The guards exchanged awkward glances. The furniture was too clean to sit upon

178

with their dusty, sweaty clothing, and so they took their positions on the neatly swept wooden floor. Minutes later, Maybelle returned with a drink tray in her hands, and their leader in tow. Much to their surprise, the leader, who had always maintained steadfast control over any emotion, seemed entirely stricken by the extremely lovely lady.

"What's taking them so long in there, Dager?" Lucia asked, with her worried face still pressed against the boards. She hadn't been able to see a thing since they'd all gone into the house.

"I don't know… I don't know what they're doing!" He looked over at Mod. "Da? Could she have changed back?" The very idea made the boy shiver with fear. Perhaps she had the men shackled and chained as she set about preparing her evening meal. Or, maybe she had them scrubbing and cleaning her wretched house. He could just picture it. Mod smiled at his wife and children.

"Oh, there's no way she's changed back, son. I would imagine that she's offered them tea or something of the like. I can smell fresh baking from here as well, can't you?" Mod was not concerned at all, with what might be going on inside the house, while Dager's eyebrows raised high upon his forehead. He had no idea what fresh baking smelled like, although this that he smelled now, was nothing at all like the usual smells that would drift about when she ordinarily baked bread. This smell was sweeter and very different from anything that he'd been accustomed to.

"Do you think we can sneak out of here, Da?" Lucia asked, and as she did so, she trembled. How she missed her home.

"Nay, child. We must wait it out a bit. I've got a mind that when we do leave here, we shall be walking and not sneaking." Goy, who had been silent until now, had become suspicious.

"What do you mean, Mod?" her eyes narrowed toward him, and she couldn't help but smile. "What exactly did you do to the hag?" Mod laughed openly, but quickly stifled it. Now was not the time to alert the hag or the guards to their presence. Dager smiled back at him, knowingly.

"Well, Maybelle P. Bonnadoolio needed some serious softening up, Goy. She's very sweet and kind now; in fact quite the opposite of how she behaved when we first arrived. You'll see it for yourself, and soon," he promised them all, with a gleam in his eye.

"That doesn't explain what the guards are doing in there, Mod. What else have you done?" and then Goy covered her mouth with her hand as she giggled.

"Well, it just so happens that I believe, that everybody needs somebody. People are not meant to be solitary creatures and whether they bond with another person for love... as you and I did," he reached over and held his wife's hand lovingly, and Goy blushed in response. The children smiled proudly as he continued. "Or they bond out of convenience or for company, it doesn't really matter. The bottom line is that everybody needs somebody. And I may have put the idea in her head, that the first man she laid eyes upon, after I left of course, she would woo and flirt with until he was of the mutual feeling. I do believe that the lead guard is well on his way to falling in love with the wonderful Maybelle P. Bonnadoolio."

# 13

## MAYBELLE FINDS LOVE

Gia led the women and children out of the forest. They took their time, finding and picking grub to replace what they'd had to throw into the middle of the pond, earlier. By the time they made it back to the Great Pond, all aprons were full.

Brand was happy to see them emerge from the shelter of the huge trees, safe and sound. All was almost as it should be, but not quite yet. There was still the matter of Mod and his family's homecoming, and of course there was a possibility that they'd have to deal with the guards who'd gone to the surface, and would eventually pass through while returning to the Village of Hurtsmire. He smiled as he looked at the shelters being built. The makeshift buildings were now being erected at twice the speed, thanks to the help of the six strong and able-bodied guards. As for these guards, they would be compensated later, in all fairness, for their services.

Brand reached down and lifted his medallion from his chest. It would soon be whole again, thanks to Dager's eventual return of the missing piece.

"I'm so hungry, Ma!" Lucia complained to Goy, as she laid her head down upon her lap.

"We all are, love." Goy replied. She assumed that the bundles of food she'd given her daughter the day before, to be long gone. There seemed to be nothing in this barn that they would be able to eat. She looked to her husband, who was leaning back against a bale of hay, resting his eyes. He didn't seem to be concerned about food or anything else for that matter. Dager stood up.

"I could get some corn. It isn't much, but it's about all we can get at, for now." he was about to do just that, when Mod reached out and stopped him.

"No, son. I've something better in mind than dried corn." Dager looked at him, surprised. What else could there possibly be? Goy and Lucia's tummies were rumbling.

"How about fresh baking, and perhaps some tea?" Goy now smiled, knowing exactly what he had in mind.

"Oh, Mod. You shouldn't! The poor woman; I'm sure she's confused enough, as it is!" Even though she protested, she hoped he would indeed go through with his plan. The fresh baked aroma from the house still wafted steadily through the old wallboards of the hay loft. Dager, having seen the powers which Mod had demonstrated earlier, allowed himself to feel his own pangs of hunger. He was convinced they would be satisfied soon enough. Lucia smiled happily.

"My dearest family," he addressed them, "I think you should all watch through the cracks of the wall." Goy and the children slid over to look out between the boards. They could barely contain their excitement.

At that same time, the guards and Maybelle were enjoying the company of each other, and the biscuits and tea. Suddenly, the hag stood up and nearly sent her tea flying in the air. The lead guard was quick to steady both her and the cup. He leapt to his feet and grabbed the woman around her robust waist. It seemed like the natural thing to do at the time.

"Why, you sweet thing." Maybelle sang out in her loving way, and in return, draped her arms around his neck. His cheeks reddened, but he did not let go. "I don't know what came over me. But look at you, coming to my rescue the way you did." Now the lead guard felt embarrassed, and he removed his arms from her large torso, and sat back down. He did not dare look at the other guards, who were at that moment, grinning from ear to ear.

"Would you lovely men excuse me, for just a few minutes? I forgot to do some quick chores in the barn, and I promise that I won't be long." she fluttered her lashes at the lead guard, as he stood again, offering his assistance.

"Lady, I would be pleased to..." She gently placed her hand upon his shoulder and sat him back down.

"Oh, no. That wouldn't do, now would it? Why! I barely know you, and it would not be right for a handsome man such as yourself to follow a woman into the barn without a chaperone!" Now the guard's face turned a deeper shade of red. The other guards had to look away. It was quite apparent to them, that the lead guard would surely follow her to the ends of the earth, if she asked him to.

Maybelle left the men and headed straight for the kitchen. She took her best basket and filled it with sugar coated biscuits, salted pork, apples, and a ladle, and held it under one arm. She filled a bucket with cold tea and looped its handle through her other arm. She pushed the back door open with her foot, and then stepped out into the hot sun.

The family of four watched as a happy, whistling, brand new Maybelle exited the house. She was visibly exultant; she gracefully skipped the distance from the house to the barn without spilling a single crumb or a drop of tea. The hag hadn't a care in the world as she stepped into the dim of the barn. Noiselessly, Dager and his family watched as she carefully set her goods upon the floor near the bottom of the rickety ladder, completely oblivious to the seeing eyes from above.

The hag's eyes glistened and her usually pale complexion had turned a healthy shade of pink. She slowly approached the hound, who still lay in the corner, tending to her newborn puppies.

"Mindy, my sweet houndie hound. How are you doing with your new wonderful babies?" her melodic voice was so unlike her old one that Dager almost felt the need to clean out his ears. Mindy flinched at first, when the hag reached a hand toward her, but settled down once she sensed that the hag meant her no harm. Clearly, even the hound was surprised at her sudden change. The hag stroked the top of Mindy's head for a few moments, and then confided, "I do believe, Mindy, that I may have found myself a man! Oh, he's such a wonderful gentleman. I think I'm in love, love, love! How about that, hound? Could it be so? Might he be the one I've waited for, all my life?" Mindy gave the woman a sideways look, and then began to lick the nearest pup. Maybelle stood to take her leave. "Well then, I shouldn't keep the sweet man waiting, now should I? Perhaps he's ready for some more tea!" With that, she winked at the hound, turned, then skipped happily away. As soon as Dager heard the door of her house slam shut behind her, he raced down the ladder, and snatched up the basket and bucket. Mod met him halfway down and helped him carry up the treats.

What followed for Dager and his family, was a feast beyond imagination. The biscuits were like nothing any of them had ever tasted, and Goy vowed that before they left, she would have to acquire the recipe. The apples were perfect and not one of them held a single bruise. The salted pork was beyond compare. The cold tea, though too sweet at first, became more pleasing, the more they drank.

It was beginning to get dark now, and Goy shuddered as the barn became even more dim. Dager climbed back down the ladder to gather some old horse blankets and burlap sacks for them to use as blankets. Mod even looked concerned at the sight of the ever darkening sky.

"It's normal, Ma and Da," Lucia was proud to reassure them. "It gets dark every night on the surface, doesn't it, Dager?"

"Aye, it does. Every night it goes dark, and every morning it gets light. I guess the sky needs to rest, too." Mod nodded in agreement.

"That's sort of right, son. It has something to do with the rotation of the sun and moon, but we'd have to do some reading on that, to fully understand. I've heard about the darkening sky, but I do have to say that last night, was the first time I'd ever seen it." Dager was now really confused. How could this be the first dark sky that his father had ever seen?

"Da and Ma, Lucia says we are from a different land. I don't understand. What land doesn't have a night time?" he asked, while trying hard to picture it in his mind, but it just wouldn't come. Mod laughed and remembered himself as a boy of Dager's age, learning about the mysterious surface land for the very first time. It too, had to be seen to be believed.

"Son, we are from the Village of Hurtsmire, which is found in the Tasman Empire." Dager nodded enthusiastically.

"I've heard of Tasmania! That's where the Kookaburras live!" Lucia laughed nervously before she asked.

"The Kooka-whats?" she was already imagining big scary beasts with sharp teeth looking for small children such as herself to eat. Dager poked her in the ribs.

"The Kookaburras! We have them here too, but not as many. They come mostly from Tasmania, I think." he watched his sister shiver with fright, and then he smiled. His explanation didn't exactly make her feel any better about it.

"Can they talk, too?"

"Oh, no. They just laugh. They laugh every morning when the sun comes up and then they laugh every night when the sun goes down. It helps if you're lost in the outback and you don't know what time it is."

"That's interesting, Dager. Tell us more about your bird," Mod suggested. Dager was pleased to tell them about the Kookaburras.

"Well, they eat snakes and lizards and bugs,

but sometimes they try to steal baby chicks from farms. That's not so good when they do that. But, where in Tasmania is our land that doesn't get dark?" and then Dager worried a little for the Kookaburras in Tasmania, for if it never got dark and never got light, how would they know when to laugh?

"It's not actually *in* Tasmania, son," Mod told him, "it's *under* Tasmania," he explained, as he watched his son's eyes narrow curiously. To Dager, that sounded similar to what Lucia had tried to tell him earlier.

"Over and under?" he asked as he looked at his sister, who nodded in response.

"Yes! There are other worlds, son. Worlds that are very separate from this one that you've been made to live on. Our world is underwater. Have you ever been swimming?"

"No, I'm not allowed to swim. There's never been time, because I always have chores to do. It wouldn't have been any fun anyway, all by myself."

"True, that's true, son. That's why you don't know then, that you can breathe underwater."

"I can what?" Dager did not think that could be. He knew that people could drown if they breathed in the water!

"You heard me. You can breathe in the water, just like you can breathe in the air. It is part of the magic that makes us who we are. When we travel back to the Tasman Empire, we will have to travel through quite a bit of water to reach it. You'll see, but don't be frightened."

"So... we live in the water?"

"Not exactly. We live under the water. Our world is protected by the water, but it isn't in the water." Dager looked at his mother, who just sat and smiled at him.

"Does the hag know? Does she know where I came from?"

"No, there aren't many surface dwellers who know anything about our world. It's just as well. They wouldn't understand. When she bought you, she more than likely assumed that you were a regular surface boy."

"And this bad man called Croy? Is he going to try to take me away again?" Mod shook his head resolutely.

"Absolutely not. We're not going back to the Village of Hurtsmire." Lucia almost choked on the bite of apple she'd just taken.

"What?" The Village of Hurtsmire was the only village she'd ever lived in. First, she'd had to go to the surface, and now she was told that she wouldn't ever be going home? The girl could not believe her ears. "We have to go home, Da. That's where we live!"

"Not anymore, Lucia. Many things have happened over the course of the last couple of days. And although we will be making life altering changes, they will not be bad. Change is not bad, my love." Lucia didn't understand. What was so wrong with their way of life? Her mother patted her hand comfortingly.

"Lucia, your father and grandfather are beginning a new village! One where girls and boys, women and men will be treated fairly. One where girls can go to school just the same as boys can!" Lucia smiled now.

"Really? I can go to school?"

"Aye, it shall be done," Mod reassured her. "You and Dager will be in the same grade, I do believe." Lucia and Dager beamed at each other. For very different reasons, neither one of them had ever been allowed to even consider going to school. Now they would be going together, and it was like a wonderful dream about to come true.

"And Granda? He won't like this very much." Lucia's eyes became downcast at the very idea. She just knew that her grandfather, whom she'd never spoken to until he spoke to her first; the man who so firmly disapproved of girls altogether, would not cherish the thought of her going to school.

"Lucia, believe it or not, it was your grandfather who first brought this idea to my attention. Granda has never been in favour of the mistreatment of women in the Tasman Empire. In this new village, you will see that he is not the nasty kind of man he's always appeared to be. Up until now he's never had the freedom to truly be himself." Lucia became extremely quiet for a few moments, as she considered all of this new information. Dager took the last bite of his apple, and then set the core aside to give to the horse later. It was really dark now, and he pulled one of the burlap sacks across his legs.

"That's a good idea, Dager," Goy said as she realized that he seemed to be settling in to go to sleep. She reached for a horse blanket, and covered herself and Lucia with it. Mod followed suit. And just before they all retired for their first evening together, Goy whispered, "We love you, Dager. It's so good to have you back." Dager closed his eyes happily, and fell into a restful sleep. He immediately began to dream. This dream was full of magic and love, and it took place in that special world, that he now knew, truly did exist.

Brand and his gathering of what now numbered a total of twenty-two people, also settled in for their first night together. Their feast was equally as enjoyable as Mod's and his family's had been. Aside from the fact that Mod, Goy, Lucia and Dager hadn't yet been able to return to the Tasman Empire, everyone was happy. The new village would have to proceed as planned, with or without them. In that uncanny way of knowing, Brand knew that everything would happen exactly when and how it was meant to. Speaking of which, there was still the matter of the man from Chadwhip, whom he'd summoned much earlier. As Brand lay upon his mat that night, he made contact with him again. The second connection wasn't as exhausting as the first, and the man was more than pleased to hear from his strange new ally once more.

*"What say you, sir? Are you well? Has your journey been a kind one?"*

*"Aye, it has. Does Gia and my child know that I'm on my way?"*

*"Nay. I've decided not to let them get their hopes up, should something go wrong, as sometimes does."*

*"I thank you for that. It was a wise decision,"* and then he paused for a moment, and looked about. He was hiding in a farm shed, on the outskirts of a small village, which was more than halfway to his intended destination. He dreaded that he'd soon have to sneak in and out of Hurtsmire; but he did not for a second, doubt his ability to do that. He too, had just bedded down for the evening, when Brand had summoned him. He enjoyed the old man's company. *"We haven't been properly introduced, although I know who you are. My name is Derk, and I am a teacher."*

*"Aye, son. And I was once the Curor for the Village of Hurtsmire. I'm sorry, but I don't remember having met you before. What you may not know is that Gia has been my handmaiden ever since you were made to leave."*

*"Oh, thank goodness. I've worried so much about my wife. I'm glad to know she's had your companionship."*

*"Nay,"* Brand laughed openly as he admitted, *"I would hardly call it companionship. All I did was lie on my mat for the last three years, and I hardly spoke a word. Gia however, did a lot of talking, and that's how I came to know so much about her love for you."*

*"Is she happy?"*

*"Your little girl keeps her happy. She is lonely; she longs for your return, but she doesn't believe it can happen. She has given up hope of it ever being so."*

*"And my little girl? Do tell, what is her name?"*

*"Her name is Pagan, and she is lovely. Gia has done a fine job with that child. She has devoted her heart and soul to raising her."* The two men continued to speak for a short while longer before saying their goodbyes. Derk's heart was in his throat as he thought about his beloved wife, and the daughter he'd never seen. He wondered what she looked like. Did she have his curls, and the almond shape of her mother's eyes? He would soon find out. For far too long he'd been forced to push the memories of his loved ones to the furthermost corners of his mind. A single tear rolled down his cheek, as he gratefully realized that soon he would have to do that, no longer.

# 14

## DERK AND BREE

The man eternally perched in the high lookout window of the Meeting chambers blew hard upon his conch shell, for far off in the distance, he had seen the strange man sneaking about, so as not to be seen. That wouldn't do! Unfortunately, he had indeed, been seen.

The guards were deployed immediately in the direction of the stranger. While they sought him out, the high council was in the process of assembling upon their pyramid. And the villagers? They came from far and wide, and only because they were curious. Something exciting was about to happen again, and they were not about to miss it. Less than an hour passed from the time the stranger had first been spotted, until the guards brought him in. His hands were bound tightly behind his back and he was forced to kneel. He bowed reluctantly and as he did so, his hat fell further down over his forehead and completely shaded his face.

"Who is this man that sneaks about our village like a common thief?" The high council member said this in such a way, that it was more of an accusation than a question. "That's what you are, isn't it? A thief? That's fine, man. We haven't had thieves in these parts for a long while. And would you like to know why?" he asked, as he tapped the stranger upon his shoulder with his brand new gavel. The strange man rose to his feet, stood straight and tall, before he replied.

"A thief? A thief? Is this how you welcome newcomers into your village?" The high council member peered closer at this man, and he could now see beyond the beard that grew heavily upon his face; he now knew exactly who stood before him.

"Derk, the teacher! May I reintroduce you all to Derk, the teacher?" As though on cue, the drums sounded and applause resonated from the audience. The high member gave the signal and everyone became silent. "You have a lot of nerve, returning to your native land. Do you think I've lifted the order of your exile? Or is it possible that you have reconsidered that devastating choice that made me banish you to begin with?" Now Derk had some fast thinking to do. His banishment years ago, stemmed from his decision to take beautiful Gia for his bride, rather than the high council member's homely daughter. The high council member had been so humiliated that he could not bear to look at Derk. And so, he was cast away and forced to live in Chadwhip. Should he return to Hurtsmire, Gia and their child would be made to suffer dearly. Now that he had been caught back in the village, would he be better off to say that he had returned for the daughter's hand in marriage? Or would it be wiser to tell the truth? The truth would mean shackles, chains and dungeons for the rest of his life. His decision was made. He would tell them whatever was necessary, be it truth or not, to regain his freedom and eventually find his loved ones. He waited for the required tap upon his shoulder, so that he could reply. But the tap did not come; the high council member had not finished ranting.

"Whatever the reason, you may be interested in knowing that Gia and her daughter have disappeared." Derk did not react. He had to make them believe that he had not come back for Gia and Pagan. His ruse was working well; the high council member was pleased. "The word is, that she fell in love with a traveling merchant and has moved on with her life." It was all Derk could do, to not lash out at the man who sat on the uppermost seat of the pyramid, telling his lies to everyone in attendance. He realized that what they thought did not matter, anyway. Not to him, Gia, nor Pagan. If all went well, soon they would be rid of the Village of Hurtsmire forever. Finally, he received his long awaited tap.

"Nay, sir. I've come to my senses. I've returned to ask for the hand of your beautiful daughter, Bree. That is, if she'll still have a man such as me."

"Still have you? Still have you, man? After all you've put the poor girl through," he paused for a moment, and twisted his moustache with his left hand. The fact of the matter was, and everyone except him knew it, that his daughter was so nasty and spoiled and unkempt, that she had never had one single suitor. She was still, very much available. "It is lucky for you, man called Derk, that my daughter loves you as much as she does. Any other woman would have gone ahead and married another. May you show her the same amount of devotion that she's shown you, even in your absence." With that, the drums sounded, and much to Derk's dismay, the daughter was summoned.

Bree soon stood at Derk's side. He forced himself to appear loving as he looked her way. She looked even worse than he had remembered. Her dress was filthy and threadbare, her hair hadn't seen a brush for weeks, and dirt was smudged up one side of her cheek. He forced a smile as the horrible young woman sneered back at him.

"What say you, man? Have you perhaps, an apology to make? A deep apology that comes straight from the bottom of your heart?" he tapped Derk on the shoulder. Real tears, tears of remorse, followed quickly by tears of fear, formed in Derk's eyes as he addressed the woman he was supposed to marry. She looked as though she'd spent the last few years doing the work of ten strong men. Her arms were so muscle-bound that they protruded abnormally from her sleeves.

"Bree, oh, Bree," Derk began mournfully. "I have realized that I can no longer live without you. Every morning when I wake, it is you I think of. And every night as I fall into my slumber, it is your face that I see..." The sneer on Bree's face faded and was replaced with a look of pure joy. His plan was working. "I am so sorry for the pain I've caused, and I've come back with the hope that you will give me another chance." Derk fell to his knees before her. This time it was she, who tapped him on the shoulder.

"Oh, Derk. I knew you'd come back. Of course, I forgive you." Tears sprung to her eyes as she yanked Derk to his feet and embraced him. The highest member of council was pleased. He summoned the drummers and they began to play a ceremonial tune. Feet stomped and hands clapped. It would be a wonderful day in the Village of Hurtsmire, after all. The high council member let the merriment continue for a short while, before he demanded silence.

"I have an announcement to make. Let it be known throughout this village and the surrounding communities that there shall be a wedding, come morning!" Applause thundered throughout the meeting chambers, and the foot stomping resumed. All Derk could think about was the coming day that would bring with it, his impending doom.

By morning, Maybelle P. Bonnadoolio had agreed to become the wife of the lead guard. They would live together, right in that house on the farm, because as she explained in her beautiful voice, who else would take care of the animals, but her? She brought him and the other guards on a tour of her property, including the barn; but thankfully excluding the hay loft, where Dager and his family remained hidden. The lead guard insisted on exploring it, but she protested with a flutter of her lashes and a hand upon his chest.

"Why, it just wouldn't be proper for me to climb up there in my dress, nor would it be gentlemanly of you men to go up there and leave me down here all by myself!" The lead guard had to agree, and so they left the barn and went back out into the hot, scorching sun. The next guard in line according to age, although ever so happy for his former leader, wondered what would happen next.

"Sir, what of the high council? They will expect to know what has become of you. And what about Mod and the others? Surely we can't return empty handed. What should we do?" The men looked at the lead guard expectantly. He shook his head in frustration, and then for the first time in his miserable life, he spoke as though he were a free man.

"Men, I think I may understand now, what Mod was going through. Would it be so wrong to live life as you see fit? Should I do as I've been told, and leave this lovely lady who has agreed to be my wife, just so I can obey the laws which govern the Tasman Empire? It's not right," he shook his head, and he believed his own words with more confidence that he'd ever known. "This is what I believe in, now." And he stuck his thumb to his chest. His men were awestruck, yet proud. They didn't know that they would ever have the courage to set forth on their own, as the lead guard was now doing. Maybelle interrupted.

"Did I hear you say, Mod? Why! He's my good friend! Mod and his son, Dager and his lovely wife and daughter! They are such lovely people, and I gave them tea only yesterday!" Movement from the direction of the barn caught her eye just then, as Mod proceeded to step out of the cool, dark shadows. Maybelle ran to her good friend and gave him a welcoming hug.

"Mod! It is so nice to have you back! You did say you would be back and now look at you all here and everything!" she bubbled over with excitement.

"Yes, Maybelle. I did say that, didn't I? And I never break my promises." Maybelle looped her arm affectionately through his, and they ambled back to the sentries and her newly betrothed.

"Mod! Do you know what, my sweet, sweet

man?" Mod smiled at her and shook his head. She was so funny to listen to now, and he could see that the guards were so surprised to see him, that they didn't know what to do.

"No, Maybelle. Do share."

"Well, it's all happened so fast, but this lovely man and I..." and she let go of Mod's arm and wrapped hers around the lead guard's waist. "... are going to be married!" In response to her happy news, Mod reached forward and offered to shake the lead guard's hand. The lead guard accepted.

"May I be the first to congratulate you?" Mod asked, genuinely. He had a really good feeling that any danger of being forced back to Hurtsmire by these men, was pretty much gone. The lead guard was now feeling no ill will toward, nor threat from this man he was supposed to capture.

"Mod, nice to see you. My name is..." he hesitated for a moment. For many years he had sadly referred to himself, only as 'Lead'. He continued, "Tad. It is nice to make your acquaintance." Mod grinned broadly, and held out his hand to the other men, who in turn introduced themselves, by their given names. Feeling great relief over the outcome of this meeting, Tad asked.

"And your plans, Mod? Where will you and your family go from here?" then he added thoughtfully, "I ask as your friend, not as a servant of the Tasman Empire."

"No fear, friend. I am not worried about your intentions, where my family and I are concerned.

We are beginning a new village, between the Clay Peaks and the Great Pond!" Mod then waved his arm toward the hayloft, signaling to his family that it was safe to come out of hiding. So they did, and after more introductions, Maybelle happily led Goy and the children into the cool and comfort of her house, and out of the hot sun. Mod and the guards remained outside, and he told them all about his plans for the new village. Goy soon discovered that she needn't have worried about Dager's reaction to seeing the hag again, for Maybelle truly had been completely and magically reformed.

Derk and Bree were separated for the duration of the day and night. She was to remain in her home preparing with her family for the main event, and he was escorted to Gia's deserted hut, where he would remain until morning. He'd been so convincing of his undying love for Bree, that the foolish high council saw no need to have him guarded.

Upon entering what had at one time, briefly been his home, Derk felt closer to Gia and Pagan than ever. He could almost smell them; it was as though they'd only left moments before. None of their belongings remained, just the furniture and housewares that must have been too bulky for Gia to take.

Derk had nothing to do now, but wait until most villagers would have their window coverings pulled tight for the night. And so he took Gia's broom and began to tidy the hut, for whomever might live in it next. He moved slowly from the kitchen and living room, into the bedroom. As he swept the corner behind the smaller bed mat which must have been Pagan's, something bright and fluffy caught his eye. He smiled as he reached down and picked it up. It was a small, stuffed handmade doll in a simple dress, with an embroidered face. Although he'd never laid eyes upon the doll before, he recognized Gia's handiwork right away. He stuffed the doll into his vest pocket and continued cleaning. As far as he was concerned, this day would not be over soon enough.

He'd just stowed the broom away when there was a knock at the door. He certainly was not expecting company. He opened the door, and a large woman, fully covered in a cape and head scarf stood before him.

"May I help you, woman?" It was so unlike a woman to be out at night, unattended as she was. He watched as she lifted the scarf away from her face.

"Derk, it's me, Bree!" His heart fell. He could be locked up for life, seeing her this way. Quickly, he ushered her inside and closed the door behind her. She was careful to keep away from the windows.

"Yes, love. What is it that couldn't wait until tomorrow?"

She grimaced as she hoarsely whispered back, "It's alright, Derk. You don't have to pretend when it's just you and I." Derk suspected that this was a trap. He was certain she was there to trick him into saying something he shouldn't. He assumed that the guards had the place surrounded, and that they were ready to pounce on him at the slightest slip of the tongue.

"I don't know what you mean, Bree. But, don't you think you should rest before our big day? The moment you and I have both been waiting for?" Bree put her fingers to her lips, indicating that he be quiet. Unbeknownst to him, she really had snuck away, and she was sure that no guards had followed.

"Derk," she began in hushed tones. "Enough of this silliness! I don't want to marry you, any more than you want to marry me!" She looked so sincere that he wanted to believe her. "I've come to you tonight because... well, because of the rumours I've heard."

"Oh? What rumours? You know I've not been in town long, and I haven't heard any village talk at all."

"There are rumours of a new village. I know that's where Gia went with your child. I want to go there, too!"

"What? I don't know what you're talking about, Bree!"

She rolled her eyes into the back of her head. She didn't want to resort to council-like tactics, but she would if she were forced. "I don't believe that you came back for me. You came back because you have somewhere else to go, where you and your family will be welcomed. I do not wish to live under the iron fist any longer. I would like to leave. I would like to start over somewhere, and perhaps I will even find my own true love, eventually."

"You can't be serious! Your family would hunt you down. More than that, they'd hunt me down and blame me for taking you away. I can't risk it, Bree. Especially not now that I'm so close..." Bree threw her hands up the air in frustration.

"Aye, Derk. Have it your way. Should I scream right now? Must I scream until the guards come? What of you then? You would never again see the light of day. Take me with you." The light disappeared from Derk's eyes. He saw no choice but to agree.

"Aye, and so it shall be. Come back here in three hours. Make sure that everyone thinks you are safe on your mat and fast asleep for the night. And then, when you come back to me, bring only what your shoulder bag can hold." Miserably, he added, "You will be carrying it yourself." Bree nodded and covered her face again, with the head scarf. Derk opened the door, and looked around to make sure there was nobody to bear witness to her leaving. And then, just like that, she was gone. Derk had nothing to do now, but wait for time to pass and wonder what could possibly go wrong, next.

# 15

## DAGER GOES HOME

"Maybelle," Goy began as she took another sip of her tea. "Would you be so kind as to share your delicious biscuit recipe with me?" Maybelle couldn't have been more flattered. She thought long and hard for a moment before replying.

"Why! You sweet woman. Of course, I would be delighted to share the secret recipe which has been handed down from generation to generation with you. But do tell, when have you ever tasted my biscuits?" She couldn't for the life of her, ever recall giving Goy a biscuit. Goy then realized that the woman had no idea that she'd treated them to a hearty feast the night before. She smiled convincingly.

"Oh, dear. No, I haven't had the pleasure of trying them. But I've heard about them. I think there is not a person on the surface who hasn't heard of the Maybelle P. Bonnadoolio biscuit!"

Poor Dager and Lucia were unsuccessful in controlling their laughter. Goy was quick to shoo them away. "Go and play outside, children. I will be with you in a moment." she ordered, giving each of them a stern look as they headed obediently out the door.

Dager headed straight for the pig pen, and leaned against the fence. Lucia followed him and did the same. Their father and the guards had moved into the shade of the barn, and were still talking. From the bits and pieces Dager could hear, it sounded as though they were discussing the new village.

"What are these, Dager?" Lucia asked as she watched the pigs root around in the dirt.

"These are pigs. The hag makes salted pork and hams and other cuts of meat from them." The pigs grunted then, just as though they had agreed with his explanation. "The small ones are cute, but when they get big, they can turn pretty nasty." Lucia shuddered as she looked at the biggest pig. She wouldn't want to be stuck on the other side of the fence with that thing.

"Do they chase you?"

"Sometimes they do, but when I'm really hungry and swat at them with a stick, they stay away most of the time." Lucia frowned as she looked at the disgusting feed trough that had been licked almost clean.

"Do you mean to say, that you eat what they eat?" Dager nodded.

"When you're really hungry, Lucia, you'll eat just about anything!" Eating the pigs' grub had been as much a fact of life for him as breathing had been. Just then, Lucia rubbed up against the fence with her apron pocket, and felt a curious lump against her stomach. She reached into her pocket, and laughed out loud when she realized she'd all but forgotten about her serpent pointer. Quickly she pulled it out and showed it to her brother.

"Look at what I've got! Ma gave it to me the other day, when I was on my way to find you. I can share it with you, if you like. It can be ours!" Dager eyed it inquisitively, and then Lucia showed him how it worked.

"Why is it in the shape of a snake?" Lucia shook her head at him.

"Oh, no. It's not a snake. It's supposed to look like the crimson serpent!" she spoke the last two words in hushed tones.

"Crimson serpent? What is that?" Lucia looked at Dager rather crossly then, for how could he not know about the crimson serpent?

"Well, that's who we pray to in Hurtsmire. Don't you pray to it? And if you don't, aren't you worried?"

"I don't pray, Lucia. The hag prays, but I don't think she prays to an old red snake." Lucia gave up on trying to convince him that the figure was a very important serpent, and not just a snake. There would be no use in that, she could plainly see. And besides; that would be a topic better covered by her parents. Just then, Mod led the other men out of the barn.

"Dager and Lucia! It looks like we'll have more men joining us in our new village!" he beamed proudly at his new recruits. He hadn't needed to use any magic to convince them; they were more than eager and willing to join forces with Mod. The lead guard, or Tad, as he would now be known, reached out to shake Mod's hand again.

"Thanks Mod, for everything." Mod smiled back at him and accepted his hand. The two men shook vigorously.

"I only said what needed to be said, my friend. For too long we've been submissive to the high council, and it is wrong."

"Aye!" The guards cheered. They were thrilled at the thought of starting over somewhere new. Each of them had loved ones to bring along; the village had hardly begun and it was already growing.

"Aye, it is wrong. I wish you the best of luck, Mod. To you and your family." Tad nodded toward the children as he spoke, and then to Goy, who had just stepped out of the house. "If there is anything we can do for you or for the new village, don't hesitate to ask."

"I know it, Tad. I will ask if there is a way for you to help. And that works both ways, you know." At that moment, Maybelle ran out, full speed ahead and swooped Tad into her massive arms. She swung him around before setting him back down on his wobbly feet. He smiled sheepishly at his loved one.

"Well, Mod! My oldest friend! You can start by attending our lovely wedding!" she fluttered her eyelashes at him, in true Maybelle fashion. "We'll have a feast to end all feasts. It'll be a celebration to end all celebrations! I can see it now!" Then, she looked up to the sky, as though she really did expect to see it there. Everyone laughed.

"Well, family. Should we make haste for home?" Goy nodded eagerly in reply to her husband. Lucia was happy to be leaving at long last, although she was still apprehensive about the new village. Dager was happy also, but he was very concerned about having to breathe in the water. For a fleeting moment, he wondered if he should stay. He laughed out loud at the thought. Of course he would go. How could he not go home? After all this time? He was willing to breathe in an entire ocean, if that's what it took.

Mod, his wife, children, and the three guards said their goodbyes to Maybelle and Tad, and started on their way. They each had stowed in their pockets, a care package from Maybelle which contained biscuits, apples, and salted pork, and slung upon their shoulders were canteens full of fresh water. They stopped at the end of the driveway and gave a final wave to the happy couple. At a glance, not a person could ever have guessed that this youthful, vibrant Maybelle P.

Bonnadoolio was the same old hag who had for years, been feared by every man, woman and child throughout the land. Those days were over for good. Just as he'd known he would, Mod had no regrets.

The point where the two rivers met soon lay before them. Mod had sent the guards ahead, and had already alerted Brand to the guards' change of heart. Brand and the rest of the villagers would welcome these men with open arms. After resting, the guards would then be returning to the Village of Hurtsmire to fetch their own loved ones.

Lucia could not resist, and so she was the first to jump into the cool waters. Her body had been covered with wet, sticky sweat and she couldn't stand it for another minute.

"Oh! This is cold, Ma!" she exclaimed as she stood near the shore, and the water rose up to her armpits. Dager just stood back and watched; he had a fearful expression on his face. Goy was next; she eased herself in, followed by Mod.

"Come, son. It's all right, see? We're all okay!" Mod danced in a circle to show the boy that the water didn't hurt. Dager kicked at the ground in front of him. "I think you'll want to take those off." Mod offered, pointing to his son's shoes. Dager slipped his feet out of the shoes and stood barefoot on the ground, but he still made no move toward the water. It was then that Mod realized what was wrong.

"Goy, you and Lucia go on without us. We'll

be along, shortly." Goy understood.

"I'll be seeing you really soon, Dager!" she told him enthusiastically, before sinking beneath the murky depths. Lucia waved, and then she too, disappeared under the surface. Mod and Dager watched the water until all the ripples were gone.

"Dager, it's okay. I understand that you've never been swimming." Dager shook his head, no. He had been feeling really brave before they reached the water, but now that they were there, any courage he'd felt was gone. The only water he'd ever actually stood in before were rain puddles, and those never even covered the tops of his feet. Mod smiled and reached up for his son. Dager forced himself to let his father take him into his arms. As much as he tried to relax, he found himself hanging on for dear life.

"It's okay, Dager. See here? Hang on to the edge..." Mod took him to the riverbank as he continued, "and slide your feet down until they rest on the bottom. Just like Lucia did, when she was standing in this very spot." As terrified as he was, Dager did as he was told. After all, Lucia had seemed pretty solid when she was standing in the water. And the water *was* cold! So cold, but fantastic at the same time. It tickled as it touched his legs, and then his knees, and pretty soon he was waist deep. He took a deep breath, and then allowed his body to drop slowly down, until the water reached his neck. Mod patiently let the boy take his time, for there was no reason to rush and cause unnecessary panic. Before long, Dager had let go of the riverbank.

"Da! I didn't know it would feel so good!" Dager laughed nervously. Mod smiled proudly at his son.

"Dager, you are not of the surface. You'll find that you will be most in your element, when you are in the water. There is nothing to fear; in fact, I'll bet you're not afraid anymore at all, are you?" Dager shook his head. He had to admit that he was not. Being in the water gave him a feeling of immediate relief.

"This is where I should be, isn't it, Da?" Dager asked.

"Aye, it is. And when you feel like going under, you go ahead and do it. And then when you feel like taking a breath..." but it was too late, for Dager had already slipped under the water. He cringed as he opened his eyes, ever so slowly. He had expected that to hurt, but gladly, it had not. Regrettably, he couldn't see much under the water, for the dirt from the river's floor swirled rapidly with each step he took. The natural thing for him to do, was to lift his feet to allow the water to clear up, and so he did. Dager lifted his feet, and in the same instant, he paddled with his arms. In no time at all, he was swimming! What had he been afraid of, anyway? Dager laughed, and as he saw bubbles leave his mouth, he realized that he'd been holding his breath. He sucked in a slow deep breath and was relieved to learn that breathing in the water really was no different from breathing in the air.

Mod soon joined his son, and watched him swim about. As he did, he imagined that there was not another living soul, that was as happy as he was at that moment. To have Dager back was life's greatest gift.

*"Son, are you ready to go home?"* Dager was startled to hear his father speak in the same manner as his grandfather had, not long before. He gave a funny, underwater nod, and then followed Mod into the darker water. It was much deeper now, so deep in fact, that he couldn't see the bottom. Dager looked up, and could barely see the light of day, and so he turned and concentrated on following Mod. Finally, they reached the bottom and Dager skimmed along it, just as he'd seen his father do. It wasn't as dark anymore, and Dager could tell that the water was becoming less deep than it had been at first. He saw all sorts of curious trinkets and shells below him, but he fought the urge to stop and explore. He would save that for another day, and perhaps Lucia would join him.

The new villagers waited excitedly at the pond, for the arrival of their guests of honour. The guards had already been there, before continuing their journey to Hurtsmire to fetch their loved ones and belongings. As far as they were concerned, the sooner they made their move to the new village, the better.

Brand was ready and waiting at the crevice, when Goy hoisted her daughter up and into his waiting arms. Lucia had no idea who this man was, as he proceeded to set her down upon her feet. As she stood wordlessly and watched, he reached in and helped Goy climb out of the water. Goy laughed out loud with pure joy, the minute she was back standing on her own dry, native land.

"Lucia! Are you not going to greet your grandfather properly?" Brand knelt down before his granddaughter; this girl that he'd been so familiar with, but in his previous condition, had never had the chance to really get to know. That was about to change. He reached a hand toward her. Ever so slowly, Lucia placed her hand in his. Could this really be her grandfather? She looked him up and down, and then up and down again.

"Welcome home, child." His voice! That didn't sound like the grandfather who hadn't spoken properly before. "Your father cured me," he explained, "and all is well with this old man, now." Lucia looked from the man who still held her hand, to her mother, who nodded reassuringly. The old man continued, "I hear you've done your family proud, child. Was Dager where I said he would be? Did you find him the market?" he knew full well that she had, but he was trying to offer her proof that he really was who he claimed to be. Lucia nodded cautiously. "Did he follow you, Lucia? And what do you think of the surface?" At last, Lucia found her tongue.

"Aye, he followed me. But I didn't know it was him at first. Just like you don't look like my

Granda. But it really was Dager, and I suppose you are who you say you are, too," Brand smiled at the young girl as she continued, "I don't think much of the surface. The people are kind of mean and the air is too hot." Brand laughed out loud.

"Aye, you are right about both things. The surface, at least in Tasmania, is rather angry. We are lucky that we are not surface dwellers. Now, I would imagine that your father is on his way here with Dager?" Lucia nodded happily. She was proud of the role she'd played in bringing him home. Just then, they heard splashing from the crevice. Brand let go of Lucia's hand and rushed over just in time to take hold of his long, lost grandson.

"Dager! You're here!" Lucia was ecstatic; she felt as though she hadn't seen him in ages. Dager nodded and smiled shyly at the man who had helped him out. In the next moment, Mod climbed out and quickly turned to conceal the opening with brush.

"Da!" Mod exclaimed happily upon laying his eyes on Brand. He hadn't seen him since the cure. The old man had come out of it even better than Mod had anticipated.

Brand embraced his son, before asking, "Will you introduce me to the young man who stands before us, Mod?"

"Of course! Dager, I'd like you to meet your grandfather." Dager did as he'd seen Mod do with the guards, and extended his hand toward the old man. Brand was impressed, and the two shook hands like regular men might.

"I am so pleased to have you back, Dager. The last time I laid eyes upon you, you were only this high!" he showed Dager with his hand low in the air, just how little he had been. Dager smiled, and immediately felt a bond with Brand. Just then, he remembered the object stowed away in his pocket. He reached in and pulled it out, offering it to his grandfather.

"I guess this is yours?" Dager handed the lost missing piece of the medallion to its rightful owner. Brand winked at the boy, and then motioned with his hands for Goy and Lucia to step closer. He kept the piece a safe distance from the medallion, until he had removed the medallion's chain from around his neck. He held the two pieces in front of him for all to see, and as he did, the earth trembled. The wind came up fierce and sudden like, and the pieces flew from his hands, straight up into the air. Dager was too amazed to be frightened, as he watched the magic playing out before him. The two pieces glowed a brilliant blue and spun in circles before finally coming together with what could only be described as a low 'pop'. The wind ceased its blowing and the ground became still. The medallion floated weightlessly back down and landed in Brand's waiting hand.

"My loved ones. It is all now, as it always should have been. The reunion of not one, but many broken pieces. Let us join the others now and rejoice in this long awaited union." he led them out of the forest. Mod and Goy held hands as they took up the rear. Dager and Lucia walked proudly behind Brand, the man whom Dager was convinced, was the most powerful and magical man that ever lived. He was in awe.

Dager's wonderment paled in comparison to that felt by the new villagers who watched as he and his family strode out from the forest. They could feel that they were indeed in the presence of greatness. It was not only because of Brand, who'd invited them all to live in this new place, and nor was it because of Mod - the bravest and most sought after fugitive-like man who held their gaze fast. They were most in admiration of the five-year old boy who walked in their midst at long last. It was his legacy and the promise of their future that they cheered the most for. He was the tangible walking, breathing, physical representation of hope and all good things that were yet to come.

16

## CROY DECEIVES

The villagers were quick to assemble themselves into neat rows, with the children in front, and in order after that, from shortest to tallest so everyone could see. Brand, Mod and his family took their positions in front of them all, behind the makeshift, temporary podium. And there was, to everyone's great relief, no dreaded gavel in sight. Excited conversations quickly faded into silent anticipation.

"My good people of... for now, let's say, the Great Pond!" Brand began, as he addressed them all happily. The people clapped and laughed in response. The atmosphere was full of relief; very much unlike that of the meeting chambers in the Village of Hurtsmire. And these attendees had come to mock no one; they were there because of their desire to be part of a bright, new future. Brand continued. "I wish you all to become reacquainted with one another at tonight's feast. It does not matter if you have known one another since the days of your birth; this is a new beginning and we will treat it as such in every way, shape and form possible." The crowd clapped again. "This new village of ours will need a name. And I ask each and every one of you to brainstorm and come up with as many ideas as you can. At our next meeting, we will agree upon the name together. It will be brought to vote." And now the villagers reacted with silence. They couldn't believe that they would be included in such an important process.

"Furthermore, this new village will be governed by laws. We will vote in a proper leader, who will lead by following the laws agreed upon by all of us. These laws, I ask each of you to think on and have ready for our next meeting as well. The rules upon which majority agrees, will be written and followed. Until the next meeting, which will take place in one week's time, will you accept me as your leader?" His request was met with unanimous applause. "And so it shall be. I thank you for your belief in my leadership. I will not let you down. Until then, let's all help one another, for we only have each other to count on. Let us rejoice!" he clapped his hands to signal the end of the assembly. Again, the villagers applauded in response to the old man who was again held in high regard. The children and men mingled together, as the women went to set up the buffet.

"Da," Dager started, after having watched the whole process.

"Aye, son? What is it?" Mod asked him, concerned by the somber look upon the little boy's face.

"Is everybody always this happy?" And Dager continued to look at all the people around him; the boys he seemed to watch the most. The boys and men were dressed in clean, earth toned vests and half pants. Dager looked down at his own stained trousers, which reached all the way down to his ankles. Mod nodded.

"Aye, son. Unless of course, high council was in an uproar over one thing or another." And then he led Dager away from the rest of the folk and they sat together near the shore of the Great Pond. "The reason we are beginning this new village is so we can live the way we choose to; happily and freely and most importantly, without fear. The high council is a group of men that rule the Village of Hurtsmire, and they are not good rulers." Dager scrunched up his brow. He thought perhaps, he understood.

"The way that the hag used to rule me, maybe?" Mod nodded. That was the best comparison, by far.

"Aye. And it's as you may already suspect, son. A ruler does not have to be wicked to keep control. He or she would fare far better ruling with a kind and just hand, than a hardened one." They watched the children play some more. Dager didn't see any boys his own age, anywhere.

"More children will come, son. There will be plenty of children who are five just like you, and before long, I bet. We have to remember that we are new, and our numbers are small. But, it will not remain that way for long." Dager nodded and continued to watch the children splash about in the water.

"It's not just the boys, Da. What about my clothes? I would like to look the same as everyone else here." Mod nodded again. He understood his son's desire to fit in.

"Aye. Your mother will take care of that in no time. She's got the cloth; all she needs is to measure you up, and in no time at all, you'll have the same kind of clothes as the rest of us." For Dager, it would not happen soon enough.

"Would you like to meet some friends of mine, now?" Mod stood up and motioned for Dager to do the same. Dager was excited to meet his father's friends. He wondered what they would be like and he hoped they would be as good and kind as everyone else appeared to be.

Rather than take him toward the area where the rest of the villagers gathered, Mod led his son to the other side of the pond. They knelt down by the shore and waited. Dager was confused. Why all the quiet and secrecy? Mod reached into his shirt pocket, and pulled from it the old, worn snakeskin pouch. Dager watched him shake it with one hand, as he held onto his medallion with the other. In a matter of seconds, three ancient frogs hopped toward them from lily pad to lily pad, and came to a stop near Mod's feet. The largest frog croaked at him and the sound was so thunderous that Dager cringed. And was he ever big! Dager had never seen such a big frog before. The ones on the surface, few that there were, had been small. Mod loosened the drawstring at the top of the pouch, opened it wide, and then emptied its contents onto the ground for the scaly beasts to feast upon. The three frogs immediately began to lick up the crippled flies.

"All is as it should be, aye?" Mod asked the frogs, as Dager watched the biggest frog nod in agreement. The two others paid Mod no mind at all, concerning themselves only with the treat laid before them.

"This is the way it will be. You've no objections, have you?" The frog again nodded at Mod, and then took another fly and stored it away in its cheek. Finally, the three frogs all croaked together, and it seemed to be their way of saying thank-you and goodbye. Mod returned his now empty pouch to his pocket. He and Dager remained at the shore and watched them hop across the pond until they were once again, out of sight.

"Magic?" Dager asked, and Mod smiled at his young son.

"Aye, in a way. The frogs have been the only occupants of the Great Pond until now. And they do not mind sharing it."

"Oh. What if they did mind?"

"To be honest, I don't know what would happen. I suppose it could rain frogs, or they would make so much noise that everyone would take their leave."

"But why does it matter, what the frogs think?"

"It's just a matter of mutual respect. Frogs and Curors go back together, to the beginning of time. We just watch each other's backs, is all. If something is wrong at the Great Pond, the frogs would let me know. They see all." Dager nodded as though he understood, and then he and his father walked back and rejoined the others at the great feast.

The table was laden with fruits, berries, nuts, vegetables and flatbreads. Dager had never seen so much grub before, and his stomach rumbled with anticipation. He stood in line to fill his plate, behind Lucia. He proceeded to load his, precisely the way she had done. If it were not for him following her example, he would not have known how much or how little he was expected to take. Everyone sat together, and in no apparent order, which was quite an amazing thing for Dager to be a part of. He was used to eating with the animals. He sat down beside his sister, and watched as she picked up a berry, smiled and popped it into her mouth. And so Dager picked up a berry, smiled and popped it into his mouth, when really what he wanted to do was shove in a whole handful at once. Lucia picked up her bread, and took a small, dainty bite of it. Dager did the same. By now, Lucia had become suspicious. Out of the corner of her eye, she could see him following her every move. Just to be sure, she took a blueberry and a strawberry, and ate them together. Sure enough, he did the same! She then squished a raspberry between two nuts, and chewed them slow and deliberate like. Dager still mimicked her. Deep inside, she was roaring with amusement, but she was careful not to let it show. Finally, she picked up a small nut, held it out in front of her, and then squeezed it tightly within the socket of her eye! Dager picked up his nut, hesitated, and then looked at her oddly. Lucia couldn't hold it in any longer, and she burst into gales of laughter. Dager was annoyed, for all he was really trying to do, was behave correctly.

"Dager!" she exclaimed, as she poked him in the ribs. "Why are you copying my every move?" She giggled again, but once she saw the look of humiliation on his face, she immediately felt sorry. She whispered, "You're trying to do it right?" He nodded glumly. "Don't worry, Dager. Just about anything goes." To prove it, she pointed to one of the adults who sat across from them, who would now serve as her unwitting example. "Look at him! He's a mess when he eats, and nobody seems to mind at all!" Dager looked at the sloppy eater, who had berry juice dribbling from his chin. And then he looked at the other people around him, and he realized that Lucia was right. Everybody was concerned only with their plates in front of them, and they paid no attention to how anyone else was eating. He relaxed a little and smiled back at his sister, and began to pick at his food.

"Thanks, Lucia. I didn't want to get into trouble," he explained, through a mouthful of half chewed nuts. She nodded, and then gave him a sisterly punch in the shoulder.

"Don't worry, Dager. You won't get in trouble for just any old thing, around here." They ate until they were full, and then went to rest on a patch of grass. It was not long before they had company. A girl about Dager's size with curly, light brown tresses bounced over to them. She looked directly at him.

"So, you're Dager, huh?" asked the little girl. Dager thought that he liked her immediately. She was his own size, and he assumed from her blunt manner, that she feared nothing.

"Aye, I'm Dager. What's your name?" She smiled a dazzling smile at him, revealing two rows of perfectly straight, white baby teeth.

"I'm Pagan. It's my ma who looked after the old man who got young." she answered in a matter-of-fact way so that he would know her great worth. Lucia laughed as Pagan pointed to the young woman who stood off in the distance, talking to their own mother. "And that's my ma, right there!" Dager nodded and smiled politely. He had seen and met so many people that he doubted that later, he'd remember which one she was. Pagan plunked herself down on the grass beside him.

"Have you seen those nasty frogs yet, Dager?" Lucia asked him. There had been a splash in the water far off, and it reminded her of the other inhabitants.

"Frogs? Where are the frogs?" Pagan asked excitedly. Dager laughed.

"I don't think we can play with these frogs, Pagan. They're really old," he replied, and Lucia frowned.

"So you have seen them! Aren't you afraid of them?" as she asked, she shivered.

"No. I think if we stay away from them, they'll stay away from us." as he spoke, he so hoped that what he'd just said, were true.

Too many hours had passed, with no word yet from any of the guards. The highest member of council who sat on the uppermost seat was to say the least, not pleased. He called a meeting. The meeting chambers was soon half-full of not only council members, but of the remaining villagers who had come because they were curious, and more so on this day than any other. They looked this way and that, and then they watched the entrance and waited. It was quite apparent that many people were missing from the usual crowd. Had this been during the days when Mod cured for

Hurtsmire, he would have been ordered to search for the missing people and guards. But now that was not to be, for Mod was long gone.

"CROY!" The high council member bellowed from his uppermost seat on the pyramid. The cave walls vibrated in response. The crowd sat stone still, waited and wondered what was happening to their beloved village. Croy's heavy footsteps could be heard far in advance of his arrival. It was not long before he was strutting down the aisle toward council. He knelt respectfully before them. The high member spoke.

"It seems that not only are we missing Mod and his family, Curor called Croy, but we appear to have fewer guards and fewer villagers. Do you know anything of this?" he tapped Croy on the shoulder. Croy stood and replied with an evil grin.

"I've been busy moving into the Curor's hut. I know nothing about the departure of such guards or people." He would not offer to search for them but he did have something else in mind. He turned and looked dramatically through the crowd, and then said, "And who is missing of the villagers, anyway? Were they important? Are they necessary for the survival of the Village of Hurtsmire?" he shook his head, no. "I think not. I think that any villagers that have left our land, we should bid good riddance to." Dramatically then, he raised his hands in an up and down motion to encourage applause, which he quickly received. The villagers feared Croy so much, that they were more than willing to do his bidding. "And the guards? Surely you have replacements. Replacements that are loyal and trustworthy, which is more than I can say for the ones who chose to leave."

The highest council member was furious now. Furious that Croy said more than was expected of him, and furious that he seemed to have so much village backing. He banged his recently replaced gavel down on the podium so hard, that it broke into pieces. The podium tipped and nearly toppled over. Croy, wise as he was, fell once more to his knees.

"Croy! As the Curor for this village, it is not your duty to tell high council what is best for the Village of Hurtsmire! Your job is to do what we tell you to do. If we require your bold opinions, we will not hesitate to ask for them," and then he leaned down toward him and shouted angrily, "are you sure you have what it takes to be the Curor for the Village of Hurtsmire?" His gavel gone once more, the high member was even more enraged. "Stand, Croy! Can't you see I have no gavel?" Croy stood.

"What is it you wish of me, sir? I shall do your bidding. I live and breathe for the Tasman Empire." Croy then hung his head so resolutely that he looked sincere. With his head bowed that way, no one could see the malicious expression on his face. His intended damage had been done; no one would forget his words easily.

Meanwhile, the high member was pleased that

he had beaten Croy down into his place, and he ordered, "I wish you to be a good Curor and go down on your knees and do what Curors do. Hold onto your medallion and find the missing guards!" Croy did as he was told, and behaved like the puppet the high member so wished him to be. His powers, however, were nowhere near as strong as Mod's, and he was unable to find the guards. His visions did not even take him beyond the village boundaries. Rather than admit this failing, he waited for a reasonable amount of time to pass, and then he stood.

"Mod has tricked them all, sir. He holds them captive in a cave not far from here. It is not the guards who have betrayed you after all. It is Mod. All of it is the fault of Mod," he looked solemn, as if it pained him to speak of such things. He continued, "The villagers too, are his prisoners and are not able to return to us. Their will is not their own." The high member frowned. He wouldn't have thought that Mod was capable of such evil. He twisted his moustache this way and that for what seemed to be, the longest time. For a fleeting moment, Croy worried that he'd seen right through him.

"I knew it." And now the high member was lying, but he wished it to appear as though this was something he had suspected all along. "Tomorrow, mid-morning, after the wedding between my daughter, Bree and the man, Derk, you shall go forth and bring them all back. Every one of them, you will return to this village. In doing so, Croy, you will become their hero. Look upon this task as though it is a favour from me to you, for that is what it really is. Save the people of the village and they will forever look upon you as their saviour and you will be held in high regard." Croy nodded and waited, until he remembered that there was no gavel. He then stood, turned and at the sound of the ill-sounding drums, left the meeting chambers. He frowned all the way back to his new hut. His recent tactics at the meeting had not gone as well as he had intended. And now it seemed that he had a trip to prepare for, and secretly he hoped that he really would learn the true whereabouts of the missing guards and villagers, well before mid-morning of the following day.

## 17

# PAGAN MEETS DERK

This was to be Dager's first time since he could remember, to be going to sleep on an actual bed mat. Like most of the other children had been, he and Lucia were sent to their hut to retire for the night. The outer shells of these huts had been constructed with slender logs, which had been placed in a circle, and they leaned into the middle until they met and joined at the tops. The logs were strapped together tightly with lengths of sinewy vines, then covered with large leaves, branches and various ferns. The end result kept out most of the light, but not all; it still filtered through in certain spots. This particular hut was more extravagant than most, being that it was built especially for the Curor and his family, and held not one, but two bedrooms. Dager and Lucia were to share the room furthest from the entrance. Each using separate rooms, they changed into nightclothes.

They wore long, identical bright white nightshirts. Lucia's reached to her knees, and Dager's fell to mid-calf. Dager marveled at the soft material that lay against his body. It felt wonderful. He lifted the neckline of his shirt up to his nose, and inhaled deeply. It smelled clean and fragrant, very much unlike anything he could ever remember having worn before.

"It can't be bedtime already, Lucia! It's not even dark, yet!" Dager exclaimed, but just as he did, he remembered what she had said about it never getting dark in the south. But now he understood, that this was not actually the south, but a completely different land that would not be considered north, south, east nor west. He recalled Lucia shuddering when it became dark, back at the hag's barn. Lucia just gave him a funny look.

"Don't you remember? It doesn't get dark in the south!" She was making fun of him now, although good-heartedly. He could tell she meant no harm, and he didn't mind her teasing him a bit. And besides, he was too tired to challenge her more experienced sense of humour.

"Aye, I remembered just at the same time as I asked. It's funny here, Lucia." She sat beside him, on the edge of his mat.

"What do you mean, funny? What is funny?" she asked, slightly concerned.

"Well, I guess it's not funny, exactly. I like it here. I haven't seen anyone get hit or tied up or yelled at. Everyone is nice to each other and they talk and play and everything. I haven't seen any bad people at all. It's a good kind of funny." She laughed at him, reached over and gave him a hug. As she got up from his mat to go to her own, she told him.

"It won't be often that you see any of those things, if at all," and almost as an afterthought, she added, "you know, Dager, for a brother, I don't think you're half-bad." He looked at her, not fully understanding the compliment. Still smiling, they each climbed under their blankets, closed their eyes and fell into a deep sleep at about the same time.

Brand, Gia, Mod and Goy wound up being the last to retire. Everyone else, adults and children included, had long ago gone to bed by the time the last four decided it was time to douse the last cook fire and call it a day.

"I think I'll be the first to bid you goodnight, my friends." Gia stood up and announced. Pagan had already been asleep for hours, and Gia felt that now would be a perfectly good time to join her. In a move that surprised not only her, but Mod and Goy as well, Brand protested. He stood up and set his hand upon her shoulder.

"Not yet, Gia. I've one more thing to ask you, before you are completely relieved of your duties as my handmaiden." She raised her eyebrows a little. She had assumed that she had already been relieved of those duties, but she would not argue. As ready for sleep as she was, she didn't mind the idea of granting him one last request. She laughed openly.

"Of course, Brand! What is it that you'd like me to do?"

"We'll need some wood for the morning's fire, to cook with. Nobody seems to like fetching wood first thing in the morning. I was hoping to send you back beyond the Clay Peaks, right about where the bush begins. There are plenty of twigs in that area, just perfect for starting fires with." Gia smiled politely, although she wondered about his odd request. She knew there were plenty of twigs close by, in the forest that lay beside them. Being the kind-hearted soul that she was, she would not dispute this minor thing with him.

"Aye, Brand. Shall I take a bag, then?" That made sense to her, to bring back as much as she possibly could.

"Oh, no. Just carry what you can in your arms. That should be sufficient." She nodded again, gave them all a little wave, and then obediently headed off in the direction of the Clay Peaks. Once she was far enough away and out of earshot, Mod gave his father a crossways look, laughed out loud, then asked.

"Pray tell me. What was that about? Certainly you are aware that we have sufficient supplies for the morning's fire?" Sure enough, there were stacks upon stacks of small branches and the like, set aside just for that purpose. Goy sat silently, and smirked at both men. She could see that a scheme hung thickly in the air.

Brand just sat back down beside his son, and with a contented sigh, told them, "It seems that right about now, there is a certain young man hiking down into our valley, whom Gia will be most interested in seeing." Goy gasped.

"You're not serious! You've summoned her husband? You've called out to Derk?"

"Aye. And he's risked everything to come to her. He's traveled faster and farther than a man who's not known true love possibly could. Can you think of two people more deserving, to be together?" Goy's eyes brimmed with tears. She quickly wiped them away, then answered.

"No, Brand, I honestly cannot," she spoke softly, as she swallowed the lump in her throat. She stood up then, and Mod joined her. It was well past time to go to their hut. She turned and added, "You never cease to amaze me, Brand. This village is lucky to have you in its midst." No more words would be exchanged between them on this day, for Mod and Goy, hand in hand, walked away. Goy looked once more in the direction that Gia had taken, before entering her hut, and smiled.

Gia's arms were laden with every single fire starting stick that she could possibly scrounge. She was still a little concerned for Brand; despite his youthful appearance, she now wondered if he were losing the aging battle. It was possible after all, for a man of his age to show signs of senility; especially after being an invalid for so long. She was thinking just that, when a man and woman suddenly appeared at the crest of the hill.

"Hello!" she called out warmly to welcome the strangers, who were still too far away for her to recognize. She was sure they had arrived to be part of the new village, for under ordinary circumstances, nobody would wander about this way. They continued to walk toward her, and she waited. The woman's face was heavily veiled with a head scarf and so it was impossible for Gia to tell, who she might be. The man looked familiar, but due to the bushy beard, which was uncommon in these parts, his facial features were concealed and it was difficult to tell whether she knew him or not.

Derk, on the other hand, knew Gia's voice. He'd heard it over and over in his beautiful memories of their short time together. This voice, he had listened to with longing in each and every dream he'd had, since his banishment. He stopped a few metres short of Gia, and turned to Bree.

"Please, Bree," he whispered, "do me this one thing and wait here for a moment. That is my wife. My beloved wife, at long last." He pled with her softly; his face so full of hope, that the usually wicked woman felt compelled to comply. She nodded at him, saying nothing. Gia watched their exchange, and for a quick moment she wondered why the woman had stopped following her man. She did not wonder for long, for now he was close enough that she could see his eyes.

"Derk!" Twigs and sticks flew into the air as she broke into a run. The husband and wife wasted no time and embraced. Tears flowed freely between them. It had been so long.

"But, how?" Gia managed to stammer though it all. "How did you know to come here? How did you get away?" Derk could not yet speak, and so he just hugged his wife harder, until he was able to regain his composure.

"It is a long story, my love. I will tell you all about it, later. It was Brand who sought me out." Gia nodded knowingly, and all at once her wood collecting errand made perfect sense. Brand had known all along that Derk would be there. She smiled, and her tears were spent. She would have nothing more to cry about on this particular day.

"Derk, who have you brought with you?"

He replied by whispering in her ear. "Trouble, I'm afraid. Nothing but trouble." With that, he waved at the woman, and she began walking toward them. "Gia, I'd like you to meet Bree, daughter of the highest member of council." Gia clenched her teeth, but politely held out her hand in greeting. She knew that this woman was the reason that Derk had been sent away in the first place. The woman called Bree pulled the cover from her face at long last. She finally felt that she was far enough away from the Village of Hurtsmire to do so.

"I am pleased to meet you, Gia." The two women shook hands, and then Gia could not help but ask.

"Why have you come?" she seriously wondered if the woman still had intentions of stealing Derk from her. Couldn't she tell by now, that a relationship between her and Derk would never be? Bree could tell immediately, that Gia did not care for her, and she didn't blame her for that. She decided to answer honestly, because after all, this was all about new beginnings.

"I wish to be free, Gia. Free like you and free like Derk, and free like Mod and his family. And just so you know, I never, ever desired to marry Derk." Gia had not known that, and she appreciated being told.

"Why was my husband forced to leave, then? Why didn't you tell anyone that you didn't want to marry him? We've been apart because of it for many years! For so long, that Derk has never even laid eyes upon his own daughter!"

"I know it. Do you think I don't know it? And I am sorry. The truth of the matter is, that I have had no more privileges than any other woman in the Village of Hurtsmire. I have no opinions and no rights as far as that village is concerned. It was to be an arranged marriage, and despite the heartache you've suffered because of it, I am grateful that Derk turned it down. If he had married me as my father wished, I would never have been able to live with myself." Now Gia understood the role that Bree had been forced to play. She felt stabbing pains of guilt. For years she had secretly blamed Bree for Derk's banishment, when by rights she shouldn't have.

"I am sorry too, Bree. Sorry for the awful things I've thought about you." Gia then smiled up at Derk, who had remained silent to allow them to work out their differences. He was now seeing Bree in a very different and positive light. The two women shook hands again, and then with the twigs and sticks strewn about and all but forgotten, the three of them traveled the rest of the distance to the new village together. Gia graciously pointed Bree in the direction of an empty hut, and then she led her husband to their own. Quietly, they crept inside, and Gia brought Derk straight to the mat where their child lay sleeping. Pagan looked like an absolute angel, lying there with her eyes gently closed and her pouty mouth slightly ajar. Her hair was splayed out like a halo around her, and she was covered in white nightclothes. Derk was speechless, as he pulled the doll from his pocket, and tucked it under the blanket next to her. Never in his wildest dreams, had he imagined that a child of his could be so beautiful. The proud couple stood for a while, watching over her, and then for the first time in many years, retired to their own bed mat, arm in arm, as man and wife.

Morning came early in the new village, and Pagan was the first to rise to greet it. She'd more than caught up on her sleep and was ready to begin the new day. With small, balled up fists she rubbed the stubborn sleep from her eyes and gave a big stretch. Then, she crawled over to her mother's mat. When she saw not one, but two bodies in it, she shrieked.

"Ma, ma! Get up! There's somebody's da got into your bed!" Pagan jumped about this way and that, in a desperate attempt to warn her mother. Gia slowly opened her eyes, and smiled furtively at her startled child. Derk propped himself up on one elbow and peeked at Pagan through his own sleepy, narrow lids. Gia laughed.

"Pagan, it's alright. You see..." But the girl would not be dissuaded. She was determined to get that man off her mother's bed mat. She climbed right over Gia and yanked on the strange man's arm.

"You have to go! You're in the wrong hut!" she grunted as she howled at him, and soon found that pulling on him was useless. The man would not budge. Poor Pagan was toiling so hard, in between heaving and fretting about the intruder, that she'd worked up a sweat. Gia tried to stop her again.

"Pagan, that's enough!" she ended up shouting much louder than she'd meant to, but she did manage to stop the girl.

"What's wrong? I'm helping you!" Pagan's eyes were as big as saucers as she tried to make sense of why her mother didn't seem to want her help. She let go of the man's arm, and it fell with a flop back down onto the covers. She climbed back over her mother and off the bed mat, then sat down cross-legged on the ground. Pagan stared defiantly at her mother. Gia swung her legs over to the edge, and sat facing her child.

"Pagan, do you remember when I told you about your father?" Pagan's eyes grew wider yet, but she said nothing. "Well, he's returned to us, love. This man is your father."

"My real da?"

"Yes, love."

"Are you sure?" she leaned over to look at the strange man again. She looked him up and down.

"Aye, I'm pretty sure this is him." Gia answered, and as she did she tried not to laugh out loud. Derk smiled at Pagan.

"But, he's got a hairy face," her voice rose in tone with each syllable she spoke. "You didn't tell me he'd be all hairy," and then the girl folded her arms across her chest and stood. With a huff, she told her mother, as a matter-of-factly. "I don't think so. I'm going to play now." Pagan stomped out of the hut, without a backward glance. Derk sighed despondently, but Gia wasn't at all worried. She tried to console him.

"She'll come around, I'm sure of it." He shook his head, then replied.

"Perhaps waking up to find me in her mother's bed wasn't the best way to introduce the two of us. It may have been better if I had walked into the village in the middle of the day."

"It's done now, and she'll come around in time. Pagan does not take kindly to change, love.

But she will. You'll see." Derk wished that he was as confident of that as his wife appeared to be.

# 18

# FOUND IN THE FOREST

Croy had no choice but do the very thing that had removed Mod from his position as Curor, for the Village of Hurtsmire. He'd much rather travel to the surface than admit to anyone that his powers were not anywhere near as powerful as he'd always claimed them to be. Why not, anyway? It wasn't as though high council would have any chance of finding out. Having made his decision, he returned to his hut and callously informed his wife.

"I've business to attend to. I won't be gone long." Quite apparently, they did not share the loving kind of relationship that Dager had just been introduced to within his own family. Keeping her eyes downcast, the poorly dressed woman nodded and at first said nothing. She was in fact, relieved to know he would be gone, at least for a while. But, she had to be careful not to show it. She was glad that their beloved son, Lor was out playing for the moment, near the edge of the forest. She detested it when the child would see his father treat her in such a demeaning manner, which was unfortunately, more often than not. After careful consideration, she replied quietly.

"That is regrettable, Croy. Shall I pack you a lunch?" He spun his face angrily in her direction and answered her with clear disdain.

"Did I ask for a lunch, woman?" She bowed her head even lower.

"No."

"Then it would be wise not to pack a lunch for me, wouldn't it?" With that, he stormed out of their newly acquired hut. Once he was clear of the village, Croy headed straight for the Clay Peaks that lay just east of the Great Pond. Unbeknownst to him at that time, he was headed straight to the new village, where he would find exactly and possibly even more than he was looking for.

Dager and Lucia had just finished their breakfast which consisted of warm porridge and fresh fruit, when Pagan came stomping from her hut. Her curls were flying wildly about her head and her arms were folded across her chest. Because she was definitely in a flap about one thing or another, Dager sort of hoped she wouldn't be heading their way. Naturally, she was. By the time she sat down beside him, her face was red with fury. Dager peeked at her from the corner of his eye, and saw that her lips were puckered tightly. He hated to ask, but by now his curiosity had gotten the best of him.

"What's wrong, Pagan?" he asked warily. Her eyes blazed as she turned and looked from him to Lucia.

"Lots is wrong. Lots is wrong, I say!" with that, she stood and pointed back in the direction of her hut. "I'm moving out!" Lucia barely contained her giggles with the back of her hand and at the same time, looked away. Dager furrowed his brows. Moving out of her mother's hut surely was not an option. He protested.

"You can't move out! That's where you live!" She stomped her bare foot harder into the dirt.

"I don't think there's even room for me, anyhow." Her angry eyes lightened and ultimately transformed into sad ones.

"But, what do you mean? Of course there's room for you." And then Dager remembered the bits and pieces of conversation he'd heard earlier that morning from the adults.

"Is it because of your father? Don't you like him?"

"But, he's not my father! Ma's wrong! I can't have a hairy old father!" the girl burst into tears before plunking her bottom back down on the ground. The fact of the matter was, she'd never seen a hairy face before, and it scared her to death. Lucia did not find this situation quite as funny as she first did, especially now that she could see just how upset Pagan was. Kindly, she offered.

"Maybe he just needs a shave! My da shaves all the time! Sometimes by the end of the day, he has lots of whiskers sticking out of his chin. But, by the end of the next morning, they're gone because he's shaved them off!" Pagan brightened immediately.

"Really?"

Lucia and Dager both nodded at the same time, although Dager hadn't really a clue as to what he was agreeing to. Pagan looked up to the sky and tried to picture that man without all the hair. As hard as she tried, she just couldn't do it.

"We'll see about that. I might stay in that hut then, but we'll see." she would make no promises in that department. At the very least, her mood had improved and Dager was relieved for her. He knew better than most, how frustrating the age of five could be. Just then, Pagan reached over and tugged hard on his arm.

"Let's play hide and seek!" Glad for the distraction, Dager happily jumped to his feet, and asked his sister to join them. "No, I don't think so. Maybe later, but I'm going to see if Ma wants me to do anything!" And she took off in the opposite direction. Just before Dager and Pagan headed into the woods, he glanced back to where his parents stood talking with another couple, and they waved back at him happily. Could life get any better than this?

Pagan took off on him at full speed. He had to work really hard to keep up as she jumped through ferns, over logs and crossed small streams. Finally she sailed into a pile of leaves, and laid flat on them, having given up on trying to lose her friend. Dager was out of breath by the time he joined her there. He flopped backwards, down onto the leaves beside her. Feigning disgust, he demanded.

"Pagan! Why are you in such a hurry?" She giggled before replying.

"Because the days aren't long enough! If we play quickly, we'll get more play time before we go to bed." And then she looked at him as though he didn't have a brain in his head. What she'd said didn't even make any sense, but he was not about to argue that fact with his stubborn, new friend. He had a feeling that somehow, she'd win the argument, anyway.

"Oh, okay, we can play fast. But don't you have chores to do? Don't you have to help your mother?" The truth was, that he felt a little guilty about not going along with Lucia, to see if their mother wanted help.

"Nopers," but then Pagan relented, after giving it more thought. "I help my ma sometimes, but not today. I don't want to, and I want to play." She had an idea that her mother realized that she needed space, especially on this particular morning. As far as Pagan was concerned, she thought that maybe, she could wish that man away. And if that didn't work, and if he was determined to stay, maybe she could at least get him to shave off all that hair.

"Aren't you even a little bit glad to have a da now?" Dager asked sincerely. "I know I'm really, really glad to have a da, and a ma, and even a sister!" Poor Dager had been without so much for so long, that he thought he could probably live an entire lifetime and never get too much of his family. Pagan pursed her lips again, as she considered that.

"I don't know, because I've never had a da. So how could I know if I'm glad?" Dager knew he was making progress, and slowly breaking through her rather icy exterior, and so he pushed a little further.

"Well, I can tell you something! I didn't have one for a long time, and now I do, and am I ever glad!" he spoke so seriously, that Pagan sat straight up and looked at him.

"Really?"

"Aye, really. You should give your da a chance." Pagan folded her arms back across her chest, tilted her head to the side, and as a matter-of-factly told him.

"Okay, but only if he shaves his hair."

"Sounds good to me, Pagan!" Dager looked this way and that. "How do we play hide and seek, anyway?" He had no idea what the game was, and so Pagan spent the next hour showing him. It was Dager's very first play date and he laughed and ran and hid and looked for Pagan so naturally, it was as though he'd been doing it for his entire life. It would seem that the poor, ragged boy who used to be known as pond scum, was gone forever.

"Can we play on the other side of the Clay Peaks, Pagan? Are we allowed?" She laughed at him.

"Of course we can!" she replied, without really knowing if they could or not. And so they kept just inside the tree line, and hiked all the way back in the direction of the new village. They circled the other side of the Great Pond, and as they did so, they could see the villagers far off in the distance. Dager waved to them, even though he knew they probably couldn't be seen, anyway. By the time the two children made their way to the Clay Peaks, both were filthy. Twigs and dirt stuck to their clothing, and their hair was messy and matted. Without a care in the world, they climbed up a hill, parallel to the very same path that had brought them down to the Great Pond in the first place. But this day, was not about sticking to paths. Dager and Pagan were more than happy to be blazing their own haphazard trails. And at about the same time that they were halfway up, none other than that nasty Croy, Curor for the Village of Hurtsmire, was making his way down.

The ground bugs were having an absolute feast on the Curor's feet and legs, and he was more than a little annoyed by it. They were so thick and frenzied that if he didn't know better, he might have thought the bugs were attempting to block his way. At the top of the hill, in fact when he stood and briefly surveyed the beauty of the valley that lie below, like so many before him had recently done, the wind gusted and almost knocked him right off his feet. The wind blew an entire sea of leaves and fallen debris straight at him, and for a few minutes he could not even see further than the end of his nose. Croy knew that none of these signs were good ones. Nonetheless, as stubborn as he was, he pressed on.

The little boy who had been frolicking near the edge of the forest, quietly slipped into it. He was so busy with his playing about; running this way and that, and dodging imaginary enemies that before long he'd completely lost his bearings. Any sense of direction was gone. He looked up and turned around and around, but the canopy of trees above him was so thick, that it was too dark to see landmarks. Not that it would have done him any good, for he'd paid no attention to them earlier, anyway. Immediately, he felt silly for having gotten himself lost. But, rather than call out for help, he decided to find his way home on his own. He pressed on, in fact at about the same time as his father did; however the boy was heading the entirely wrong direction. And when he finally realized that he'd gotten himself into a bigger fiddle than ever before, he began to cry. He sat down on his bottom in the middle of a large group of ferns and he felt more frightened and alone, than ever before.

Finally, Dager pushed his way in front of

Pagan, and he took charge as the leader of their game. The whole time they'd been playing, she'd insisted on being the boss, and now he was more than ready to have his turn. Pagan was tiring anyway, and by the time Dager took the lead position, she was more than content to just follow along behind.

The whacking stick he held in his right hand, was about five feet long, and fairly straight. He'd succeeded in peeling most of the bark and small branches from it, so in the end it appeared fairly smooth, and almost polished. It worked well for what he needed; clearing a path through the ominous, endless branches which tried earnestly to block their way. They traveled to a clearing and found themselves standing directly in front of a large group of ferns. These wild stalks were so tall that they reached Dager's neck, and with his trusty tool, he began knocking them right down flat to the ground.

"STOP!" Pagan yelled out. At the same time, she swiftly grabbed onto the end of Dager's stick, while it was still in mid-swing. Dager was so surprised at her sudden outburst that the stick flew from his hand. He looked at her angrily, but stopped short when he saw the look on her face. She retrieved his stick and handed it back to him.

"Don't you hear it?" she whispered, and fear blanketed her face. It was just at that moment, when Dager did indeed hear it. Whimpering that was becoming louder by the second. It was the whimpering of a child.

"Who's there?" Dager demanded to know. The ferns which remained standing ahead of them rustled a bit, and then a boy's head popped out from them. Dager trembled. Two more whacks with his stick, and he would have nailed the boy for sure. Maybe even poked his eye out. The boy was bleary-eyed and quite obviously, had been crying for some time. His face was tear-streaked, but he smiled weakly. He'd been all alone for too long, and was very glad to have company in this scary, unfamiliar territory.

"I'm here." he answered, in a quiet, shaky voice. "It's me, Lor." Pagan folded her arms across her chest, and stomped her foot down in the dirt.

"Well, I don't know any Lor. Where are you from?"

"The Village of Hurtsmire." he replied, to which Pagan harrumphed, loud and clear. She didn't believe him.

"Well, that's where I used to live, and I don't know you at all." The boy didn't know what else to say. Should he tell her that he hadn't ever been allowed to see other children, or was it better that he remained silent? Just then, Dager intervened.

"Are you lost, Lor?" The boy nodded enthusiastically. It didn't seem to matter what he said to the girl, as she'd already made up her mind about him. But this boy on the other hand, was a lot more pleasant to talk with. Dager smiled brightly, for Lor's benefit.

"You can come back to our village with us, if you'd like." Dager offered, hoping to be of some help to him. The lost boy looked nice enough, and he might even be the same age as he and Pagan. But, it seemed that Pagan would have none of that.

"What? No lost boys. Those are the rules." Pagan coolly informed them both. Dager looked at her in wonder. How could she be so mean as to not want to help the lost boy? He looked back to Lor, whose face had immediately become downcast.

"Pagan! What if you were lost in the forest, and two boys came along and wouldn't help you because of a stupid "No Lost Girls" rule?" Pagan thought about it for a moment, without once realizing that Dager had her figured out. Lor cheered up again, when Dager winked at him on the sly.

"Well, alright then. I guess we can break the rule," she then gave Lor a look that meant, just this time. Lor immediately disliked the girl called Pagan, and decided that Dager had more than earned his friendship. He smiled again at Dager.

"Come on, Lor! We can play on the way to the village." The idea sounded like fun to the newcomer, but Lor would be sure to stick close to Dager, and keep more than a few paces between himself and Pagan, for however long it took to get there. The new trio found the beaten path and crossed it. They then began a new adventure together through the forest, on the opposite side of the path, and picked their way ever so slowly down into the valley.

Croy's wife had begun to panic. She could not find five-year old Lor, anywhere. There was no one she could turn to for help; she had no friends to speak of, and her relatives were back in the village she and her husband had been cast from, years before. The last thing she wanted to do was alert Croy; and she didn't know exactly where he'd gone, anyway. Her voice was hoarse from yelling her son's name repeatedly, and now the only thing left for her to do, was search for him on foot. She so hoped she'd find him soon, and with any luck she'd learn that her son had come to no harm. She had a pretty good notion that he'd wandered into the forest, and that he simply could not find his way out again. He was lost is all, she tried to convince herself. Another huge lump formed in her throat, and like the others before, she swallowed it down, hard. Hours had gone by, and poor Lor could be a long way from home by now. She began making her way into the forest, and lucky for her, she found a path that looked very well worn. Perhaps this was the way her son had gone? Well, there was only one way to find out. She wiped away the tears of worry and frustration, and began her journey. If the serpent was on her side on this day, surely she'd have Lor back safe and sound, long before Croy's return.

# 19

## FULL CIRCLE

What a sight you are, my love!" Gia exclaimed proudly to her freshly shaven husband. She wiped the blade clean, and hurried back into her hut to return it to its safe place, as far as her hand could reach, underneath her bed mat. Derk reached up and felt his smooth cheeks, upper lip, and then chin. He was very pleased with this wife's skilled hand. And when she returned, he replied.

"Aye, and I thank you for it. I feel much better without the extra warmth." Gia shook her head at him.

"May I ask whatever possessed you to grow such a thing in the first place?" she looked upon him lovingly, as a newlywed might look upon her brand new spouse. She could tell by the look in his eyes, that his love for her had not dimmed, either.

"To tell you the truth, Gia, I just couldn't bring myself to take it off. Everything had changed for me. My life, my village, and my job. I didn't think that growing a beard would matter. And believe it or not, in Chadwhip, much unlike Hurtsmire, bearded faces are very common." Gia was surprised to hear that, for beards in the Village of Hurtsmire, were considered an oddity. Nonetheless, it didn't matter anymore, anyway. They were all out of danger now, and most importantly, the three of them would be together. It was finally the way it always should have been.

Just then, Bree spotted the couple and hurried over to them. The Bree of today looked very little like the Bree of the day before, and as a matter of fact, better than all of the days before then. Her hair was clean and neatly arranged at the back of her head. She'd obviously bathed, and she was dressed in fine clothes. One might have claimed, that she even looked pretty.

"Oh, Derk! How can I thank you for agreeing to bring me along?" she looked entirely sincere as she spoke. She'd spent all morning and most of the afternoon getting to know the other villagers, and helping out in any way she could. She'd done it all without her controlling father looking over her shoulder. Derk laughed out loud at the woman, albeit in good humour. He couldn't resist teasing her, just a little bit.

"As I remember it, Bree, I had no choice but to bring you along! Do you not recall threatening to scream and bring the wrath of high council down upon my head?" Bree looked at him coyly.

Gia silently watched their exchange, and as she did, she discovered that the woman who had caused them so much pain in the past, was really not so bad, after all. Circumstances beyond Bree's control seemed to have, at least up until this point, dictated her whole entire, miserable life.

"Aye, and I'm sorry for it. You see, I had to leave. No matter what!" Derk reached over and kindly patted her shoulder.

"I know it. You won't have to use such drastic measures, here. Although, I do fear what's to become of us, once your father discovers your whereabouts." Bree sighed, and nodded in response.

"Aye, it's all true, and you should worry. We should all worry. However, I think that I may know how to handle him, when the time comes." This time, Gia spoke up.

"We hope you're right, Bree. We sure hope you're right. It's no good to begin our new village with strife. Let's hope it can be worked out easily." Even though the three spoke positive words about the unfortunate, impending coming of the high council, a dark cloud continued to loom high overhead. It was as though none of them truly believed that any good could come of Bree's recent arrival in the new village.

"Brand!" Brand had been taking an afternoon nap, when he heard his name being called. He sat up on his mat and rubbed his eyes. He easily recognized Mod's voice. His son waited patiently outside the opening of Mod's hut, for him to answer.

"Aye, I'm up. You can come in, son." Mod did as he was told. He sat on the ground, across from him.

"All's well in the village, Da. You've done wonderful things in a short period of time." But, Brand shook his head. There was no way he would accept the credit for all that had been done.

"No, that's not all true. All I did, was set it in motion. Everything that has been done here, from the building of the shelters to the gathering of food, has been done by each and every one of them," he waved toward the door, indicating to the outside population. Mod knew the depth of his father's modesty, and he would not disrespect him by pressing the issue.

"Just the same, I fear trouble is brewing. Croy makes his way to our village as we speak. The ancient frogs have alerted me. He's just about here." Mod stated worriedly. He didn't want to see any mayhem in his paradise. He didn't wish to be remembered for it; trouble was not how he wished to make his mark as Curor for the new village. He was so done with the Village of Hurtsmire, that the news of Croy's visit saddened him. Brand suddenly smacked his hand against his knee, and smiled at his son with glee. He had the gift of foresight that Mod would still not realize for many years to come. Mod felt relieved to see the worry free expression on Brand's face.

"Full circle, Mod. That's what is about to happen. Life has fallen into place, in more ways than you could ever imagine. I'm not going to tell you, and ruin it, oh, no! You'll see it for yourself, soon enough. In the meantime, do not fret. Croy will do no damage here." Mod nodded at Brand as he got up to leave.

"Are you coming then, too? To see it for yourself?" The old man laughed out loud.

"Aye, I will come. Although, I've already seen it." he tapped the side of his head then, and indicated toward his precious medallion. Brand rose to his feet, and he and Mod walked out of his dim hut together. Just as they did, they looked beyond the Great Pond, and off in the distance, they could easily make out Croy's looming form coming toward them. Goy, who'd been sorting nuts nearby, snapped her head suddenly in Croy's direction, the moment she saw the look of concern cross her husband's face. She dropped her nuts, panicked, and rushed to Mod's side.

"No! No! Where's Dager? Croy's done it again, hasn't he?" she covered her face with her hands and began to sob. No sooner had she gotten her long, lost son back, and now she's lost him, again? It wasn't fair. It just wasn't fair at all. A reassuring hand began to rub her back. Surprisingly, it did not belong to her husband. It was Brand who soothed her.

"Do not cry, Goy. Sit back and watch," he

then took the startled Lucia, who stood back a ways, by the hand, and urged her to join her mother's side. "Dager is absolutely fine," Brand told her. "In fact, he's been having the time of his life, all day!" Goy sniffed back her tears and convinced herself to believe him. She had to trust that all he'd said was true. After all, it was Brand, who'd said it; he, who had never said anything that did not need to be said.

The nearer Croy came, the more the villagers huddled together in groups. The ground began to shake with each step closer the Curor took. Idle chatter came to a dead stop. Breaths were held. Young children were ushered to be near their parents. Thankfully here, there were no drums to celebrate Croy's arrival, and no automatic stomping of feet. Finally, Croy stood within speaking distance of where Mod and Brand waited.

"What can we do for you, Croy?" Mod did not bother to address him properly, as he formerly would have. If he were to follow protocol, he would have said, "Croy, Curor for the Village of Hurtsmire, of the Tasman Empire". This however, was not Hurtsmire. Croy's blood instantly boiled at the insult, and he replied with an evil sneer.

"I've come to bring the villagers and guards back to Hurtsmire. You're a fool, if you think you can keep them here indefinitely."

"A fool? Nay, Croy. It is not I, who is the fool here." Croy took a step closer to his foe. Mod wasn't about to show fear by backing down from this man. After all that Brand had told him earlier, Mod had time to put this dilemma into proper perspective. The man called Croy would have no power here. For in this village, that was all Croy was. A man and nothing more. Croy was about to respond with a cruel remark, when he eyed up the man standing next to Mod.

"Who is this man that stands beside you? Have you enlisted someone of great importance to help you in your treachery?" Mod was about to retort, but stopped suddenly when he saw Brand raise his hand toward Croy.

"Treachery! No treachery has been committed. Don't even think that we didn't see the look of surprise on your face when you saw us gathered here at the Great Pond. You were about to commit the same so called treason, by going forth to the surface yourself!" As he accused Croy, he stared straight into Croy's eyes. He held his gaze fast. Croy found himself unable to look away. He realized that this strange man held powers even greater than Mod's. There was no way to defeat either of them. He shook with anger, and both of his massive hands balled into tight, angry fists. If necessary, Croy was prepared to use physical means to fight his way out of this particular mess.

"There is no need for violence, Croy. You'd do best to gather up your wife and child, and return to the Village of Hurtsmire." Now it was Croy who laughed. He laughed heartily at the powerful, yet obviously senile, old man.

"What makes you think my wife and child are here? They are back at our hut." Croy then nodded at Mod. "Surely you know the one." Mod knew exactly which hut Croy was referring to. He did not need reminding. Just then, there was a commotion at the perimeter of the forest, and three children spilled out from it.

"Dager!" Goy cried out in alarm. Gia ran forward and scooped Pagan up into her arms. She rushed with the child, back to her husband's side, and the moment she did, Pagan noticed his freshly shaven face. She smiled at him, and he was pleased. Had he known before, that was all it would have taken for her to warm up to him, he would have asked Gia to shave him right away. All this while, Croy just stood looking dumbfounded, as he stared at his son, who stood beside Dager. How could it be, that his son was at this place?

"Da!" Lor exclaimed. But he did not hurry to him; rather, he took a step back out of fear. Dager, on the other hand, was completely oblivious to the lines of tension which were so thick, that they were nearly visible to the eyes of the adults who knew better. Dager was very happy with the day's events. Naively, he took his new friend by the hand, and led him over to Mod and Brand.

"Da! Granda! This is Lor. He's from Hurtsmire, and we found him lost in the forest!" Lor, still avoiding eye contact with his own father, nodded to the two men, and added with his own enthusiasm.

"Aye! They saved me, for sure. I was lost and alone and I didn't know which way to go!" Brand's eyes shone with glee. He smiled to himself, and repeated quietly, so only Mod could hear.

"Full circle."

Mod recognized an opportunity, and took it. He clapped his hands with delight, and spoke loud enough so all could hear.

"Well, Dager and Pagan! Wasn't that kind of you to save a little lost boy? Don't you think so, Croy?" Croy shuddered as he learned that his son had been missing; even though it could only have been for a relatively short period of time. He stuttered.

"Aye. Son, come here." Lor did as he was ordered to do, and dragging his feet, he approached his father. He was hesitant, for he was sure that he was about to be scolded in public. Dager looked at Croy, curiously. He did not yet remember anything about the man who had stolen him from his land and his family, and had then proceeded to sell him to the hag. Chances were, that even if he had, he would have harboured no resentment. That was just the kind of boy Dager was.

Just then, a wave of confusion overtook him. Croy? Did his father say, *"Croy"*? The conversation he'd had with Lucia days earlier, filled his head: *"Ma and Da didn't sell you! An awful man named Croy who lives in our land stole you! Our granda, whose voice I think you heard this morning, has been looking for you the entire time!"* Dager's face fell. He was no longer smiling at Croy. Goy sucked in a deep breath. The moment she'd been dreading was coming to pass right before her very eyes. Dager took a step toward him.

"You?" Dager scowled, then bravely spat on the ground between him and Croy, as though marking his territory. Croy cleared his throat, and for the first time in his life, began to feel extremely uncomfortable. He shifted his bare feet this way and that, before answering. He'd never expected to lay eyes on this child, ever again. Lucia braced herself for the worst, for she was the only person who had seen Dager behave that way before, and she knew that he would not easily back down.

"Aye, it was me," the depth of the wrong he had so willfully committed years prior, suddenly hit him like a brick. He felt twinges of shame. He looked from Lor, to Dager, and then back to Lor again.

"What was you, Da?" Lor asked him, innocently. "What is Dager asking?" the boy was clearly baffled as he looked from Dager to his father, then back to Dager again. The rest of the villagers watched quietly. Regret consumed Croy as he attempted to explain.

"Well, son. It was a long time ago..." But just then, Dager stepped in. He was wise for his years, and he saw no need for more pain or suffering. Especially for Lor. What would he think if he knew the awful truth?

"Aye, it was a long time ago. When I was smaller, your father found me in the forest, and helped me, too!" Lor's face lit up with pride.

"You did, Da? You did? Just like Dager and Pagan helped me?" Croy didn't know how to react, and he was speechless. He realized immediately, the kindness and maturity that was being granted to him; by a five-year old boy, nonetheless. He was amazed that a man such as himself could be shown such compassion.

"Aye. That's how it was, boy." Brand answered for him. Lor had never been more proud of anyone in his entire life. He was unaware that his father could be so kind. He was beaming as he wrapped his arms around Croy's legs and hugged, good and hard. Mod stepped forth, and offered Croy his hand to shake. Croy was still in shock as he accepted it.

"I'd say we're even now, fellow Curor. Wouldn't you?" Mod asked as he nodded toward their two boys, who had fast become friends. "I'd say that all debts have been repaid." Croy nodded, having grasped the finality of their longtime feud. He found his voice.

"Aye, fellow Curor, it is." Croy stammered, as he acknowledged the villagers now, who had slowly inched closer, and had heard all that had been said. They could sense that in an instant, he was a softened man that now stood before them. "Good luck to you, Mod, with your new village. I see it is off to a fantastic start." Mod agreed.

"Aye, it is. More people should be arriving gradually, day by day. By the way, we can always use allies such as yourself, from surrounding villages." He remarked, hinting that perhaps Croy, would consider himself one.

"And so it shall be done. What of the guards, then?"

"The guards have all decided to remain here, with us." Mod purposefully chose not to tell him about Tad, the lead guard who'd chosen to stay on the surface and marry Maybelle P. Bonnadoolio. That minor detail would not matter anymore. No guards or villagers for that matter, would be accompanying Croy back to the Village of Hurtsmire on this day. Croy nodded. His mind was racing, for what would he tell the high council, now? But that, he knew, was his problem and his problem alone. Croy looked again at the man that stood beside Mod. The more he considered it, the more he realized fully well, who the old man really was. Croy was smart enough to not pry into matters such as this, that did not concern him. The less he knew, the better it would be for everyone.

"Can we go home now, Da?" Lor asked him. "I think Ma may be worried by now." the small boy was genuinely concerned for his mother. He was picturing her hunting for him, high and low. Croy and Mod shook hands again, and the Curor for the Village of Hurtsmire and his son, turned and walked away. The ground no longer shook with each step Croy took. His gait was lighter now, and it was as though the weight of the world had been lifted from his shoulders. In a large way, indeed it had; for he had just received the gift of forgiveness. Silence ensued as the father-son pair headed for home. Every set of eyes laid upon them, as they made their way toward the Clay Peaks, hand in hand. On the other side, they would be reunited with Lor's mother, who really had been searching for him as her son had assumed, high and low.

Everyone in the new village felt immense relief. The idle chatter began once more and children were again allowed to roam beyond an arm's length away from their parents. Mod, Goy, Lucia, Dager, and Brand sat down together on the stumps arranged beside Brand's hut. Goy addressed her son.

"Dager, I was so afraid for you! Weren't you afraid of Croy, son?" Dager thought for a moment, before replying.

"Not at all. I thought I would be, if I ever met him. But, I wasn't. I know that he's already done the worst thing to me that he ever could do. He can't hurt me anymore, Ma." his words held such meaning that for a moment, not another word was spoken by anyone.

"Well, I was sure scared enough for both of us!" Lucia exclaimed, and she was happy now that it was over. The adults laughed good-naturedly. Brand smacked his hand against his knee, which was an indication that he was about to speak.

"I, for one, am proud of how you managed that, Dager. I don't think it could have been handled better, even by an adult." Mod and Goy nodded in agreement. It was rather sad, though, to think that their son had been through so very much that little could ever really frighten him again. He was certainly a brave young man. Dager flushed as he wondered what the fuss was about. Mod clapped his hands together, breaking the silence.

"Well, now!" We've only one more thing to contend with, I think." Goy furrowed her brows in concern as she looked to her husband. Dager and Lucia looked on quietly.

"What might that be, my love? Naming the village? Setting rules?" she quite obviously was, at the moment not aware of the woman that was presently consuming her husband's and father-in-law's thoughts. At the moment, Bree was far from Goy's mind.

"High council," Mod answered, "they'll be coming, you know!" He whistled into the air, knowing full well that this new village was not quite out of the woods, yet.

"High council? Why would they come here?" Goy had no idea what Mod was talking about, and though it did not happen often, she thought her husband might be mistaken.

"For Bree, of course!" Goy's mind whirled. Bree? Mod continued. "Bree, as you know, is the daughter of the highest member of council. She wanted so badly out of the Village of Hurtsmire, and out from under her father's rule, that she kind of made Derk bring her along!" Goy laughed nervously. It all sounded absurd, and it brought with it, a certain element of danger.

"Will she stay, Mod?"

"I think so. She wants to, and by rights this should be a free world. That's why we began the new village. For freedom. Freedom to choose. That seems to be exactly what she's done."

"Aye, love. She's made her choice. I've worked with her today, and I do think she'll prove to be an asset to this community." Even Brand nodded in agreement. It would not be a good sign to have one of the newcomers forced out by the very hand they had fled from. If such a thing ever came to pass, then what exactly was the point of beginning the new village in the first place?

# 20

# DAGER AND THE BABY HOUND

A week went by, and there was still no visit from Bree's father. Every day, she paced this way and that, and she fretted over it so much that she thought she might go completely out of her mind. Goy consoled her to the best of her ability. Bree and Gia had managed to strike up quite the friendship, despite their troubled history, and Bree had been able to keep herself somewhat busy when various needs arose. But, after all the morning chores were done, and meals were prepared, and the chores were done again, she still found too much time on her hands and she would worry some more.

Dager could not have put into words, how perfectly content he was. There was no expression nor word, at least to his limited knowledge, that could be used to describe the emotions which he was now feeling on a daily basis. Such happiness, at one time, he would have never thought possible. From time to time he thought about his past, but never with remorse. He preferred to remember Maybelle P. Bonnadoolio as the woman she now was, rather than as that mean, nasty hag that she used to be. And it filled his heart with joy. However, as happy as he was, he really did miss the animals. One day, broached that very subject, with his father.

"Da?" Dager asked him one morning, after a hearty breakfast. The ladies were scurrying around, picking up dishes after their children were through with them. The men were making sure the cook fires had been extinguished. His mother was huddled together with Gia, off to the side. Lucia was playing with Pagan and Derk. Brand sat in the thick of the woods on his own, thinking.

"Aye, son? What is it that troubles you on such a beautiful day?"

"I've been thinking about Mindy and her babies," he hesitated for a moment. "And the horse and the pigs. And the black of night." Mod nodded. It was quite a thing, for his son to have his entire world change in an instant right before his very eyes. He could hardly expect the boy to forget all about his old life. He took note, that not once had Dager mentioned missing the stinky, noisy hens.

"Aye. They were your friends for a long time, weren't they?"

"They were," Dager admitted easily, "and

when it got dark at night, I knew my day was done. It's hard to know here, when my day is done. And will I have no chores?" It was as though the hard working little boy was waiting for the nonexistent boom to drop. Surely, something more than breathing in and out, playing, sleeping, and eating was expected of him.

"Aye, you'll have your chores. Once we stake out a yard that will hold our permanent hut, there'll be so much to do that you'll wish you'd never asked!" Dager was relieved to hear that, and to know that he would someday have some sort of responsibility.

"As for the dark of night, I'm afraid it will never happen in our land, son. But, once our permanent home has been erected, we will be able to block out the light far better than we have so far, with these quickly built shelters." Dager felt comfort in hearing that, too. It had proven to be incredibly hard for him to close his eyes and fall asleep in the daylight.

"As far as the animals go, we may have a remedy for that, as well." Dager scrunched up his nose as he thought about that. He really wasn't keen on the wallabies of the Tasman Empire, and he couldn't imagine ever having one of those for a pet. The frogs would certainly never agree to it either, he was sure.

"What can we do about that, Da?" he asked when he couldn't wait any longer.

"I don't think it would hurt to visit the hag

now and then, and when we do, surely you can spend time with your animals." Dager smiled politely. He supposed that would have to do, then. But, Mod continued.

"After a certain amount of time has gone by, and the baby hounds are old enough to leave their mother..." Dager's eyes opened wide and he sucked in a deep breath. He looked at his father expectantly. "...we may be able to bring one home for you!" Dager could hardly believe his ears.

"Really? Do you mean it?"

"Aye, I mean it."

"But, how..." Dager wondered how a baby hound could ever swim down to the Tasman Empire. Could it be taught to hold its breath? Mod heard each and every single thing his son thought.

"I've already discussed it with your grandfather, son. I can cure the baby hound to the point, where he or she can survive the trip." Dager smiled the biggest smile, ever. He was so excited to know that he would soon have a hound of his own. He knew that he wouldn't be able to wait.

"When, Da? When can the baby hound come home?" It did Mod's heart good to hear his son refer to the Tasman Empire, as his home. How quickly he had adapted.

"No sooner than eight weeks old, son. The baby hound has to be big enough that it can eat food, without the help of its mother. And we must be sure to not take the baby hound from its mother too soon."

"I saw the baby pigs," Dager offered, as a matter-of-factly. His father's eyes looked blank as he looked back at him. Dager reminded him, "The little pink animals that grunt!"

"Aah." Now, Mod knew which animals his son was referring to.

"The baby pigs, when they get bigger, they start to root around on their own more. Sometimes they go to their ma for a big, long suck but the bigger they get, the less they go to her."

"Exactly!" Mod was impressed by just how much Dager had studied them. But then, what else had the poor boy to do with is time? "Then I think you already have an excellent idea, of just when your baby hound can come and live with us." Dager was thinking ahead. He was now thinking beyond the point in time of when the baby hound would come.

"A name! Can I name it? Can I?" Dager bubbled over with excitement.

"Aye, I think you'd better name it, son. I couldn't think of anyone better to name the first hound of our new village!" Dager reached over and gave his father a hug.

"Thanks, Da, thank you!" Mod hugged the boy back. How proud he was of him.

"Aye, it's alright. Off you go now, to play. We have some time left, before the big meeting." And so Dager did. He, along with Lucia, Pagan, and other children, headed over to splash about in the Great Pond. Mod watched as Dager led the group in what looked like a miniature version of follow the leader. Mod had begun to laugh out loud, by the time Goy finished her chores and joined him. Together, they watched the children, and then turned their attention toward the villagers all around them.

"Can you believe it, Mod?" Goy asked. Her cheeks were flushed with happiness. Her eyes glistened, and a contented smile formed upon her lips. There was no discrimination here. Men did chores; women did chores. Boys and girls played peacefully together as equals. And soon, there would be schooling; she was ecstatic. Mod reached over and held his wife's hand.

"Aye, I can. This has been our dream for years and years!"

"Why have you not said anything to me about it, until recently, then?" Goy queried him. Hadn't he trusted her with that information, before? She had to admit that her feelings were hurt. Mod sighed.

"It was my plan to, Goy. Right before Dager was taken. Had that not happened, we would have started this village back then. The timing was right... but then, all of a sudden it became very wrong." Goy nodded. She understood now. "Everything was put on hold, while Brand spent all of his energy on finding our son. And his tireless searching just about finished him for good." Goy knew it. Shortly before Mod had cured Brand, she had felt that his time was near its end. She was glad that everything had fallen into place, before that ever came to pass.

"But, now look at him!" Goy marveled. Her husband's father had been completely regenerated. Still, she worried. "Will that kind of cure last long, Mod?" It pained her to ask it, almost as much as it pained him to answer.

"Hard to tell, love. It really does depend on destiny. When it is his time to leave us, he will go. And it will be a sad day." Goy nodded. She didn't even want to think about life without Brand. Especially now that Lucia was free to address him at will, and he took a genuine interest in her, as well. Mod added, "Something tells me that he will not be ready to go, for some time." And to that, Goy breathed a huge sigh of relief. She happened to look toward the forest then, at the same time that Brand came wandering out of it. His expression was grim, and he appeared to be in deep thought. He was quick to join his son and daughter-in-law as soon as he spotted them.

"Da! Good morning!" Mod greeted him in the customary manner. Brand sat across from Mod, and replied.

"It is a good morning," he replied, nodding to both Mod and Goy.

"Are you ready to call the meeting, then?" Mod asked. He had assumed that was what his father had been preparing for, all morning.

"Perhaps after I've eaten my porridge. I had other matters to attend to, first thing." Brand's expression had started to soften, from the serious one he'd originally arrived with. Mod was glad to see it.

"Matters like..." Mod inquired.

"For one, Croy and I were engaged in quite a discussion." Now Goy's interest was perked, and she became really intrigued by the men's conversation.

"Aye. High council will not be visiting us for some time. There was to be a wedding last week, between Derk and Bree." Mod and Goy laughed, for they'd already heard about the ill-fated union.

"And how did Croy explain that to the high council?" Brand's eyes gleamed. He was more than pleased, that his earlier prediction regarding the full circle was truly coming to be.

"When Croy returned to the Village of Hurtsmire, a meeting was held at the meeting chambers. And as you can imagine, even those who were not summoned, were in attendance." Goy frowned, as she pictured the scene in her mind. The villagers that were curious, would never pass on such an entertaining opportunity. "And when Croy told the highest member that never would the villagers and the guards be returning to Hurtsmire, he flew into a rage." Mod grimaced and interrupted.

"Of course he did. That is what he does best." He was being sarcastic now, but he felt that he'd more than earned that right over the years. "And then what happened? Surely he wants to retrieve his beloved daughter?"

"I would imagine any father would. However, when he flew into his fit, he hit the gavel so hard upon the podium, that it broke in two!" Mod roared with laughter, now.

"But, that is not unusual! How many gavels has he had to replace in this last year, alone?" Brand smacked his hand against his knee.

"It was different this time, Mod. This time, the biggest piece of the gavel flew up, and hit him right between the eyes!" Goy's hand flew to her mouth and she squealed with delight. Quickly, she recovered.

"Surely, he was not injured?" To which Brand shrugged his shoulders.

"It doesn't sound as though it is serious. However, he spends most of his time sleeping these days. He has been coherent only long enough to eat!" Mod and Goy and Brand giggled until they could giggle no more. They could see even more clearly than before, how ridiculous Hurtsmire, and the people in it, were. After a few minutes, Brand cleared his throat. It was time to become serious again.

"I need to speak with Dager." Mod jumped to his feet and walked over to the Great Pond to fetch his son. Only a few minutes passed by the time they returned together. Once Dager had taken a good, long look at his grandfather, he could tell that the older man had something important on his mind.

"Aye, Granda!"

"Good morning, son. Are you having fun this fine day?" Dager nodded up and down excitedly.

"I sure am," he looked at the older man quizzically. "What's wrong?" Brand shook his head.

"Nay. Nothing is amiss. Sit down a while, will you? I have something significant to talk to you about." Dager nodded again and did as he was told. He looked to his parents, and judging by their expressions, it appeared that they didn't know what Brand wanted to discuss, any more than he did.

"I need to talk to you, son; tell you things. The time is now."

"Okay. Is it a secret?"

"Sort of a secret. You shouldn't share matters like this, with anyone else. Consider it the first step onto your road as Curor." Goy stood up then, as she felt that this was her cue to leave. She had been a Curor's wife for a long time, and knew exactly which discussions she would not be welcome to. Were her feelings hurt? No. This was a rule she had no desire to break, as it was a matter of utmost respect. She kissed her husband on his forehead, and then followed suit with her son. The men smiled as she walked over to join the other women who were visiting and planning their futures. Goy was pleased to see that Gia was one of them gathered about, and that Bree was another. Brand took a long drink of water from his earthenware cup, before he continued.

"You're not meant for this land. Not really." Mod was just as surprised as Dager was, when Brand said that. But, Mod remained silent. This was not his conversation, and he had no desire to interfere.

"Aye!" Dager snapped hotly, "I am so!" Brand smiled kindly at him.

"For now, you are. And for many years to come. But, you must know your importance and worth. You are destined to do a great many things." Dager raised his eyebrows.

"I am?"

"Aye. And not all of those things require curing. There will be a time when you're older, when you must hide your true identity."

"I will? But, why?"

"The reasons will vary. You will have a family of your own to provide for one day, and you will use each and every one of your life experiences to help you do that to the best of your ability." Dager frowned, as he couldn't imagine ever wanting to marrying a wife. But, he already knew better than to argue with his grandfather.

"Oh." Dager wondered why he had to know all that his granda was telling him, but he did not ask. "Will I go back to the surface to live, then?" Dager assumed as much, for he did not know very much yet, about the underwater empires and kingdoms.

"Nay. Your travels will keep you under. You

will never be a surface dweller again." Upon hearing that, Dager was relieved. He had no desire to live in that hot land ever again. "But you will marry and you will at first have a son. A son to whom you will pass the gift of curing to."

"I will?" Dager almost found it amusing. It was hard for him to fathom. Mod only looked on in silence, and maintained a very solemn expression.

"Aye. Many years will pass, and then you will have another child. I cannot say at this point, whether it will be a boy or girl. However, it is the first child that will be very much like you, his father." Dager worried about this.

"Will he get stolen and have to live with a mean, old hag on the surface?" he shuddered at the very idea.

"Fear not, son. Nay. He will travel to the surface, for sure. He will have many adventures with his friends, when he is just a boy, twice your age. He will be a hero in his land."

"In his land?"

"The land you will move to, Dager. It is an underwater kingdom much grander than the Tasman Empire. It is not governed by a cruel, self-appointed council, and those who live there, are for the most part, a good and happy lot." Brand watched Dager look to his own father, with sad eyes. He was quick to reassure him. "You will still see your family here, often, Dager. You will never be on your own, again." Dager brightened immediately. He was very glad to know that.

"Do you know his name? My son's name?"

"Aye, I do. But it is not my place to tell it to you. You will learn it when the time is right. That's all for now, Dager. You know enough for today." Dager was eager to go off and play again with his friends, but when he did, he couldn't stop thinking about his future. He would have a son who would become a hero?

# 21

# WELCOME TO UNITY

Six weeks following Dager's return to the Tasman Empire marked the day of a very special meeting, to which all the villagers were invited to attend. Dager was most excited, for later that very morning, he, along with his sister and father, would be visiting the surface. Ordinarily such a trip would not cause his heart to skip mid-beat as it was now doing. This particular trip would be the one he'd been waiting so impatiently for. This was the glorious day, that he would carefully select and bring home a new, lifelong friend. He was about to have a baby hound of his very own.

Pagan was panting by the time she'd caught up to Dager and Lucia. The three of them continued toward the meeting place together. Dager could tell that she was in one of her nasty moods again. Cautiously, he asked her what the matter was.

Through clenched teeth, she replied, "I'm

moving out again!" Lucia chuckled and then stopped abruptly, upon receiving a sharp nudge in the side, compliments of Dager's elbow.

"But, I thought you liked your father, now!" Dager protested, feeling more than slightly surprised. At least it sure seemed that way to him, the way Pagan paraded around on Derk's shoulders most of the time. Pagan folded her arms across her chest and glared straight ahead.

"Aye. Da's fun now that he got rid of his extra face hair. But, now him and Ma expect to give me a brother or a sister! I didn't ask for one or the other. And besides that. Where would they put it?"

"What?" Lucia asked skeptically. "Are you saying that your ma is pregnant?" Pagan turned and looked at her as though she were a complete idiot.

Pagan's voice was high pitched as she replied, "I never said nothing about pregnant. I said they want to give me a brother or a sister. They don't even know yet, what kind it's gonna be." Pagan took a deep breath. Dager was at a total loss over what he could possibly say to soothe his friend, and so he remained quiet. He knew Pagan well enough to realize that once enough time had passed, she'd get over this fit, as she'd done the others before, which he'd had the privilege of bearing witness to.

"And..." she huffed as though she was about to reveal the absolute worst. "They never even asked me first what I think about the idea. They just went ahead and decided it all without me." Lucia felt helpless as she patted the younger girl's back. No more words would pass between them, as they'd just reached the meeting place. Both sets of parents were standing off to the side with Bree, chatting amongst themselves quietly, and they had become the unknowing recipients of occasional hard looks from Pagan. Gia and Derk were unaware of their daughter's insolence, which only served to infuriate her even more.

Brand raised, then lowered his hands, which signaled silence amongst his people. He looked down upon forty-some expectant, hopeful faces. Women and men alike shushed and stilled their anxious youngsters. Childless couples stood arm in arm and the older generation observed everyone else wistfully. The sky was clear violet, and the light breeze whisked gracefully about, leaves of many colours.

Unanimously agreed upon laws had been set in place weeks before, and assigned duties had been accepted and were already in motion. What primarily had begun as a gathering of assorted stragglers had swiftly blossomed into a thriving new community. Brand began.

"I have exciting news to share!" as he spoke, his smile never once wavered. Not one of his eager listeners, young or old, dared make a sound. It was clear that this news would be good.

"Of all the names you have submitted, the majority of our population has indicated that our village shall go by the name, 'Unity'!" Thunderous applause rippled throughout the people. Brand was not finished yet, and so he raised, then lowered his hands, again.

"Also, you have decided that from this day forth, you shall look upon Mod as your leader!" Mod smiled, lovingly squeezed Goy's hand, and modestly bowed his head. He was proud to have been selected to act in such an honourable role. "The next step will be to nominate a party of five councilors whose job will be to assist him. These appointments must not be made in haste. You must choose from amongst yourselves, those who are sound of mind and clear of conscience. These people will have the best interests of Unity at heart. Take this next week to consider those of you who are worthy of playing such vital roles in our community." Brand hesitated momentarily and scanned the many faces before him. Even though he knew exactly who the chosen few would be, it was not his place to speak it out loud.

"Now it is time to mention a serious matter which needs immediate address. I speak of the crimson serpent, whom you've all been taught not only to idolize, but to fear as well." A hush fell over the people of Unity. Brand knew that he'd just struck a sensitive chord among them. Even the children, who'd been steadily growing impatient, now sat still with their ears cocked intently in his direction. "Let it be known, that there is no giant, red snake. It is a myth. There has never been such a creature in the Tasman Empire, nor anywhere else for that matter. It has been said, that some surface dwellers, pray to a red serpent. That has been their belief and was never meant to be ours. Let your conscience be your guide, from now on. Never again in our land, fear the wrath of a nonexistent reptile." Brand saw waves of relief wash over his captivated audience. There would be many questions, he knew, but the answers would come later. Too much information too soon, could bring about too many mixed feelings. "That will be all for today. Thank you for coming." The meeting dispersed quickly, and as it did the low murmur of everyday chatter began again. Brand summoned his family to join him at his hut, and so Dager and Lucia had to bid Pagan farewell for now. She huffed off in the direction of her parents' hut; the one Dager knew she'd never move out of, despite her many threats to do just that.

"Congratulations are in order!" Brand announced as he heartily shook Mod's hand. Lucia and Dager were both a little too young to grasp the importance of their father's new position. They stood next to Goy, who beamed proudly at her husband.

"Thank you, Da," Mod replied, and then he winked at his wife and children, "we mustn't stay long this morning, however." Brand looked from him to Dager knowingly, and sat down and gestured for the boy to sit upon his knee. Dager happily complied.

"Is this the day, then?" Brand asked him.

"Aye, today I get my baby hound!"

"Good. Pets are good for children. Perhaps you can lead by example, and before long Unity will be run rampant with all sorts of pets." there was a twinkle in his eye as he spoke. He turned to Lucia.

"And you, child? What kind of pet might you wish for?" Lucia was caught off guard for a moment, because she really had not considered having a pet of her own.

"Well, Granda! I haven't really thought about a pet for me. I've been so excited about Dager getting a hound..." her voice trailed off thoughtfully. Brand nodded at her.

"It's as I expected, Lucia. I have something you may be interested in looking after for me." This excited her, but she wondered why he couldn't look after whatever it was, himself. She was about to ask just that, when he continued, this time addressing his entire family. "I've a journey to embark on, and very soon."

"A journey!" Mod gasped, for this was the first he'd heard of it. He'd had no idea whatsoever, about his father leaving. Goy furrowed her brows; she was extremely concerned. Regenerated or not, he was still an old man, after all.

"Brand! Do tell us it won't be a dangerous one!" He shook his head as he replied.

"Nay, it shan't be. I've received word that my niece needs to relocate, and so I've invited her to join us here."

"You can't mean Stormy, do you?" Mod inquired, knowing full well that Stormy was the only niece his father had. It was beyond belief, that after all this time, she'd want back into the fold.

"Is she the one you've spoken of, Mod?" Goy asked. "The cousin that lived with you like a sister?" Goy's eyebrows rose. She too, was surprised. She knew it had been many years since they'd had any contact with the woman at all.

"Aye," Brand answered gravely, "it sounds as though she's trying to change her ways. The least her family can do for her is give her a chance." Mod laughed sardonically, which for him was completely out of character. But then, if anyone could ever possibly bring out the worst in Mod, it would always be Stormy.

"Tell me, Da. Just how many chances will she get, this time?" Brand gave his son a long, admonishing look.

"Just this last one, son. I've already sent word attesting to that. But for now," he added, before gently nudging Dager from his lap, "I do believe you have a trip of your own to make!" he winked at Dager, and then motioned toward Lucia and Goy. "Lucia, would you mind staying back with your mother and I?" Lucia was grateful for the excuse to not have to return to the dreadful surface, and so she nodded eagerly. Mod narrowed his eyes at his father. "Why you? Why must you go for her?"

Brand answered simply. "Because I am the only one."

"Will you be here when we return?" Brand shook his head, indicating that he would not. Mod resigned himself to the fact that there would be nothing he could do to change his father's mind, and so he extended his hand toward him.

"Good luck to you, then. May you have a safe and successful journey." Brand smiled.

"Aye, and you. Dager, take good care of your new little friend." Dager just nodded and smiled back. He could feel the tension which had steadily mounted between his father and grandfather, and it made him feel uneasy.

A few minutes later, he and Mod made their way for the tallest willow that stood in the clearing of the forest, beyond the Great Pond.

In the meantime, Brand led Lucia and her mother to a makeshift cage, which sat in the shade against the backside of his hut. It was well hidden beneath some brush; so concealed that Lucia had never noticed it there before. Weak, laughing sounds could be heard from within the wooden slats. Lucia giggled nervously. Brand moved the branches away, and then lifted the lid from the cage so that Lucia was able to peek inside. What she saw, was a small bird, which was presently looking right at her! There was a curious dark stripe across its eyes, and its large bill looked heavy. The bird's tail feathers puffed up as the bird began to pace about. Lucia could see that the edges of its tail feathers were brownish, with the colour fading to an off-white toward its body.

"What is it, Granda?"

"It's a small kookaburra. I am not sure how old she is, but when she is fully grown, she should be three times bigger than the size she is now," he explained, as he indicated with his hands, just how big the bird might get.

"How do you know it's a girl?" Lucia peered closer at the creature.

"By looking at her tail feathers. Male kookaburras will have light feathers at the top of their tails. As you can see, this bird's feathers are dark brown."

"Oh! I didn't know that! What does she eat?"

"For the time being, mostly insects. But, as she grows and begins to venture out on her own, she'll probably look for worms, mice, newborn rats, or snakes to eat, in addition to the bugs." Lucia wrinkled her nose at the very idea of eating such strange things. Brand told her to hold out her hands together and flat, palms up. In the next instant, he scooped the bird up and set it in her hands. The baby bird was adorable, and Lucia was speechless.

"You'll need to name her, of course. That will be up to you, Lucia." Lucia cupped her hands protectively around the delicate creature.

"But how did you get it? Aren't kookaburras wild?"

"Aye, they are. This one, I happened to come

across during one of my early morning walks. I do believe it was abandoned by its mother, which sometimes happens if she already has too many chicks to feed. As for being wild, they usually won't go near people at all. But, if you raise her well and love her, she'll be your friend forever." Lucia smiled at that, though she worried.

"But, I don't know how to look after a baby bird. What if I do it wrong?"

"Don't worry so, child. If I thought for a moment, that you weren't up to the task, I would never have asked you to take care of her for me."

Goy, who had been standing silently in the background, agreed. "You'll see, Lucia. Babies of all kinds need love more than anything else in the world. We know you've got a lot of that to share."

As the bird laughed again and gently tried to flutter its little wings, Lucia smiled. She, just like her brother would soon have, now had a new best friend to love and protect.

Leftover early morning mist still hung heavily in the air by the time Dager and Mod reached the surface. It was an uncommon occurrence to see so late in the morning, especially considering how arid this particular land usually was.

"Have you settled on a name for your baby hound?" Mod asked him as they trudged down the road toward the farm.

"No, I can't seem to come up with the right one." Dager looked rather disappointed about it, as well he should. He'd been mulling names around, over and over in his head for weeks now, and still couldn't decide on one. His father quickly reassured him.

"I think you'll be able to name it, once you're holding it in your arms, son." Dager smiled up at him.

"Aye." They walked the rest of the way in silence. Dager's mind was filled with visions of baby hounds, while all Mod could think about was his father's journey and his awful cousin, Stormy.

Just as Maybelle P. Bonnadoolio's driveway came into view, Dager asked him. "How come you don't like Stormy, Da?" Mod was taken back. He hadn't realized that his disdain for the woman was so clear, that a child Dager's age, would notice. He tried his best to explain.

"It is not so much that I don't like her, but that I don't trust her. She was often nasty as a child, and would say things that weren't even true, or things that she didn't mean."

"Oh." Dager said in response. To him, Stormy didn't sound a whole lot different from Pagan.

Mindy barked out a warning welcome the moment she saw Dager approach. She was laying on her side in the shade near the barn. There was a gradual dip in the ground there, and it was so misty that Dager could barely make out the baby hounds that were struggling to nurse upon her.

"Mod and Dager!" Maybelle P. Bonnadoolio screeched, the second she saw them. She could hardly believe her eyes! Two of her favourite people had come to pay her a visit. She set her egg pail down gently on the ground beside the chicken coop and ran like the wind toward them. She swooped Dager right off his feet and spun him wildly around. He couldn't help but laugh. She set him down, and proceeded to hug Mod.

"You sweet man!" she sang out. "How thoughtful of you to come and keep me company while Tad is off to market!"

"Aye," Mod replied, even though he hadn't known Tad was away. "We can't have you getting lonely, Maybelle. How is the happy couple doing these days?" as he asked, he looked beyond her to what had once been a ramshackle house. He could see that Tad had been an extremely busy man in the last few weeks. The shingles on the roof had been replaced with new ones, and he'd done away with the hazardous steps, and had instead installed a wraparound veranda. Dager headed for the hounds, while his father and Maybelle talked.

"Hey there, Mindy," he greeted the dog as one would greet an old friend. He knelt down and cradled her head in his lap, the way he often used to do. She snuggled in closer to get the full effect of his gentle touch. The baby hounds were all over the place now, running and stumbling this way and that. All that is, but one.

"Are you the shy one?" Dager asked it directly. It made no move toward him, as the others had done. The baby hound shyly turned its head down, and tried to ignore him. Dager would have none of that. "I'll bet you're the last one to feed, aren't you?" Dager could see that this was the smallest of the litter. As he leaned closer, it tried to shrink back against the wall, but it was already as close to the wall as it could get. Dager reached over and picked it up by the scruff of its neck, and laid it on his lap next to Mindy's head. He could see now, that this baby hound, with the white toes and chest, was a girl. Mindy licked her face. Cradling it then, as a mother might cradle an infant child, Dager knew without a doubt, that this was the one. This small, dejected creature, that preferred the background to the limelight, was the one Dager would be taking home.

Mod and Maybelle approached him then, walking arm in arm, like two long lost friends.

"Dager, is this the puppy you're taking with you to the south?" Maybelle asked him so sweetly, that he didn't bother correcting her.

"Aye," and then he asked Mod, "What do you think, Da?" Mod smiled with approval.

"You've made a good choice, son. Have you decided on a name, then?" Dager looked around as he held it in his arms. The mist had completely evaporated in the few minutes he'd spent with the hounds. Mist, he thought. His eyes brightened and he raised them to meet his father's own.

"Misty. My baby hound is named, Misty."

Not long afterward, Mod and Dager said

goodbye to Maybelle and the animals, and then headed for home. The sun was shining and the cracked, hard ground was burning their tender bare feet. Dager's discomfort was the least of his worries. His concern lay only in the soft black bundle he protectively carried with him. Misty was asleep now, nuzzled against his chest, and every now and then, she'd let out a contented sigh. Dager now had everything he could ever possibly need or want. He had a family that loved him. They lived together in a happy, magical land which was often filled with laughter. And last, but not least, he now had a best friend with whom he just knew, he'd share many fantastic adventures.

# ABOUT THE AUTHOR

The author works, plays and writes in the beautiful Cowichan Valley on Vancouver Island, British Columbia, Canada.

While writing for children has been and likely will always be her primary focus, she's found a little niche in writing memoirs aimed toward the adult audience, beginning with *Memoirs of a Pakhtun Immigrant*.

More books by Teresa Schapansky:
*Imogene of the Pacific Kingdom*
*Some Christmas*
*Coinkeeper series,* books 1-4
*One Little Coin*
*Along the Way series,* books 1-12

For more information
about the author, please visit:
www.teresaschapansky.com